# DOG GONE LIES

# Ted Clifton

**Dog Gone Lies**
Ted Clifton
ISBN 978-1-927967-65-2

**Produced by IndieBookLauncher.com**
*www.IndieBookLauncher.com*
Editing: Nassau Hedron
Cover Design: Saul Bottcher
Interior Design and Typesetting: Saul Bottcher

The body text of this book is set in Adobe Caslon.

**Also Available**
EPUB edition, ISBN 978-1-927967-66-9
Kindle edition, ISBN 978-1-927967-67-6

# CONTENTS

—

*Free Preview:*
*The Bootlegger's Legacy*

—

# PROLOG

"Hello, Ed."

"What the hell do you guys want? Look, I didn't tell them anything while I was in jail. Fuck, man, I don't know anything."

"Why don't you shut the fuck up and come with us before you make us mad."

The two goons gave Ed a shove toward the door. He was terrified, trying to calculate what would happen. How the hell had he gotten mixed up with these animals? He'd been depressed and lonely. Then he'd found drugs and life had seemed okay for a while, although things weren't always real clear. But this fucked up world just wouldn't leave him alone to be a loser drug addict. It cost a goddamn fortune to illegally self-medicate. If he'd been rich he'd have been under the care of some asshole psychiatrist, getting all the drugs he wanted.

As the morons shoved him into the back seat of their ratty car, Ed began to wonder if he should just run. These fat bastards would never be able to catch him—would they shoot him in broad daylight on a city street? He decided they would, mostly because they were too stupid to understand how dumb that would be.

They were probably just going to hurt him some, anyway,

like last time. All they wanted was money—kill him and he
could never pay anything again. He felt calmer once he realized they were just going to beat him up, maybe break an arm
or a leg. If things went too far he could tell them about the
evidence that would go to the cops if he turned up dead. But
then they might force him to tell them that he'd mailed it to
his mother, in which case they'd probably just kill him and
then kill his mother, too.

"Ed, you must be the dumbest fuck who ever lived. Why
did you get your mother involved in this shit—what kind of
asshole son are you anyway?"

"Jeez, man, I don't know what you're talking about. My
mother? She isn't involved in anything. Sometimes I say things
that aren't right—no way my mother's involved in anything—
you assholes better leave her alone."

The goon turned around in the seat and popped Ed a
good one right in the jaw. The world became suddenly less real,
more distant, and he keeled over in the back seat. He seemed
to be dreaming about his mother and father. He cared about
them so very much. Why had he hurt them? He'd done it re-
peatedly over a lot of years. He wasn't sure why. He certainly
didn't mean to—it just seemed to happen. So much in his life
just happened, without any obvious reason.

Ed drifted back into semi-consciousness, unsure of where
he was. Then he remembered the goons. He didn't raise himself
up, just stayed still and hoped that everything would go away.
He'd decided against telling them anything about his little surprise package. He'd stay quiet and everything would go away.
That's what was going to happen. It would all go away for Ed.

# 1

*Friday, 1988*

*1988: The Hubble Telescope goes into operation, exploring deep space. A bomb explodes on Pan Am Flight 103 over Lockerbie in Scotland. Prozac is sold for the first time as an anti-depressant. Hit movies include* Rain Man, Die Hard, *and* A Fish Called Wanda. *Cell phones and internet technology are in their early stages. The top-rated television show is* The Cosby Show. *The U.S. president is Ronald Reagan. Roy Orbison dies. And CDs outsell vinyl records for the first time.*

Ray Pacheco had been the sheriff for Dona Ana County New Mexico for twenty years when he retired and took up fishing. He'd been good at his job, but he wasn't driven. He thought of the people who lived in his county as friends and the kids of friends. The new breed of law enforcement seemed to see enemies everywhere, from terrorists to druggies. Everyone was a suspect. He couldn't work that way and decided he'd rather just quit.

Ray had made a deal for an old abandoned cabin close to Elephant Butte Lake outside the oddly named city of Truth or Consequences, New Mexico. He'd retired from being a cop and, to some extent, from being around people—he'd decided to just hide out for a while. It wasn't that he didn't like people—quite the opposite. He liked them fine, he was just tired of dealing with the bad ones, and one of the hazards of being in law enforcement is that you come in contact with a lot of bad ones.

So here Ray was, retired to a remote cabin by a lake with nothing to do. After a few months of doing very little he was getting jumpy. Well, hell, there was fishing. He'd never fished in his life. He knew it didn't fit the stereotype of a rural county sheriff, but he'd just never been much of an outdoorsman. Under the circumstances, though, it seemed like the thing to do.

Ray drove down to the lake and stopped at the largest bait shop—*Jack's Bait, Boats and Beer*, the triple B. He sat in the Jeep for a while, wondering if he even wanted to go in—it was like entering a different world. Even before he got through the door, the odor was a little off-putting. Not real sure if it was the bait, or maybe the beer, but it didn't smell good at all. He entered what had to be the most cluttered store that ever existed. There were things hanging from the ceiling that could easily have been there fifty years before—and he wasn't real sure what some of that hanging stuff was.

Even finding the sales counter took some time. Once Ray reached what he thought must be it—after all, there was an old cash register sitting on it—no one was there. As a matter of fact, he couldn't see anyone anywhere. While he wasn't sure there was much here anybody would steal, he couldn't believe that there wasn't somebody around somewhere. At that moment he heard noises out back, and he followed them out a back door onto a dock area, where several men were occupied loading things into a boat.

One man looked up. "Hey, be with you in a minute—soon as I get the rest of this shit loaded." Must be the store owner. He looked to be in excess of three-hundred pounds and was chewing on an unlit cigar that seemed a likely source of the offensive odor.

The man finished his task, thanked his customer, and headed towards Ray. "Sorry, I didn't hear you come in—guess I had my head up my ass. As usual. What can I do for you?"

"My name's Ray Pacheco. Just moved up here a few months ago and I'm mostly looking for some information."

"Well, hello, Ray Pacheco, name's Big Jack—I own this pile of shit business and also give out free information on almost any topic you can dream up." Big Jack's smile was big. *Everything* about Big Jack was big. Ray sensed that he'd be more than willing to share his opinion on almost anything—the problem would be deciding which parts were true. There was a twinkle in the man's eye that suggested he found merriment in being a little off-center. Ray wasn't sure how anyone could tell when Big Jack was lying or telling the truth—he was willing to bet that most of what Jack said at least stretched the truth some—but at the same time there was something about his manner that suggested he might be a lot smarter than he looked. My god, he'd almost have to be.

They shook hands. "Nice to meet you, Big Jack. I've retired up here and decided that I'd take up fishing. I've never fished in my life and I'm looking for some guidance."

"Oh my, I think I just caught something on my line." Big Jack started laughing so hard Ray was a little worried he might topple over.

After several minutes of enjoying his own humor, Big

Jack started to quiet down. "Sorry, Ray. Just couldn't resist. Okay, so you want to be a fisherman. First thing is don't buy anything. Do you see a little tear in my eye, Ray? Yep, that's what I said—the first thing you need to do is go fishing. Just borrow or rent some stuff and figure out if this is something you really want to do."

Son-of-a-bitch—honest advice. Ray was impressed. "That makes sense, Big Jack. But I'm going to need someone to help me get started. What should I do?"

"Just gettin' to that. There are several fishing guides who work this lake. All but one are not worth shit. The problem with the one who does know shit is that he's almost always drunk. But my advice is go see this guy and if he can stand up at all, hire him to show you how to fish. And don't believe the dumb Indian schtick—it's an act. He'll charge you some money, but it'll be a whole lot cheaper than buying the stuff now. Especially from someone like Big Jack, who enjoys screwing with most people." Jack was amused with himself again and Ray waited for the fit of laughter to pass.

After Ray left with the fishing guide's name and directions to his camp site, he thought a while about Big Jack. The guy was loud and obnoxious, and claimed to be untrustworthy and out only for his own benefit—but his actions seemed to say the exact opposite. Told Ray not to waste his money until he knew he was actually going to enjoy fishing and maybe knew something about what he needed to buy—all in all, very good, honest advice. The opposite of what Ray was used to dealing with, which more often than he liked was crooks pretending to be good guys. This guy was all bombast, but genuinely good underneath. He smiled. He was glad he'd stopped in—plus the smell was starting to go away.

Finding the campsite took a lot longer than Ray had anticipated. While there were occasional signs, most of Big Jack's directions were based on landmarks. Eventually he found some people in an RV who showed him where he'd gone wrong. They added some details to Ray's map and said they knew exactly where he wanted to be. He'd been pretty close, and with the revised information he quickly found the right spot.

Ray parked in an area that had been cleared for that purpose and headed down the trail that was supposed to lead him to the fishing guide's camp. He'd already had more activity in this one day than any time since he'd moved up to the lake, and it made it clear that he had to get out more. He felt better, and his bones felt better—if he just sat in that cabin all day he'd rot away.

As Ray rounded a large mesquite bush, he found himself at a fairly large campsite. There were two tents, plus two more areas covered by tarps. Under one of the tarps it looked like there was a boat. On one of the tents was a handwritten sign that read, "Tyee Chino Fishing Guide." *This must be the place.*

"Hello? Anyone about?" There was no response. Ray wasn't sure what campsite etiquette required after yelling. He went over to the tent that bore the sign and yelled again. "Hello, anyone home?"

"Fuck you evil white man—leave me in peace."

Okay—not the response he'd been expecting. "Sorry to bother you. Big Jack said you could be hired as a fishing guide."

"Fuck Big Jack."

Well, this was starting to feel like he was on duty again. A lot of people had told the sheriff to fuck off.

"Look, if you're not interested in work that's fine. I'll just leave. Sorry I bothered you." Ray had yet to see anyone—the whole exchange had taken place without anyone emerging from the tent.

Ray turned around and headed back to his car. Figured he'd go by and ask Big Jack about the other two guys, the ones who didn't know shit—maybe they'd at least be a little easier to deal with.

"Wait. I need work—I'm best fishing guide in whole damn country. You should hire me—even if I tell you to fuck off." Standing outside of the tent was an Apache Indian. He was over six feet four inches and appeared to be very muscular. His long hair hung in a braid. He was frowning—which might've been his natural look—but Ray thought he saw a mischievous intelligence in the man's eyes. He also appeared to be quite drunk.

Ray wasn't real sure if this was some kind of strange sells pitch, or if Tyee Chino was just the dumbest fishing guide who ever lived. "Tell you the truth, I'm not sure you could guide anyone to anything right now, Mr. Chino."

"I drank too much. Come back tomorrow morning at seven—I'll be ready. I'm best damn fishing guide in whole damn country."

Ray wasn't sure what to do. What the hell—maybe he *was* the best damn fishing guide in the whole damn country. "You know tomorrow's Saturday?"

"Fishing guide works weekends—come back tomorrow."

"Okay, I'll be here at seven tomorrow."

Tyee Chino grunted and went back inside his tent. Ray went to his car.

As Ray drove back to his cabin he made notes on the map, which was by that time covered in scribbles. He was a little concerned about finding Chino's tent again the next day—he sure the hell didn't want to be late and have this strange, very large man mad at him.

# 2

*Friday*

Monica Jackson pulled off the interstate at T or C to get some gas and make a phone call. Her 1985 Subaru Wagon was her pride and joy and got excellent gas mileage, but it did have a small tank, making frequent gasoline stops necessary. She was still a very active sixty-three, but even so the frequent stops were a convenience for her as well as the car. She needed bathroom breaks and to limber up her joints.

Traveling with Monica was her best show dog, an Icelandic Sheepdog named Bruce. Monica bred the friendly dogs, and she showed them at regional dog shows to increase her visibility. She lived not too far off of I-25 just south of Albuquerque in an area called Bosque Farms, in a small place with plenty of room for her fifteen dogs. Bruce was the smartest dog she'd ever raised. He seemed to know as much about the dog shows as she did—he was a showman, or a show dog, and he loved being in the spotlight.

He was a wonderful dog, but he wasn't a perfect specimen. The judges at the dog show events were some of the snobbiest people Monica had ever met. Most of the top prizes went to the same owners over and over, and everyone knew it was politics that won, not necessarily the best dogs. If a judge decided who was going to win in advance, then it was easy to find flaws in the others since there was no such thing as a perfect dog.

Most of Monica's life she'd been an elementary school teacher. She'd become a teacher mainly because that's what had been expected of her. It hadn't been exactly what she'd wanted in a career, but she'd gone along with what her mother and her husband advised her to do—always taking the path of least resistance.

Then Monica's whole world had turned upside down, about ten years ago now, when she divorced her husband, Mike Jackson, who was a dentist. Mike had had a silly affair with his young—maybe better to say very young—dental assistant, Terri. There was no doubt in Monica's mind that Mike had been pursued and lassoed by the little tart—who had nothing better to do than capture old men as prizes. Like it was some kind of national contest. The consequences of her actions and use of her unbelievable body were beyond anything Terri could comprehend. Actually, she seemed not to comprehend much except screwing. Maybe Monica should have forgiven poor old weak-willed Mike, but she was tired of always being the understanding one so she divorced him instead. Then she quit her job. Everyone says she retired early, but of course that's bullshit—she just plain quit. Used some of the divorce money frivolously, purchased a home south of Albuquerque, and became a dog breeder.

Now, it would probably have helped if she'd known something about being a dog breeder beforehand—but too late. Suddenly she was one. Since then Monica hadn't been very successful financially. On the other hand, she'd never enjoyed herself as much as she had these last ten years. The dogs were wonderful to be around and, except for the judges, most of the dog people were generous and thoughtful.

After getting gas, Monica headed down Main Street looking for a place to get a quick bite and to use a payphone. She spotted the Lone Post Café and parked in front. She made sure Bruce had his water bowl and food, then patted him for a minute before going inside.

The aroma of the café was fantastic. Even if Monica wasn't hungry, she was going to have some of whatever smelled so good. She was shown to one of the booths, served water immediately, and given a menu.

"Hello, how are you today?"

"Just fine. What's that wonderful smell?"

"Does smell good doesn't it? Mostly what you're smelling is green chilies. And those chilies can go on most anything we serve—including pancakes. Although I don't think I'd recommend that."

"Maybe I'll have the small green chili breakfast burrito and a glass of iced tea."

"Very good. My name's Sue. I'll put your order in and it'll be ready in just a minute."

Monica thanked her and had her point out the restrooms and payphone.

Monica called her ex-husband and got his voice mail. "Hey Mike, I'm in T or C, at a little diner, and wanted to let you know I think I'll stay an extra day in El Paso. Made some last minute plans with Betty. If you can, could you go by the house and check on things? Really appreciate it. I'll call you from El Paso, probably tomorrow, and let you know my exact schedule. Thanks."

The angry part of Mike and Monica's divorce had been over for a long time. Mike's girlfriend had taken off as soon as Monica filed for divorce. Mike had been very remorseful and underwent extensive therapy to deal with the consequences of his actions. About five years after the divorce, he'd sold his dental practice and retired to an assisted living facility in Albuquerque. He had aged significantly, to the point that Monica and their children were worried about his health.

Mike seemed to adapt to the assisted living home and soon was feeling better, but he'd changed in many ways. Monica and Mike had three grown children and two grandchildren. In a complete role reversal, Mike had become more involved with the children and grandchildren as Monica became more and more withdrawn.

Placing another call, Monica waited for an answer.

"Hello."

"Hey, Betty. It's Monica."

"Where are you?"

"I'm in T or C and should be in El Paso in about three hours or so. Maybe we could get together this evening for dinner?"

"Well, I don't know, Monica. These damn dog show people are such gossips. Lately it seems all they want to do is sneer and point at us like we're harming them in some way."

"To hell with those creeps. Come on, Betty. This is just dinner—you were going to eat anyway weren't you?"

"Okay. Sorry. For some reason I seem on edge lately. When you get checked in give me a call. I'm in room 607—see you tonight."

Monica and Betty had become close friends over the last

few years. They went to the same dog shows and liked to talk about the same sorts of stuff, so they enjoyed each other's company. But recently they'd become aware of some gossip going around amongst some morons within the dog show organization, suggesting that they had more than just a friendship. At first they were shocked. Then, as they both gave the rumor thought, they realized there probably was more to their relationship than just friendship, but neither of them wanted to deal with what that meant so they'd been avoiding each other the last couple of shows. Monica had decided this was stupid and was going to make an extra effort to have a conversation with Betty about their relationship. If it turned out to be sexual, so be it. If it wasn't, to hell with those narrow-minded bastards.

Returning to her table, she settled in just as her food was being served. Her first thought was: *thank goodness I only ordered the small.* It was enough food for four. But Mexican food was one of Bruce's favorites, so she could consume about a third of the meal and Bruce could enjoy the rest.

As she was leaving with her doggy bag, she took a moment to thank her waitress, who'd seemed especially nice.

When she reached the car she was surprised to see a note or something stuck under the windshield wiper. She first opened the side door and arranged Bruce's special Mexican treat—he really appreciated the food and rewarded her with tail wagging and dog smiling. Then, with her hands free, she retrieved the paper.

It was a handwritten note.

*You need to know I've been watching you. You can't call people names and accuse them of immoral behavior and get away with it. People like you think you're better than everybody, but you're not. I'm going to make sure you don't hurt anyone else the way you've hurt me. You'll be sorry. Very Sorry!*

What the hell was this? Monica looked around, as if the author might be standing by to answer questions, but there was nobody about. Then she noticed that her car was leaning. She went around to the other side and saw that both tires on that side were flat. Shit.

Monica checked on Bruce. She made sure there was plenty of air flowing through the windows, which were rolled down about three inches. She relocked the car, although she wasn't exactly sure why. Then she went back into the restaurant.

Sue greeted her at the register.

"Well, that was quick. Decide you needed dessert?"

"No. I have a problem with my car. I have two flat tires and I guess I need a tow to someplace that can help me out."

"Two flats. Now that sounds like bad luck big time."

"The tires are fairly new so I think maybe someone cut them or something—it looks like there are slash marks on the sidewalls."

"What? I can't believe that! Right downtown in front of the café—no way."

"Yeah, seems strange to me too. But that sure looks like what happened. Anyway, do you know of someone I could call?"

"Of course, dear. Let me make the call. I'll get Tom Yates—he has the only tow truck in town—and then I'll call Bill Lopez, who runs the Firestone store. Just give me a second, and we will get some things movin'.'"

Sue came back and told Monica that she'd called everyone and the tow truck would be there any minute. She also said she'd called the sheriff's office so that they could take a report about someone slashing her tires.

"Thanks, Sue. I guess that's okay. I don't want to make any trouble for anyone."

"Sure it's okay. That's what the deputies are for. And believe me, nobody in T or C wants someone slashing visitor's tires. The town lives on tourists. They'll take this stuff seriously."

About that time the tow truck arrived, closely followed by the sheriff's deputy's car. Monica went out and talked to both the tow truck driver and the deputy. They agreed she would get her dog out and ride with the deputy over to the Firestone store while the tow truck driver hooked up the car and brought it along. Monica waved to the waitress through the window, and with Bruce in tow got into the deputy's vehicle.

It was a short ride to the Firestone store. The deputy parked in front of the store and Monica related what had happened, giving him the note. He asked her if there was anyone who might wish her harm. She said she wasn't aware of anyone specific who'd do something like this. She explained that she was on her way to a dog show in El Paso and that she didn't know anyone in T or C. He took extensive notes as they sat in the car, while Bruce made himself at home in the rear seat as usual.

"Well, not sure what to tell you Ms. Jackson, but that note indicates someone who knows you and has some kind of grudge. I consider this a genuine threat. Slashing your tires is an act of aggression. If someone's angry, they often start with this type of thing and then progress to more serious acts. Before you leave town I'd like you to come by my office and let me take a more formal statement. Would you do that?"

Monica hesitated. She was looking forward to getting to El Paso and relaxing tonight. It was already early afternoon, and she still needed her car fixed.

"I'll do my best. I don't know though if I believe someone is really threatening me. If for some reason I can't make it by, I'll call. Okay?"

"Well, I can't force you to come by, but you should take this threat seriously. Here's my card."

Monica thanked the deputy and opened the door for Bruce. She had seen the tow truck take her car around to the side of the building and she walked back to that area, where she talked to Bill Lopez, the manager of the tire store. He didn't have two tires that would fit her car—said they didn't have many Subarus in town. He could change out all four tires using a different size or he could order two tires and have them by the next day. The day wasn't getting better for Monica. She couldn't justify buying two additional tires, especially if they weren't even the recommended sizes. It seemed like she had no choice but to wait until the next day.

"Is there a place around here you'd recommend for me to stay?"

"Best place in town is the Hot Springs Inn," Lopez said immediately. "Matter of fact, I'd be happy to run you up there if that's where you'd like to go."

"Well, that'd be very nice of you Mr. Lopez. When do you think you'll have the car ready tomorrow?"

"First thing, ma'am. The truck from El Paso should be at

my shop by eight thirty or so and it'll take us only about thirty minutes to get everything fixed up. Matter of fact, I'm sure the Inn has a van—they can run you down here about nine and everything should be ready."

So far Monica had only encountered nice people in this town—except, of course, for whoever had sliced her tires. It was a quick trip up a slight hill to the Hot Springs Inn. She left most of her luggage in her car and brought only a small case for the night. She unloaded the case and Bruce in front of the Inn and said goodbye to Mr. Lopez. As soon as she turned around there was someone there to assist her.

"Good Afternoon, ma'am. Checking in?"

"Yes. Thank you."

He carried her small bag into an impressive lobby. The exterior of the building needed some attention, but once inside she was impressed. The lobby was very large, and off to one side she could see an enclosed pool. It had been designed for soaking, so the entire pool was shallow, and there were benches placed in the water where people could relax. She walked up to the registrations counter, which was massive and very ornate. At one time the place must have done a lot more business than they were now.

"Hi. I had a little car trouble and I'm in need of a room for one night."

"Well of course, ma'am. Hope it wasn't anything serious?"

"No not really. Two flat tires, but the store here didn't have the right size so the car won't be ready until the morning."

"Too bad. Is it at Firestone?"

"Yes."

"Well, Mr. Lopez will take good care of you. Now let's

see. I have a single queen bed, a single king bed, or a two-room suite."

"The single queen will be great. Also I'll need a ride about nine in the morning to the Firestone store. Can you do that?"

"Of course. As soon as you're ready in the morning, let us know and we'll run you down there."

The very efficient desk clerk had presented her a registration card and quoted her a price as they were talking. Monica handed over her credit card.

"While you're with us, Ms. Jackson, you've got complete pool privileges. We have the large community pool, which stays open until eight in the evening, and we have more private spas that you can schedule for any time. There's no charge for whichever one you prefer, but the private spas have to be reserved and sometimes aren't available. But for today that shouldn't be a problem. We have one dining room that will be serving until eight this evening. The menu's limited, but all the items are very good. There's also a small bar just off of the dining room serving drinks and snacks. Thank you for staying with us. Your room is 125, which is directly down this hall to your left. Can I help you with anything else?"

"No, you've been very helpful. Thanks so much. Did I mention that I have a dog with me? Is that okay?"

"Yes, ma'am. I saw your dog. He's very beautiful. Is he a show dog?"

"He is. That's where we were headed, to a dog show that starts tomorrow in El Paso."

"There's no problem with the dog staying in your room. We would request that if there are other guests in the public areas that you limit the dog to going or coming from the room.

But since we're a little slow today he can more or less have the run of the place."

Monica thanked the man again and headed to her room. It sounded like she might be the only guest, which felt a little spooky, but it would be nice for Bruce.

Once in the room, Monica called the El Paso hotel and spoke to the desk clerk. She told the woman that she wouldn't be needing a room for that night since she was stuck in T or C with car trouble—she confirmed her room reservation for the next night. She then dialed back to the hotel and asked for Betty's room. Getting voice mail, she left the message that she had some car trouble and wouldn't be in El Paso tonight but expected to be there before noon tomorrow. She apologized to Betty and told her not to worry. She also left the name and number of the Hot Springs Inn.

# 3

*Saturday*

Ray arrived at Tyee's camp right on time. Scary huge fishing guides can make you very punctual. He searched the camp site area but didn't find Mr. Chino. Thinking that he might have headed down to the lake, Ray began the small hike toward the water. After going a short distance, he spotted Tyee working on getting gear into a small boat.

"Good morning, Mr. Chino." Ray waved as he called out.

"Yet to know if good morning. We will see soon."

The response wasn't warm and friendly, but compared to the day before it was a hearty welcome.

"I didn't introduce myself yesterday. I'm Ray Pacheco." No response from the guide.

Ray went on down and helped as much as he could, which was limited since he didn't know what needed to be done and Tyee wasn't saying anything.

"Are there basic things I'll need to know before we get started?" Ray asked, thinking *what the hell, might as well ask this mute mountain of a man something.* Depending on the answer he might not want to go out onto the lake with this guy.

"Yes."

Great, they just had a conversation. This wasn't going to

be easy. Ray decided that there would be conversation when Chino wanted it, so Ray should just shut up and wait.

"First will talk about boat safety. Even if you good swimmer, you wear life vest. Is small and should not bother you, but it could save your life. I not wear vest because I'm Tyee and not fall in water."

Ray was thinking the first lesson seemed to be along the lines of: *you're an idiot and I'm not.* Of course when it came to boats and fishing, maybe Ray was an idiot.

"Second we talk about equipment—what it does, how to handle, and make sure isn't damaged."

Tyee began a discussion of the various rods, lures and baits he had already stowed on the boat. His descriptions were clear and precise. After some time, Ray started to understand some of the equipment and how it was used. Tyee made it clear that types of lures and bait choices were dependent on the type of fish you were trying to catch, time of year, time of day, lake temperature, sunny or cloudy weather, personal preference, and a host of other considerations. Ray was starting to get overloaded. At first the man said nothing—now he wouldn't shut up.

"Mr. Chino, I was wondering— "

"Please call me Tyee."

"Sure, okay. Tyee, I was wondering how you can possibly remember all of the variables you just described to decide what to use?"

"Good question—uh."

"Please call me Ray."

"Ray, the more you know the better—but the best fishermen develop an instinct about what to use. Some of this is experience, some is just guess work. Some maybe magic, I'm not sure."

This would be what Ray had always called bullshit. Tyee wasn't a fishing guide, he was a magician. He was starting to regret his decision to take up fishing—maybe he should look into getting one of those big satellite dishes instead.

Tyee finished packing the boat and shoved it a little further into the water. There was a very old wooden pier that extended out about twenty-five feet into the lake which allowed them to step in the boat without having to wade into the water. That was good, because Ray hadn't brought the right shoes to go wading. Ray noticed the boat trailer up under some trees. Apparently Tyee had launched the boat by himself. It wasn't very large and probably didn't weigh that much, but it would have been fine with Ray if Tyee had asked for his help. The man was obviously self-sufficient.

The boat was a Pro Craft, with a Mercury motor. There were two tall chairs, no doubt for the fisherman to be able to cast while sitting. It crossed Ray's mind that the boat couldn't have been cheap, and he wondered where Tyee got the money. He didn't think about it for long, though—none of his business.

They settled into the boat and Tyee started the motor and headed out onto the lake. Ray had been around the lake on several occasions, and when he'd been sheriff of Dona Ana County he had assisted in law enforcement operations at the lake, but he'd never been on the lake in a boat and the perspective was totally different. They had been running for about ten minutes and weren't even close to the middle of the lake yet—it was huge.

Tyee stopped the boat close to the middle of the widest section of the lake. It suddenly became quiet. The vastness of the water was intimidating.

"We work on basics this morning. First casting—so we are in middle of lake to make it less likely you get line caught. Most fishing done along the shoreline, or areas where there're lots of hiding places under the water. There're fish here but the water much deeper and volume of water to fish not good for catching."

Made sense to Ray—more water, fewer fish, less likely to catch something. Tyee got one of the rods and began to show Ray how to hold the pole and operate the reel. Once Ray got started, he was doing pretty well for distance but doubted he could hit any sort of target. He was just happy to get it into the water.

Their first day of five hours on the water was tough but satisfying. Ray worked hard and seemed to have made a noticeable improvement by the time they called it a day at a little after noon. Once they got back to the shore, Ray helped Tyee load the boat onto the trailer and secure it tightly. He settled up with Tyee with his agreed-upon hourly rate for guidance. They seemed a little bit more comfortable with one another and even shook hands as Ray left.

Ray was beat—as in totally exhausted. This had been the most physical work he'd done in months. Being out on the water in a rocking boat and casting again and again was very tiring. And the sun had contributed to a washed out, I'm-going-to-fall-down feeling. Plus, on top of everything else, he was starving.

Ray decided to head to the Lone Post Café in downtown

T or C. He'd eaten there many times when he was sheriff in the neighboring county, and had heard from almost everyone that it served the best food in all of southern New Mexico—and he didn't disagree.

After he'd moved into the cabin, Ray had purchased a lockable upright freezer that he managed to install in one of the outbuildings on the property. It was stocked up with all kinds of food. For the last few months he'd been fixing his own meals, and thought he was a pretty good cook—but today he was in the mood for someone else to fix him a meal.

It took about fifteen minutes to get into T or C and park across the street from the Café. He didn't bother locking his old Jeep. The poor thing was a great vehicle, but it was so dog ugly that he just couldn't imagine anyone going to a lot of effort to steal it. Ray thought he and the Jeep might be a perfect match.

At about six-feet-one and just slightly on the heavy side, Ray was generally described as burly. The mustache he'd grown when he first arrived in New Mexico gave him an old west cowboy appearance. Most days he dressed in comfortable jeans, an old work shirt, and a cowboy hat. Some days he wore cowboy boots.

Ray was originally from Macon, Georgia. It's where he'd met and married his wife, Loraine, and his first years in law enforcement were spent there. He'd spent a short time with the police force in Jacksonville, Florida, before he answered an ad in a law enforcement magazine looking for a chief deputy sheriff in Las Cruces, New Mexico. Ray and his wife had debated the craziness of moving to New Mexico—the distance, the difference in cultures-- just the overall risk involved for

Ray and his family. They were both excited about the change and the opportunity for Ray to advance in his career, but still concerned about moving so far from their roots.

When the Dona Ana sheriff's office responded to Ray's resume and offered him a job, Ray and Loraine had mixed feelings. But they moved anyway, and they fell in love with Las Cruces and Dona Ana County. Loraine became active in civic matters almost at once and began to feel at home.

Ray had lost Loraine to cancer more than six years ago now, and his only son, Michael, had moved to Boston to take a job with a top notch law firm. Ray was proud of Michael, but harbored a deep resentment that he would move so far away from his home. After Ray's wife died, he didn't hear from his son very often—a phone call on major holidays was about it, and even then they didn't have much to talk about. He hadn't seen him since his wife's funeral.

Now that Ray was retired, he toyed with the idea that Michael might make a trip out to the boonies and see how he was doing—but he didn't really think it was going to happen, just like he wasn't going to Boston to visit. He wasn't exactly bitter—he understood getting involved in your work and not being able to find the time for other things, so it was okay—sort of.

Entering the Lone Post Café, Ray was overwhelmed by inviting aromas. He'd forgotten how wonderful this place always smelled. It was mostly the wonderful fragrance of green chilies—the famous Hatch, New Mexico, green chilies.

The hostess recognized Ray and seated him in one of the Café's old wooden booths, rubbed smooth by many a rear end.

"You retired didn't you, sheriff?"

"Yep, been almost six months. Moved up here to an old cabin. Just relaxing and enjoying myself." Ray could be real folksy when it suited him. The hostess said his waitress would be right with him.

A very attractive waitress in her mid-forties came over with water and a menu. "Good afternoon, my name is Sue and I'll be your waitress today; would you like iced tea or coffee?"

Obviously said hundreds of times a day. Still it seemed to Ray that there was a very special smile that went with the spiel. He liked it.

"Well hello, Sue, my name is Ray. I think I'd like some sweet iced tea."

"Good choice, Ray. I'll be right back."

Okay, he was old, not dead. He watched her walk away and enjoyed the view.

Ray ordered the Mexican lunch plate special—somewhere close to twice the amount of food he needed. He ate it all. He'd always heard that the red chili sauce was addictive and believed that was true—every so often you just needed your red chili fix. He leaned back to relax just as Sue appeared with more tea.

"Anything else today, Ray?"

"I think that has pretty well done me in for today, Sue. Guess I need the check and someplace to take a nap."

She smiled. Ray liked the smile. You never can be sure with waitresses if they're flirting or not; but Ray sure thought so.

"I don't remember seeing you in here before, Sue. Are you new?"

"Boy, I wish I was new—but mostly I'm old and tired.

As far as the Lone Post, I guess I'm new. Started about two months ago. Moved out here from Florida and before that I was in New York City. Just can't seem to find where I belong. I was driving through on the highway thinking I might stop in Albuquerque or maybe drive on to Denver when I got off at T or C looking for lunch. Decided this local place looked like it would have good food. There was a sign in the window that they were looking for a waitresses, and presto here I am." With that she gave a little curtsy.

Sue was very attractive and no doubt had some interesting history. Ray thought he should be careful. She had the look of someone who had seen some troubling times.

"Well, nice to meet you, Sue. I used to be the sheriff of Dona Ana County which is the county next door where Las Cruces is located. Retired a few months ago and moved into one of the lake cabins up here—still not all settled in, but getting closer."

"You moved up here with your family?"

"No. My wife died about six years ago and our son is an attorney in Boston—so it's just me." Ray knew she was fishing, but he didn't mind.

"Well Ray, you'll have to come back in and let me wait on you again. I'm here Tuesday through Saturday from six a.m. to four p.m. I wish you luck with your retirement."

"Thanks, Sue. I'm sure I'll see you again."

Ray left and went to his Jeep. He sat in the car a minute pondering what had just happened. He knew she had invited him to come back, but was that just for good tips or was there something going on here? Ray thought: *you crazy old man, you need to go home and take a nap.* Not prone to ignore advice from his inner voice, he went home and took a long nap—he was actually very tired.

It was getting dark when he woke. He was a little embarrassed that he'd slept that long. Being out on the lake in the sun had really taken it out of him. Something had made a noise to wake him, but he couldn't remember what it was and couldn't hear anything now. Maybe just part of a dream.

Even after that huge lunch, he was giving thought to dinner—something a little lighter would be in order. Pan-fried fish would be good with brown rice. The fish was frozen but he could thaw it some in cold water and then fry it in a little olive oil. He headed out to the barn-like outbuilding.

The cabin and the outbuildings had been abandoned for almost thirty years before the relatives of the owner had discovered the cabin. The owner's son hadn't known that his father owned the cabin and, for his own reasons, the father had ignored it for many years. Ray had purchased it from the son and learned that during part of that time an illegal drug running operation that involved the local Sierra County sheriff had used the outbuildings for storage.

The drug dealers had made significant improvements to the outbuildings, with new floors and new power lines. It made some impressive storage for Ray. He located the fish he was looking for and headed back to the cabin. As he approached, Ray caught sight of movement on the wraparound porch. He couldn't make out what it was, but was sure that it was some kind of animal. He hadn't taken his old service revolver with him to go to the outbuilding, so he was hoping that whatever it was would be more afraid of him than he was of it. Maybe it could just be scared off.

Ray approached the porch cautiously. As he got close, he heard a *thump-thump* sound, like something being hit against the wall or floor in a rhythmic beat. Even though it wasn't completely dark yet, he couldn't make out what was on the porch or if it was the source of the sound. Ray was a cautious man after spending many years in law enforcement and never invited unnecessary risk, but he didn't sense danger. Maybe this was like Tyee's magic, but Ray trusted his gut when it came to danger. He thought all people had this instinct—it was just that most lost it because they didn't use it. So with an inner signal that it was safe, he climbed the steps to the porch.

As Ray stepped onto the porch, he could hear the *thump-thump* sound very clearly. He looked down and there was a beautiful all-white dog. Could be part Labrador or some kind of sheepdog—he wasn't sure—but he could tell it was a very expensive dog and didn't belong out in the woods alone. The dog looked up at Ray and wagged its tail, beating the floor: *thump-thump, thump-thump.* Ray could have sworn the dog was smiling at him. He reached down and petted the dog and got a double time *thump-thump* in response.

Ray knew there was a problem with people letting dogs go in the countryside when they didn't want them any longer, but this dog was obviously a purebred and very valuable. Made no sense that someone would just dump him off in the woods. He got the dog some water, which was noisily appreciated. He had no dog food, but managed to find some cans of Vienna sausages that were well received. If Ray had thought the dog was smiling before, now the animal was almost laughing. He petted the dog and found him to be very friendly. When told to sit, he did. Ray walked away and told the dog to stay—he did. So the dog looked expensive, was well groomed, and had been trained. That's not an animal that shows up loose in the wilds. He would have to visit the sheriff's office tomorrow to see if anyone was looking for it.

Ray debated, but eventually decided to let the dog into the cabin. Not being an outdoor dog could mean he was at risk, being on his own in this remote setting. The dog sniffed everything for some time and finally found a comfortable place in front of the large fire and went to sleep.

Ray wasn't sure what to think about a dog just showing up. As he sat there watching, he realized that having the dog sleeping in front of the fire made him feel happy.

# 4

*Sunday*

Ray's schedule with Tyee was three times a week and no Sunday, so he wasn't fishing today. First thing he did was let the dog out. The beast ran off in something of a hurry, and Ray thought maybe he was gone for good, but about five minutes later he was back at the door, giving a small bark of request. Ray opened the door and he came in and returned to his spot in front of the fireplace and went to sleep.

After making his coffee, Ray found some more Vienna sausages—although he wasn't sure if it was really an appropriate food for dogs. He decided that there had to be some kind of resolution this morning—if the dog was staying, Ray needed to get some dog food. He went about getting ready to leave for the day.

When he headed out the door, the dog followed. He opened the back of the Jeep and the dog jumped in like he'd done it a thousand times. The old blanket in the back was perfect, and the dog nuzzled around on it and finally lay down.

Ray headed to the Sierra County sheriff's office. The county was currently without a sheriff since the last one had been arrested for drug smuggling. Ray had been involved in that matter, and no doubt the old sheriff, Hector, wasn't a fan of Ray's. He understood that they were holding a special election in a few months to find someone to take Hector's place.

Ray pulled up in front of the sheriff's office. He opened the car door and the dog jumped out and went with him. He didn't run off or appear to be dangerous, so Ray let him tag along.

"Good morning, my name is Ray Pacheco. I had a stray dog come to my cabin yesterday and I was wondering if you've had anyone looking for a dog."

"Well good morning to you, sheriff. I'd heard you were living up here now—welcome."

"Hey thanks."

"My name's Cindy. I was an intern in your office a couple of years ago when I was going to college."

"Oh, Cindy, of course. Sorry, my old brain sometimes doesn't remember much of anything. Hey, that's great. Looks like you graduated and got a job in law enforcement."

"Yes, sir. Just been here a few months and with the old sheriff having his problems things have been a little hectic."

"Yeah. I bet. Well, it's good to see you. I wish you lots of luck."

"Thanks, sheriff. About the dog—is it the one that's with you?"

"Yeah, that's him."

"He's beautiful. That can't be a stray. My goodness, his hair's in better shape than mine." Cindy was a very cute girl, probably in her early twenties. She knew she was cute and gave Ray a perky smile.

"Well, don't know about that—but he doesn't look stray to me either, so I figured someone would be looking for him."

"Nobody's been by here. We don't have animal control officers in the county anymore. Everything's run out of the sheriff's office—oh my goodness, look who I'm talking to. You already knew all of that."

"Yeah, I did. So nobody's been looking for a dog in the last few days? Sure couldn't have been lost for very long—look at him. Looks like he was brushed this morning. He sure hasn't been out in the boonies for long."

Ray gave her his address. He didn't have a phone, but gave Cindy the number at Big Jack's to call. If someone showed up looking for the dog, they could leave a message. He said his goodbyes and once again wished her the best in her career.

The dog followed right along beside Ray. When they got to the Jeep, the dog went around the back to get in. Ray was impressed—this was one smart dog. Before leaving the downtown area, Ray dropped in to the local market, Smith's Grocery, where he purchased a few things for himself and a huge bag of dog food. He told himself there was no reason to buy a small one since it was so much cheaper per serving to buy in bulk. Once he got everything into the car, the dog spent an incredible amount of time smelling the dog food bag—like he knew it was for him.

They headed back home. One of the big problems with the cabin before Ray purchased it was access. The road leading up to the area had washed out years before and the county had decided, since there was no longer anyone living in the vicinity, not to repair the road. Ray had known this, and it had helped him get something of a bargain price for the cabin. After he moved in, though, he complained to the county. One day, about a month before the dog turned up, they'd come by with heavy equipment and made some improvements. The road went from being more or less impassable to just being very bad. It felt like a major victory.

Bouncing along on the new and improved road was still a little bone-jarring, but the dog didn't seem to mind, happily hanging his head out the window. Ray unpacked everything and found bowls for the dog's food and water. His new friend was most pleased and consumed significant quantities of both, demonstrating his satisfaction with some enthusiastic tail-wagging.

Among the purchases was a dog brush. Ray went out on the porch and called "dog" to join him. He gave him a good brushing, and this time there was no doubt—the dog was smiling. Ray chuckled a little bit at how good natured he was. For someone to ditch him just didn't make sense.

"You know dog, calling you *dog* all the time doesn't seem right. You're obviously handsome, well-bred, and have good manners. You deserve a name. I think I'll call you Happy." The dog perked up. If Ray hadn't known better, he would have said he recognized his name. Happy had a new home.

# 5

*Monday*

The next day, Ray was about to head to Tyee's when he realized that he didn't know what to do with Happy. "Boy, not sure I can leave you here, but not sure I can take you with me. Damn sure you can't go on the boat—I don't think Chino would like that. So what to do?"

He decided to go by Big Jack's and see if Happy could hang out there for a few hours. He began practicing his sales pitch to Big Jack before they arrived. When Ray and Happy entered the store, Big Jack was sitting out back on the porch drinking coffee. They joined him.

"Hey what you got there Ray—looks like a show dog."

"Well, I actually think he's a stray, but a very smart, handsome stray. His name's Happy." The name got the tail to wagging super-fast. Happy went over and sniffed around on Big Jack a little and, in a big shock to Ray, seemed to find the smell okay.

"Happy just showed up at my cabin. I checked with the sheriff's office but they haven't had anyone looking for a dog, so I guess he's going to stay with me for a little while. The problem is that I have my fishing lesson with Chino today and I'm sure he wouldn't let a dog on the boat. Is there any way you could let him stay here for a few hours while I'm out on the lake?"

"Fuck no. What do I look like a fucking kennel?" The outburst resulted in spilled coffee, and the dog scurrying to the side of the building, followed by uproarious laughter from Big Jack. Ray must have been getting used to Big Jack's ways, otherwise he might have been startled.

"Sure your damn dog can stay here. What the hell. Maybe I can sell him or something." This brought new gusts of heart-threatening laughter.

Big Jack went into the store and came out with a bowl full of something foul-looking and foul-smelling and offered it to Happy, who went from happy to ecstatic. Whatever the horrible stuff was, it made Big Jack a friend for life. Ray told Happy to be a good dog and he'd be back in a few hours. Happy had found a comfortable spot on the dock and seemed content. Ray felt a tinge of something as he left—as if Happy should be more upset that Ray was leaving. He quickly erased the thought, feeling a slight tinge of embarrassment.

Big Jack was still something of a mystery to Ray. He knew the guy lived next door to the store in an old double-wide trailer that couldn't possibly meet any code requirements for an appropriate housing structure, but that seemed to fit his needs. Big Jack was fond of saying that it was a double-wide just like him. Ray had never seen inside and was sure he didn't want to. Big Jack was always at the store or in the double-wide—he never left. Guess he didn't want to.

Ray was curious about Big Jack, but since he'd only known him a few days it didn't seem polite to start asking nosy questions. Plus, all indications were that Big Jack would tell Ray to mind his own fuckin' business. He knew from past experience that a lot of the people who chose to live around the lake had histories that they preferred to keep to themselves.

The second session with Tyee was much friendlier and the time passed quickly. He showed Ray all sorts of things about combinations of lures and baits. Ray practiced more casting and listened while Tyee told him about lake maps and instruments to measure depth. Some of this tangible information was becoming more and more linked to the magic Tyee had mentioned the first day. Ray couldn't believe how many complications there were in the world of fishing.

Close to the end of their second day Ray asked Tyee how it was that he came to be at Elephant Butte. Well—wrong question.

"I'm fishing guide and damn good fishing guide. My past my business."

Any warmth Ray had been sensing must have been just the sun—the guy was still a very unpleasant companion. Ray settled the fee just like he had the first day, but Tyee didn't shake Ray's hand. He had no idea why it was such a crime to ask a man about himself, but lesson learned. Ray had also noticed that several times the stereotypical movie-Indian patter had dropped away for a moment before returning. It was apparent that there was much more to learn about his new fishing guide.

They agreed that the next lesson would be from Big Jack's dock on Tuesday. Tyee said he was going to have Ray try various tasks related to handling fish—unhooking them and such—and Big Jack always had some live fish on hand. For the first time, Ray realized he hadn't really thought about what he would do if he actually caught a fish. He wasn't squeamish by any means, but handling fish wasn't something he would seek out as a hobby.

He headed back to Big Jack's and found Happy more or less in the same spot he'd been in when Ray had left. Happy jumped up and made his day with a tremendous, joyful greeting. Ray thanked Big Jack for his help and Big Jack flashed what appeared to be a genuine smile, saying that Happy could visit him anytime he liked. Happy went over and gave Big Jack a lick—one brave dog.

# 6

*Tuesday*

Ray and Happy were at Big Jack's bright and early the next morning, and to Ray's surprise the place was doing a booming business. All this fishing stuff being new to Ray, he hadn't realized that Big Jack did almost all of his daily business in the early morning hours. People came in to get their supplies for the day, to purchase gas at the dock, and to shoot the shit with Big Jack about where the best fishing would be that day—and of course Big Jack always had an opinion.

Ray and Happy stepped around people as they squeezed through the store's tight aisles and headed out onto the dock. Ray saw Tyee working on some equipment out toward the end of the dock—he headed that way.

"You have dog now?"

The man just radiated warmth.

"Well, he's maybe just visiting—not sure. His name is Happy."

"Good name for dog."

Tyee knelt down and gave Happy a scratch behind his ears. Happy responded and decided to stay close to Tyee in case the man decided to rub him again. Tyee smiled. Well—that might just be a first.

Tyee began showing Ray various items that should be in any tackle box. He pulled out a few things, explaining how they were used. This went on for some time. Happy had found a quiet corner of the dock and went to sleep—a primary dog function.

"Hey Ray. You've got a call from the sheriff's office." That was Big Jack yelling from the store's back door.

"Be back in just a minute." Tyee may have grunted something, but Ray wasn't sure.

"Hello, this is Ray Pacheco."

"Hello, sheriff, this is Cindy at the Sierra County sheriff's office."

"Well hello, Cindy. Did something happen about the dog?"

"Sort of—Deputy Martinez was wondering if you could come by the office as soon as possible. He'd like to talk to you."

"Well sure. I'm kind of in the middle of something how about in a couple of hours—would that be okay?"

"I guess so, Sheriff Pacheco. I think the deputy was pretty anxious to see you, but I'll tell him it will be a couple of hours." She hung up. Some of her perkiness was missing today.

Ray walked back out to where Tyee was still working. He no doubt had a concerned look on his face as he tried to figure out what the call was about.

"You look worried Ray. Problem?"

"Well not sure, could be or could be nothing. When Happy showed up at my cabin I could see he wasn't an ordinary stray and the next day, yesterday, I went to the sheriff's office and filed a report in case someone was looking for him. That was Cindy at the sheriff's office saying Deputy Martinez wants to see me ASAP. It could be about the dog, but she didn't say. So maybe I should postpone our session today. Of course I'll pay you for the hours we were planning today."

"No need to pay out for nothing. I will go with you. See what they want."

Ray wasn't sure what to think about that—being nosy was one thing he never would have guessed about Tyee Chino.

"Sure come along."

They picked up all of the equipment and stored it back in Tyee's boat. Tyee didn't have a car, according to Big Jack, but could get most places with his boat and a little walking. They got into Ray's Jeep with Happy in the back and headed towards T or C.

"You know Deputy Martinez is an asshole?"

An actual conversation with Tyee? Ray wasn't sure how to respond. "Actually Tyee, I've only met Deputy Martinez once and that was some time ago. I don't really remember much about him. He was kind of Hector's assistant wasn't he?"

"Martinez was more like a lackey. Sheriff Hector Hermes was a drug dealing useless human being and Martinez was his trainee. Every bad thing the old sheriff was back then, Martinez is now, plus some new ones. Starting with him being the mayor's son. The only reason he was ever hired was that his dad, no doubt, had something on Sheriff Hermes. These backward people run this little town like it's their own little fiefdom."

What in the world was this? Tyee speaking in full sentences with nouns, verbs, and everything. What happened to the fishing guide speak?

"Tyee, what happened to your old way of speaking?"

"Most of that's an act. Some of it's just me being lazy.

Before life kicked me in the gut I graduated from UNM with a degree in computer science and a second major in English Lit. Then things started going bad for me—bad marriage to a good person—and suddenly I was a drunk. I'm still a drunk. But now I'm a fishing guide competing for tourist business and the man-of-few-words Indian act is a good front. Everybody knows Indians know everything about fishing, hunting, tracking—you know, all that Indian stuff. And a drunk Indian speaking in a monosyllabic way—it just fit right into everyone's narrow perception of what an Indian fishing guide should be. I mostly just use it on tourists and the occasional asshole. And I don't mean you're an asshole, Ray. I thought you were a tourist since Big Jack sent you."

Ray looked over at Tyee and it was like he was seeing a different person. He laughed. "Well, that's something. I'm not sure I like this turn of events. I'd grown real fond of your Hollywood Indian ways."

"Don't worry, Ray. It's still there when it's needed—it's become part of who I am. But I have to be careful—if some of my relatives from the rez saw my act they just might shoot me."

"Well I guess that means Big Jack knows all about this charade?"

"Listen, the whole Big Jack persona is complete bullshit. Big Jack used to be a lawyer in L.A. Had his own drinking demons, along with women problems, and he was disbarred or something. Pulled up stakes and headed east. Stopped here for god knows what reason and stumbled into Big Jack's place. Apparently he left L.A. with a pile of money—he offered the real Big Jack more money than the place was worth and presto he was suddenly Big Jack—never to be found by ex-wives or the IRS."

"Fucking amazing. That's hard to believe. He's the perfect Big Jack and it's all made up. I'll be damned, I seem to be the only person who really is who they say they are." This caused Ray to start a deep, genuine laugh—then Tyee joined in, and then Happy wagged his tail even harder.

"So who is Big Jack really?"

"No can tell, swore secrecy."

This generated another round of laughter. Ray felt like he was part of a conspiracy—or maybe it was a family.

They pulled into the parking lot at the sheriff's office.

"Hey Cindy. I got away a little early. Is Deputy Martinez available?"

"Oh hello, sheriff. Let me see." Cindy seemed uneasy. She picked up the phone and pushed a button, then said something into the phone that Ray couldn't hear.

"Sheriff said he'll be with you in just a minute."

"Thanks, Cindy."

"In just a minute" turned out to be more like twenty minutes. Ray was annoyed because this felt like one-upmanship on Martinez's part. He hated these kinds of games. He knew it went on in almost every human encounter, but it was still a waste of time and energy.

Martinez entered the room like he was running for political office and was there to greet voters: big smile, big handshake, big phony.

"Good morning sheriff. Glad you could come down and visit." They shook hands, and Ray introduced Tyee. Martinez didn't shake Tyee's hand.

"The Indian can wait out here."

"Tyee is with me. If you don't want to meet with us, we'll leave." This was said in a voice that would make it clear to anyone, even a jerk like Martinez, that there was no room for discussion.

Martinez looked at Ray, then at Tyee. There was a dull look in his eyes, as if he didn't really understand what was going on.

"Yeah, well come on back to my office." He showed Ray and Tyee, along with Happy, into his small, cluttered office.

"So this must be the dog you found."

"Probably more accurate to say he found me. Showed up in the evening three days ago. Let's see—that would have been Saturday evening."

Martinez continued, "We believe the dog belongs to a woman who was staying at the Hot Springs Inn Friday night. She apparently went missing on Saturday. The Inn called in a missing person report Saturday morning, but for some reason nothing was done until her ex-husband and the El Paso police called on Monday looking for information about her. Any chance you happen to know this woman, Monica Jackson?"

"Nope. Never heard of her. Was her car still at the Inn?"

"I'll ask the questions, Mr. Pacheco."

Okay, ask away asshole. Ray knew this guy was a jerk and probably didn't have a clue about how to investigate a missing person, but he just shut up anyway and waited.

"Look Sheriff Pacheco, I didn't mean to be rude. Her car was at the Firestone store getting some new tires. That's why she was staying at the Inn—they had to have the tires brought up from El Paso. No doubt for some reason her dog was let out in your area on Saturday, the day she disappeared. We probably should have been on top of this earlier but one of my deputies, and Cindy out front, dropped the ball. At this point we have no evidence as to what happened with her, so we're just asking questions to see if anything turns up."

"Well, Deputy, I don't know anything except what I've told you. Are you going to take the dog until this is resolved?"

"Actually, if you're willing, it might be best if you could keep him until we either find the owner or have someone show up wanting to take possession—is that agreeable to you?"

"Sure, I suppose that's okay with me." Ray stood to leave. Martinez didn't seem to be done.

"Since you're living up here now, maybe you know we're having a special election for sheriff—just wanted to make sure you knew I was running. It would be great to have your vote and support." This was accompanied by what appeared to be a practiced smile that by all appearances was painful for Martinez to use.

"I'd heard about the special election but I'm not real familiar with the candidates. I'll look into it and see who should get my support. Thanks for your time, Deputy."

Ray had previously had no interest in who became sheriff of Sierra County, but he did now—pretty much anyone but this guy. As they left, he could tell that Cindy had been crying—no doubt after a good reprimand by Martinez. Ray guessed it was because she'd failed to create a report about Ray reporting the dog he had found. While he felt sorry for Cindy, having to deal with such a pompous ass, it was one of the basics of law enforcement to make sure information was reported and shared.

As they neared the Jeep another Deputy approached Ray.

"Hi, I'm Deputy Clayton. I know you've been in talking to

Deputy Martinez about the Jackson woman and I just wanted to let you know that I met the woman and there was a threat made against her on Friday."

"Deputy Clayton, nice to meet you. Actually, weren't you part of a joint task force between Sierra and Dona Ana counties a few years ago?"

"Yeah, I was Sheriff Pacheco. I really learned a lot on that task force."

"I'd ask you what's going on but I have a feeling Deputy Martinez wouldn't like you talking to me."

"No, he wouldn't. But I don't give a shit what he likes. I'm running against him for the sheriff's job. In a month or so I'm either the sheriff—not very likely—or I'm fired, which is way more likely. He can't fire me now because it's against county ordinances as long as I'm his opponent. But I'm gone as soon as he's elected. So I'm more than pleased to talk to you about this matter with Ms. Jackson."

"You sound a little defeatist about the election—is Martinez that popular?"

"Not with anyone who works with him—he's one-hundred percent asshole, maybe even a little more. Has been since he became a deputy. Sheriff Hermes ignored all of the complaints about Martinez because his father's the mayor. That's also why I have no hope of being elected sheriff—his father has all of the political pull and influence to convince people to elect his son—and those people don't want to make an enemy of the mayor."

"Should go after people vote. Let assholes vote for asshole." This was Tyee in his most Indian-wisdom-conquers-all manner.

"Deputy, this is my friend Tyee Chino." There was a slight smile when Ray described Tyee as his friend.

The Deputy nodded towards Tyee. "What do you mean people vote?"

"Lots of people live around the lake and not in T or C who are eligible to vote for county sheriff and don't care about small town politics—my guess is that they outnumber townspeople about three to one—if me, I would seek that vote."

The deputy was obviously open to suggestions. They stood around and talked some more about the election. Ray was wondering how he could help this young deputy defeat Martinez.

"Deputy, would you be available to meet this evening at Big Jack's to talk about strategy for your election?"

"My god, sheriff, does that mean you'd help me?"

"That's exactly what it means."

They agreed to meet at eight at Big Jack's. Now Ray just had to tell Big Jack about the meeting—the one that would be at *his* place.

"Deputy, you mentioned earlier that the Jackson woman had been threatened—what was that about?" Ray asked.

Clayton told Ray everything he knew, including the contents of the threatening note. He said the woman hadn't seemed all that worried and had assumed it was some kind of mistake. Clayton's impression was the exact opposite: he thought the note and the tire slashing were definitely directed at Ms. Jackson. The deputy also thought that whoever left the note and slashed her tires was behind her disappearance, but he said that Martinez had basically instructed everyone to just drop it unless something new happened.

Clayton told Ray that Jackson's car was still at the Firestone store and that her belongings had been left in her room at the Inn. No one at the Inn had seen anything suspicious Friday or Saturday. She was supposed to get her car that morning and the Inn staff was going to drive her to the Firestone store. Around nine they had called her room and there was no answer. They waited until about 9:30 to try again—then got worried when she didn't answer. They opened her room and discovered she was gone.

The Inn called the sheriff's office and Clayton had gone there to investigate. He'd found nothing—no evidence of a forced entry or a struggle—she was just gone.

"Thanks, Deputy. Sounds like there are a lot of loose ends on this case. Guess your sheriff isn't going to do much of anything except blame other people for screwing up. If you can do it without getting in trouble, keep me informed."

Ray and Tyee headed back to the car.

"Do you think we can help Clayton become sheriff?" Ray asked Tyee.

"I do, Ray. Obviously you have all of the experience of running for sheriff, you know what he should talk about in meetings and things like that. What I can do is get a list of all of the eligible voters in the county. Then we can figure out how to meet with as many of them as possible and ask for their vote."

"How can you get a list of voters?"

"Couple of ways. One, public information is available as to who's registered—so we can request that. I think the big thing is that we need to get people to register who haven't before. That information we'll have to resource ourselves. I've got some computers and modems that are still functional-- if I can hook them up, maybe in a back room at Big Jack's with access to his phone line—I think you might be amazed at what I can uncover."

"I seem to remember that the turn-out for Sierra County elections was incredibly small. I bet the election's decided by fewer than a couple hundred votes. If we could get some of the non-town county citizens to become active Clayton might win in a landslide." Ray was getting excited.

Big Jack was excited, too. He allowed how he'd love to beat that asshole Martinez and his crooked old man. He agreed that his store could be campaign headquarters and Tyee could hook up anything he wanted. Clayton showed up and was impressed with the ideas and plans that Ray, Tyee, and Big Jack had devised. Time was short, so they agreed to meet again on Thursday evening.

# 7

*Wednesday*

Ray woke up energized. The discussion of the election and the possibility of putting a good guy in office instead of a jerk made his blood flow a little faster. He wasn't a do-gooder, he was a practical man and thought people should mostly be allowed to do as they saw fit—unless, of course, it harmed other people. People like the Martinez family, who used cronyism to make other people miserable, got Ray fired up.

Ray let Happy out for his morning business. He was sure that once something was discovered about Ms. Jackson's disappearance that someone would be along to claim the dog. It had only been a few days, but he had to admit he was going to miss him. He wouldn't get anywhere worrying about what might happen, though, so he concentrated on what he could do to maybe unravel the mystery of Ms. Jackson. After getting dressed, he decided he would go visit the Hot Springs Inn. He doubted much would come of it, but maybe there would be something he could learn.

Happy took his now familiar spot in the back of the Jeep and went to sleep. Ray hadn't been around many dogs, and he was astounded by the number of little naps they took during the day. As he approached the Inn, he recalled a few visits he and his wife had made to enjoy the healing waters. He liked the place a lot and was somewhat surprised that they were not doing better business. There were very few cars in the lot.

Ray entered and went to the registration desk.

"Hello sir, may I help you?"

"Hi. My name is Ray Pacheco—used to be sheriff down in Dona Ana County."

"Well sure, sheriff, I remember you. You and your wife have stayed with us a couple times. Nice to see you."

"Thanks—we always enjoyed our stays here. I'm no longer sheriff, I retired, so this maybe a little out of line. I was wondering if I could ask you some questions about Ms. Jackson, the lady that disappeared."

"It's great with me. Our sheriff has decided to do nothing, apparently. What can I tell you?"

"Just tell me what you know about her checking in and if you saw her at all after that."

"She was a very nice lady and she had a dog—wait a minute, that's the same dog with you."

"Yes, somehow the dog was let go or something up in a remote area of the lake where I have a cabin. That's one of the reasons I have an interest in finding Ms. Jackson—returning her dog." Not completely true, but close enough.

"My gracious, that sounds ominous. Anyway, she just checked in—nothing abnormal at all. Asked if we could give her a ride in the morning back to her car, which was being worked on at the Firestone store. We made arrangements for her to leave about nine the next morning and we would drive her to the store. I don't believe anyone at the hotel saw her again—I know I didn't. I called her room in the morning about nine and didn't get an answer. I thought maybe she was still in the bathroom, so I waited a while and then called again about 9:30—still no answer. At that point I got worried that something was wrong. I was thinking maybe she was ill or something, so I decided to go and check. I knocked but she didn't answer. I'm always reluctant to just go into a room, but I thought there must be something wrong so I used my key. Everything looked normal except that she wasn't there. The things she had with her when she checked in were still in the room. At that point I called the sheriff's office."

"Had the bed been slept in?"

"Yes, the covers were pulled back and it did look like someone had slept in the bed."

"Does the room have an exit other than the front door?"

"It does. Those rooms along that section all have sliding doors that take you out to an area that has outdoor spas."

"Was that door open or shut."

The manager paused a bit as he thought.

"Now that you ask, I believe that door was open a few inches—she could've gone out that way."

"Did she make or receive any phone calls?"

"The first deputy, Clayton, I think was his name, asked me that question. So I looked, and she did make three phone calls, and looks like she received two."

"Do you have the numbers?"

"Only on the out calls. We currently don't capture the phone number of someone calling in."

The manager gave Ray the two numbers Ms. Jackson called, indicating that she had called one number twice. Ray thanked him for his trouble and wondered if it was okay if he looked into the room. The manager gave him the room number and then walked down the hall and opened the door for him. He told Ray to just shut the door when he was finished. Ray examined the room, but there was nothing he could see. As he was leaving, though, he noticed something sticking out from under the bed. Reaching down, he put it into his pocket— probably nothing, but it was more than he had before.

He went out back and looked at the area just outside the room, then walked around the area that had the spas. He could see that they hadn't been used in a while. Heading back toward the parking lot, he noticed a groundskeeper working on a flower bed at the corner of the building.

"Good morning."

"Morning, sir."

"Don't mean to interrupt your work. I'm looking into the matter with the woman who went missing and I was wondering if you saw anything last Friday or Saturday that might help me?"

"I heard about the missing person. Really strange—nothing like that ever happens around here. I think I did see that lady very early Saturday morning. She had her dog with her and was walking along the north path. I'd come in around five that morning because I was going to dig up another flower bed and wanted to leave early in the day, so I'd guess this was about five fifteen or so. That path goes up over that little rise and then back down next to the parking lot. Didn't think anything about it because she was walking her dog, so I went back to my truck and got some more soil and continued to work. I didn't see her come back. Figured she had already gone back in while I was out to the truck."

"Did you happen to notice if the sliding door was open or shut?"

"No, I don't remember looking over that way at all. I finished up that bed and then moved around to the other side of the building."

"Hear any cars or anything at that time?"

"No. Didn't hear or see anything else."

"Okay thanks, you've been helpful."

So she could've taken the dog for his morning walk, someone was waiting for her and forced them both into a vehicle. While a little farfetched, it was reasonable that she'd be out with the dog fairly early in the morning—Ray had already seen the demands of that schedule. If someone knew she was staying there, waiting for her outside in the wee hours of the morning would be a perfect opportunity for something. Still didn't know what—but at least it helped to create an outline of what might've happened.

Ray looked around the parking lot, especially the area along the north path. There was nothing unusual that he could see. He did notice that there were security cameras in the parking lot. He went back in and asked the manager about the cameras and learned that they were dummies—a cheap security measure designed to scare off the completely stupid.

The paper Ray had found under the bed seemed to be a partial phone number. Not much help. He was becoming increasingly convinced that Ms. Jackson and her dog had been kidnapped Saturday morning. The kidnappers must have headed out toward the lake, for reasons that Ray couldn't yet guess at, and the dog escaped, or he was let go in the hope he wouldn't survive. So did that mean Ms. Jackson had been killed and dumped or buried in the same area? He had no idea, also had no idea how to find out. Beginning to look like a dead end. Martinez's dumb-headed plan of doing nothing unless something happened might actually be the only plan available. But he wouldn't accept that—there had to be other options.

Ray decided to stop by Big Jack's on his way home. He found the proprietor out on the dock with a beer and his infamous unlit cigar, more or less asleep. As he walked up, Big Jack stirred, took a sip of his no-doubt warm beer, and welcomed his visitors. Happy returned the greeting with licking and tail wagging. Since this was obviously Big Jack's afternoon slow period, Ray decided to fill him in on the missing woman's story.

Ray laid out everything he knew and offered his speculation. The big question was: is she still alive? And if so, where is she?

"My guess is she's dead. The note and the slashed tires—as the deputy pointed out, those are acts of aggression. While most people don't recognize it, it's not a huge step from that kind of aggression to actually committing murder—especially if it's based on hatred. The note suggests it's someone who hates her for some real or imagined injuries that the missing lady caused this person. People with that much hate can't hold it for long—they'll want to hurt the person who's the focus of all that emotion. Regarding the dog apparently being let go, my guess is that this person could kill the woman, but couldn't bring himself to harm the dog."

Big Jack knew his stuff. Ray agreed completely. "That suggests that it's someone she knows. It's probably someone who has a similar connection with dogs—probably someone involved in the dog show or the dog breeding business."

"Most murders are committed by someone you know or your relatives—usually the relatives. That's why I stay far, far away from all of my relatives."

"Maybe your relatives are avoiding you?"

"Now, you're just getting nasty Ray."

"Sorry, didn't know you were so sensitive. I think you're right, though. She's buried somewhere up around my cabin and the dog escaped or was let go when the deed was done. Whoever did it has had more or less four days to disappear and could be in a foreign country by now, or back home in Cleveland. Who the hell knows?"

Ray and Happy headed home. He didn't like the conclusion, but he'd be astounded if he discovered that it wasn't right. Of course Ray had been astounded a lot in his career—people often did the unexpected.

# 8

*Thursday*

Ray was meeting Tyee at Big Jack's dock so they could have a lesson out on the lake. He was somewhat nervous about actually catching a fish. Their previous lesson had been intended to cover aspects of handling the fish, removing the hook, and other things Ray didn't know how to do, but it had been postponed when they cut the lesson short that day. He could only hope he didn't catch anything too big.

Walking around the side of Big Jack's store, Ray saw Tyee out on the dock getting everything ready. It was shocking to Ray how his impression of Tyee had changed over just a few days. While Tyee still called himself a drunk, other than at their first encounter Ray hadn't seen Tyee drinking at all. And now he had to absorb the fact that Tyee had a computer science degree and an English Lit degree. He wasn't even real sure what an English Lit degree was. Despite everything that was going on, Ray felt like he had discovered a unique person whom he wanted to get to know better.

"Guess I'm ready to actually catch a fish, I think?"

"Good thing fish can't hear you, you sound scared of fish—not good for macho fisherman to be scared of fish."

"Well, Tyee. You've taught me a bunch of things I want to

try out, see if I can catch something. Also my macho ego isn't as large as some, so I say *watch out fish here I come!*"

"Good save, sheriff. I believe you are starting to pick up on this fishing stuff."

They loaded the remaining gear and headed out onto the lake. It was a cool morning, slightly overcast, and Tyee said this could be a good day for fishing. He went over the map of the lake with Ray and explained various reasons why one area would be better than another, based on depth and the shape of the shoreline. Tyee pulled them into a cove and killed the motor.

Ray got his gear ready and took one of the casting seats. He had to admit he was a little excited. Surprisingly, as he started casting and concentrating on what he was doing, he experienced an unusual calmness and sense of well-being. Tyee said very little as they each went about their tasks.

Within about thirty minutes, Ray got a strike. Tyee immediately pulled his own line in and started giving Ray instructions. It appeared to be a large fish and Ray was absolutely amazed at its power. He was using all his strength trying to reel the fish in as Tyee reminded him to let the line out and let the fish tire out. With much prodding from Tyee, he started to get the feel for reeling in and then letting the fish run. After what was probably a short time, but felt like hours, the fish began to tire. Tyee got a net and approached the side of the boat. Ray continued to reel the fish closer. Tyee reached out with the net and, with obvious skill, scooped the fish into the boat. The fish seemed huge. Tyee said it was a medium size bass, but still one hell of a catch. Tyee showed him how to hold the fish and release the hook. Then he gave the fish to Ray to hold while he took a picture, after which Ray released the fish back into the lake. Ray was exhausted, thrilled, and hooked on fishing.

They had little luck the rest of the morning and decided to call it a day. Tyee aimed the boat back toward Big Jack's.

"Tyee, I want to thank you for teaching me fishing and helping me understand the beauty of these skills. I'd never have guessed this would be something that would give me so much pleasure. Thanks again—it means a lot to me."

"Hey, satisfied customer testimonial. Must get this in writing."

Both men sat back and enjoyed the boat ride. It was a pleasant afternoon with more sunshine than there had been in the morning. The breeze from the movement of the boat, and the warmth of the sun, gave the experience a comforting quality—it was easy just to live the moment, smile, and say nothing. When they reached the dock, Tyee jumped out and secured the boat.

"Something I'd been meaning to ask you Tyee. You know I'm kind of poking around looking for evidence or information regarding the missing lady, Ms. Jackson. I have some phone numbers and a partial number, and I was wondering if you could help to try and identify who the numbers belong to."

"Sure, no problem. Sometimes that can be easy, and of course sometimes it just can't be done. Do you have the numbers with you?"

Ray handed Tyee a piece of paper that had the two outgoing calls numbers written on it and told him that the Inn knew that Ms. Jackson had also received two calls but that their system didn't capture those numbers. However, when he'd been searching Ms. Jackson room he'd found a torn piece of paper that seemed to have a portion of a phone number written on it. He wasn't sure if this was related to Jackson or not.

"I just about have my computer systems up and running in Big Jack's storeroom. I'll do some research on these numbers this afternoon. Also should have some information on resident lists for the campaign at tonight's meeting."

Ray said that sounded good. They went into the store and related Ray's fishing experience to Big Jack. It was hard to tell who looked the proudest Ray or Tyee. Big Jack said maybe he should sponsor Ray in the annual fishing competition on the lake. At first they all laughed, but after a moment's thought they decided that maybe it was actually a good idea.

Tyee went to work in his computer lair and Ray, along with Happy, headed home.

As Ray approached his cabin he could see a car in the driveway, possibly the first time anyone had driven to the cabin since he'd moved in except for Ray himself. The condition of the access road was terrible, and unless you had a good map it was hard to find the entrance. He pulled in and parked next to the car. As he got out of his Jeep, a man got out of the car and waved.

"Hello, you must be Ray Pacheco. Sorry to just drop in on you, but they said you didn't have a phone. My name's Mike Jackson, from Albuquerque. I'm the ex-husband of Monica Jackson—the lady who disappeared from the Hot Springs Inn."

"Hello, Mr. Jackson. I'm Ray Pacheco, and dropping in is just fine. Sorry about the condition of the roads, but this is a remote part of the county and they don't get a lot upkeep. How can I help you?" Ray was concerned about the man—he looked very tired, or possibly ill.

"Please call me Mike."

"Okay Mike, and call me Ray."

About this time, Happy came up and greeted Mike like a long lost friend. Mike was pleased to see Happy, too, and gave him a good rubdown, which prompted a great deal of tail wagging.

"It's great that Bruce is looking so good. They told me at the sheriff's office that you had him. This is wonderful, I was so worried about him." Greeting the dog had added much-needed energy to Mike's demeanor.

"Are you here to get the dog?"

"I don't think so, Ray. Mostly I'm here to ask for your help. I called the sheriff's office numerous times and talked to Sheriff Martinez several times. To be blunt, I don't think they know what they're doing. The sheriff has even gotten to the point of telling me not to call anymore. Well, at that point I decided to head down here and see what the hell was going on. I met with the sheriff this morning and he as much as told me that I was wasting his time and if I didn't like it, tough shit. He's one rude person."

"Yeah, I'm afraid our sheriff's in over his head a little. But Mike I have to tell you I'm not real sure what he could do— other than be more polite."

"I kind of guessed that—even though he was being all self-important what I sensed was that they didn't have any leads and didn't know what to do next. Well, I had a chance to chat with Deputy Clayton, who seems like a very nice young man, and he said he thought my best hope of finding something was you."

"Not sure about that, Mike. I guess someone told you my story. The ex-sheriff from Dona Ana County who moved up here some months ago to retire. I have absolutely no authority to interfere with the sheriff's investigation and no desire to do so. I was curious to some extent because of the dog, so I stepped into the fire a little and asked some questions. But it's the sheriff who has the responsibility and the authority to find out what happened to your ex-wife."

"Look Ray, I can see the political mine fields lying all around here. And of course I don't care—all I want is to find my ex-wife and make sure she's okay. We're divorced, but we're good friends and I'm terribly worried about her. Is there any way I could hire you to conduct a private investigation with me as your client. I don't have tons of money, but I can afford to pay for a few weeks of investigation if you'll do that."

"Mike, I'm just a private citizen. I'm not a private investigator. Plus, I've already butted heads with the sheriff—he wouldn't cooperate with me now no matter how I approached him. I think your best bet might be to contact the El Paso police department and see if you could get them interested."

"I have called them, and they said there was no evidence that Monica was in El Paso. Everything they had learned said she disappeared from T or C and I should contact the sheriff there."

"Well, I sure understand your frustration with the sheriff. One of the hardest parts of being in law enforcement is dealing with the families and their concerns. Many times there are no answers and that can be very difficult to accept."

"Well, Ray, you know that as much as anything else you

want the people in charge to show that they care. I'm afraid the T or C sheriff's office hasn't done a very good job of that."

"I know it's very difficult." Ray filled Mike in on what he'd learned and what he suspected might have happened, with someone taking Monica and the dog from the parking lot in the early hours Saturday morning. He feared that the dog had escaped in the area of his cabin when something happened—either an accident or maybe murder—although he had no evidence apart from the fact that Happy, or Bruce, had showed up at his cabin.

Ray showed Mike into the cabin and fixed some coffee. Mike was obviously dealing with some health problems and almost fell into the chair. They drank their coffee and continued to talk about what might have happened to Monica. The afternoon wore on, and Mike gave no indication of leaving.

"Mike, I've got a meeting I'm going to in an hour or so. Would you like to stay here this evening? There's an extra bedroom and it wouldn't be a problem for me. You're looking a little tired and I thought it might be difficult getting back to T or C in the dark. What do you say?"

"Oh, thanks Ray. That's so kind. I am a bit tired. My health hasn't been real good lately and I tire so easily. I don't want to be a burden, but at this point I'm not sure I could drive back, so thank you very much. By the way, you asked if I was here about the dog. If Monica was here, I bet she'd ask you to keep him if you wanted to, and I'd offer him to you as part of your fee if you decide to discover what happened to Monica."

Ray showed Mike the spare room and the extra bathroom, told him to make himself at home, and said he'd leave Happy there while he went out for a little while. Regarding his taking on the investigation, he told Mike that he would think about it and they could talk again. Ray made sure Mike was comfortable and secure, then headed to Big Jack's.

The meeting of the Clayton campaign was attended by Deputy Clayton and his wife, Ann, Cindy from the office, her boyfriend Sam, Tyler Boyd, who was a clerk in the mayor's office, Ray, Tyee, and Big Jack. Clayton made a few remarks about how much he appreciated everyone trying to help. Ray stood after Clayton and spelled out the challenge. It boiled down to getting people who weren't usually involved in county politics to register and vote. The plan was simple. Tyee would identify people who were registered, as well as residents who hadn't registered. They would hold meetings for the non-registered residents and try to get them to register. Ray went on to explain that the approach that he thought would work best for Clayton would be straight talk about the nepotism and cronyism that existed between the sheriff's office and the mayor's office. Clayton would spell out the things he would do differently to run an honest sheriff's department that would treat everyone equally. No one cheered, but there was a lot of head nodding—it looked like a consensus.

Tyee stood up and, in a commanding voice, explained how he had developed the lists and how he thought they should be used. He thought it would be better to have more meetings with fewer people as opposed to large events. Everyone seemed to agree. The lists were divided up, and everyone went to work trying to develop the ideal list of people to invite to the meetings. They ended up with twenty-two lists of about 150 people. Their plan became clearer with the goal of having twenty-two events, inviting the 150 people from the lists. They decided that Big Jack would host eleven meetings and Ray would host eleven. As they worked into the night, the overall strategy started to take shape. They would need materials to hand out, and people to do a solicitation campaign by telephone and door-to-door. The entire group became energized, with people suggesting others who they thought would want to join to help organize the meetings. Big Jack suggested that some of the meetings should be barbeques, and everyone was enthusiastic in theory, but it was clear that it was going to cost a lot. Big Jack said fuck the cost, he would pay, and on that profane and uplifting note the meeting was adjourned.

As the group was breaking up, Tyee signaled to Ray that they should talk.

"Thought the meeting went well. Really looking forward to seeing if we can make a difference. Just wanted to let you know that two of the Ms. Jackson's numbers were fairly easy to identify. One was her ex-husband in Albuquerque—a guy named Mike Jackson. The other was to the Camino Real El Paso Hotel. I checked it out and found that was where the dog show was held. I can't tell if she called someone in particular or just called the hotel. The other partial number I'm still working on."

"Let me tell you something Tyee. The stuff you've put together for Clayton is terrific. I have no idea if we can change anything or not, but I'm happy that we're trying. The call to Mike Jackson doesn't surprise me. He's actually at my cabin as we speak. Just showed up out of the blue wondering if he could hire me to find his ex-wife. They're apparently good friends and he's very worried. I'll need to ask him about the call, but I'd say he's not a suspect. The other one I'll follow up on and see what I can learn."

"Did her ex-husband hire you?"

"I said no. Mostly because I'm not sure what he'd hire me as—a PI, or just some guy checking stuff out? Plus, I've got fishing duties to fulfill."

Ray said his goodbyes and headed out. He thought about all of the things that were going on in his world and started to chuckle. This wasn't how he'd envisioned retirement in the backwoods.

# 9

*Friday*

Ray and Mike enjoyed a simple breakfast of coffee with toast and Welch's grape jelly. Why the simple things tasted the best wasn't a mystery to Ray—they just *were* the best—no mystery.

At this point in the morning Ray hadn't planned his day. He wasn't fishing today, so it felt like he should do something to help learn more about Monica's disappearance. He was reluctant to bring that up with Mike because he was concerned that Mike might take it as an implied agreement to be hired as an investigator. "Ray, I want to thank you for your hospitality last night. It was very kind—not sure I could've made it back to town. I was exhausted. This morning I feel much better. I think I'll head back to Albuquerque today so I can check on the rest of Monica's dogs. Our oldest son was supposed to have done that yesterday and today, but sometimes he's not very reliable." Mike had a pained expression on his face when as he talked about his oldest son.

"Also Ray, if there's any way you could help with this matter with Monica, it would be great. I know this isn't your business and there's no particular reason for you to do it, but I have nowhere else to turn. If you don't push this, I think the sheriff will just let it drop."

"Mike, I think it's good that you head back to Albuquerque. You're just going to wear yourself out waiting around here for something to happen. I'm going to look into this for my own reasons. Not ready to be hired as a PI for many reasons, so let's just say I'll do this based on our new friendship."

Ray could see that his words had an emotional impact on Mike.

"That's wonderful Ray. I really appreciate it—you really don't know how much." He seemed on the verge of tears.

Ray needed to change the subject before he broke down too. He said that Mike should get his stuff together and get on the road before the day got too old. They shook hands, and both men seem pleased to have found a new friend. After Mike packed and gave Happy a good rub, he headed toward his car.

"If anything comes up, you have my contact information. I also left information on two of my sons who are living in Albuquerque, it's on your kitchen table. If something does happen and you aren't able to get ahold of me, please give them a call. Thanks again, Ray, for everything."

Mike got into his car and started the bumpy ride down the so-called road.

Ray decided to head over to Big Jack's with Happy and see if Tyee was around or if anything was going on in general. When he pulled up in front of the store, he was surprised to see a lot of cars. It was almost noon and this usually wasn't a very busy time for Big Jack. Ray went into the store and could see several people milling about. He didn't see Big Jack or Tyee. He looked out back and still didn't see them. One of the people who'd been standing around came over.

"Are you a local?"

Ray was about to say no—when he realized he was. "Yes, sir. My name is Ray. Is there something I could help you with?"

"Well, we've been here quite a while and nobody's shown up to help us. Just wondering if maybe this is some sort of crazy honor system or something?"

"Pretty sure Big Jack hasn't implemented an honor system. Let me look in the back, maybe he got busy on something and just lost track of time. If I can't find him I'll come back and help you myself." Although Ray wasn't sure he knew how the antique cash register worked, he figured he needed to reassure the customer. He let Happy out onto the dock so he could find his favorite spot and begin his afternoon nap, then headed to the only place Big Jack and Tyee could be: the new computer room. Ray opened the door and saw them both, engrossed in something on the computer screen.

"Big Jack, you've got a store full of customers who are threatening to clean the place out."

Big Jack looked up with a smile. "Doubt very much anyone could clean out that store, at least not anytime soon. Thanks Ray, guess I lost track of time. I'll go out and see how I can help them."

"What was so interesting on the computer?"

"Just confirmation of what we were saying about the numbers. There are almost three times the number of non-townspeople to townspeople. I think this gives Clayton a very good chance of winning. Also we were wondering if we could get enough invites out to have a barbeque on Sunday. What do you think—free food and beer on Sunday afternoon?"

"That's pretty quick. But free beer ought to have some appeal, so why not? I guess we'd need to invite 300 or so people to get a good number who actually show up. Have some ideas on a flyer or something we can hand out?"

Tyee said he had worked up a simple flyer and thought they should concentrate their distribution on the lake area. They could pass them out and then have the people talk to their neighbors about it. Ray looked at the flyer and was impressed with Tyee's skills once again. They talked about calling Clayton and getting some more people to hand them out the next day.

"What's going on out there in the store—you said there were customers?"

"Yeah, surprised me. When I showed up there were three cars out front and maybe ten or more people in the store. They're not local, so not sure what it was about."

Ray and Tyee went into the store and found there were now even more customers than before. Big Jack was smiling and ringing up sales on the old cash register. When he had a break, he joined Ray and Tyee.

"Seems there was an article in the El Paso paper about the fishing tournament week after next. These people were in El Paso on some kind of church mission, saw the article, and decided to come up and see the lake. They didn't know there was such a large lake in New Mexico. Anyway, just a freakish thing. Normally we only get about twenty or so fishermen entering the tournament, so it's never attracted much attention from the press. Also looks like I have about thirty messages on my machine, presumably something to do with the same article."

"What would you do, Big Jack, if you had this kind of

business all day long?"

"Lock the door."

Big Jack wasn't a devoted business man. Part of his daily routine was an afternoon nap on the dock, weather permitting, and it would be absurd to have it interrupted by customers. As it turned out, the church group could probably have been trusted to make their selections and leave the money, but the next group to come in might take all the beer. Big Jack didn't seem too concerned one way or the other, though.

After the invaders had satisfied their curiosity they loaded into their cars and headed back to El Paso. Ray suggested they stop at La Posta in Old Messila to have dinner, highly recommending the food.

Once the quiet of the store returned, they went back to the plans for the meeting on Sunday. Tyee started printing flyers, and Ray called Clayton and told him their plans. Clayton was excited and said he would get his wife, as well as Cindy and her boyfriend, to distribute the flyers the next day.

Pretty soon Big Jack suggested it was time for a beer. Ray and Tyee joined him on the dock and sipped their beers. Well, Ray and Tyee sipped—Big Jack was doing something closer to gulping. Happy was well pleased to have the company and settled down as close as he could get to the group.

"I think Big Jack's should sponsor you in the Elephant Butte Fishing Tournament—what do you think Ray?" This was Big Jack speaking in between gulps of beer and chews on his cigar.

"Do you ever light that cigar?" Tyee seemed curious about the ever-present, disgusting cigar.

"That'll teach me to give an Indian a beer."

Ray thought this was good natured banter, but decided it was best if he changed the subject.

"Exactly what would that mean, Big Jack, if you sponsored me in the tournament?"

"Mostly it would mean I'd provide you with a Big Jack's hat and vest. If you win I would get half your earnings and free publicity. If you lose, I'd be out a hat and vest and the fifty dollar entry fee."

"If I win, what's the prize?"

"First place prize is three thousand dollars."

"Why not sponsor Tyee?"

"Well, he won the first three tournaments, so the executive committee, which is actually just me, decided on a new rule the next year that doesn't allow professional fishing guides to enter."

"White man fuck Indian once again."

"Yeah, doesn't feel right, just because he won to stop him from entering."

"Okay, maybe it wasn't right, but nobody else would enter if Tyee was fishing. So the tournament wouldn't exist. So what do you do? Piss off one guide or stop the tournament? I went with pissed off guide. Hell, he was already pissed off about something all the time, so what was the harm?"

They pondered the complications of fishing guides in fishing tournaments for a minute. "Okay, I'll enter the tournament—and I'm going to win!"

Tyee didn't look too convinced about the last part. "You've only caught one fish in your life—how are you going to win?"

"I'm going to use old Indian wisdom and cheat."

"White man very wise."

From this point on, most of their attention went to drinking beer.

# 10

*Saturday*

Ray woke up a little groggy. He decided he'd probably had a couple of beers too many the night before—but he'd sure had a good time. He enjoyed Big Jack and Tyee's company in a way he hadn't experienced in a long time. He got up slowly and let Happy out for his morning activities, then headed toward the kitchen and coffee.

Ray fixed a cup of instant coffee and decided to get dressed, a fairly simple process for Ray since he wore basically the same thing every day. He washed his clothes often, it was just that everything he had looked the same. This wasn't an issue for him, and so far nobody else had mentioned it. While he was showering, Ray decided he would head into town and treat himself to breakfast at the Lone Post, very much aware that Sue would be working that morning.

After dressing, he exited the bedroom and realized there was no sound at all in the cabin—Happy hadn't returned. He felt a sudden fear. Happy wasn't used to all the things he might encounter around the cabin. Each time Ray let him out he felt concerned. He started out the door to see if he could find Happy, when the dog appeared on the porch of his own accord. Ray noticed that as time had gone by, Happy had become a little more disheveled than when he'd first arrived. He felt bad that he wasn't brushing him as much as he should, but it was reality: the days of getting show dog treatment were over. He gave the dog a good rub, went back in the cabin to get his jacket, and then locked the door. As he was turning to leave, he noticed something. Reaching down, he realized it was a woman's shoe.

This felt like an ominous sign. It could belong to Ms. Jackson. Ray figured that Happy had found it somewhere and brought it home. What seemed odd to him was that Happy wasn't acting like it was his owner's shoe. Ray decided he was going to search the area immediately around his cabin that day and see what he could find. With that in mind, he headed toward Big Jack's to see if Tyee might be there and to ask if he'd assist in the search.

He and Happy got to Big Jack's quickly. It was apparent that Big Jack was having another good business day, which would put him in a foul mood for sure. Ray and Happy went around back and looked to see if Tyee's boat was there, but it wasn't. No boat, no Tyee. Ray decided they would head into T or C and have breakfast—he was starving.

Ray parked in front of the café and made sure Happy was comfortable and had plenty of air. The Lone Post was also doing a brisk Saturday morning business, so there weren't any tables or booths available, but there was a small counter and Ray took a stool. He'd barely sat down before Sue appeared.

"Good morning, Ray."

"Good morning, Sue. Looks like you're busy today."

"Yeah. Somebody said there was an article in the El Paso paper yesterday, and now we have a few more visitors than normal."

Ray placed his order with Sue, then went out front and got an El Paso paper from the box. He read the sports and glanced at the rest of the news. His breakfast was served and he enjoyed every bite.

"Well, we didn't have much time to talk today." Sue was looking disappointed.

"Sue, this may be an oddball question. I'm going to do some searching for a body that may be up around my cabin later on this afternoon and I was wondering if you'd like to help?"

Sue laughed. "Well yeah, that's an oddball question."

"Sorry, I guess that was more like stupid than oddball." Ray couldn't believe he had just tried to make a date to search for a dead body. Even for him that was bizarre.

"What time and how do I find your cabin?"

Ray was a little surprised. He told her Tyee would probably be there part of the time, but maybe after they searched some he could fix her dinner. She smiled. Ray wasn't sure what he was doing, he was just doing it. He gave her a map and said that three o'clock would be great. He said they would wait until three to start the search, and if she arrived later to just wait on the porch. She continued to smile and said she would take off a little early and be there by three. He hadn't realized he'd asked her to take off work early—now he was embarrassed all over again.

"Look Sue, I'm sorry, I wasn't thinking. Why don't you just come for dinner? I'm such an idiot about some things and just didn't realize I was asking you to leave work early."

"Ray, it's okay. I'll be there at three—if I'm not I'll be there at five—how's that?"

"That's great Sue. See you later." Ray got up and paid

his check at the register. The lady there gave him an I-know-what-you're-doing look while she counted out his change. Ray couldn't get out of there fast enough. Back in the Jeep, he let his breath out while petting Happy. He felt like a teenager who'd just asked a girl for a first date. Well, hell, maybe that wasn't such a bad feeling. He was grinning.

Ray stopped by the market in town and picked up some things: bread, wine, and one of those pre-made salads. He had steaks in the refrigerator. He also got more food for Happy. Then headed to the far side of the lake to drop by Tyee's camp. This took a bit of time, but soon he was parked just above the campsite. He went down, accompanied by Happy, and yelled out to Tyee. There was no response. Ray found some paper in his truck and left a note explaining that at around three he was going to do some searching in the vicinity of his cabin to look for clues about the missing woman. He mentioned the shoe and asked if Tyee could join him.

After a brief stop to get gas, Ray decided to bypass Big Jack's and head home. He was still deeply embarrassed that he'd invited Sue to search for a body—what in the world had he been thinking? He'd wanted to see her and that was what he'd been planning on doing so he'd invited her—it just didn't occur to him how stupid it sounded until he'd said it.

It seemed like a really long time before he finally reached home. For the first time since he'd moved to the lake, he wished he had a phone so he could call Sue and cancel their meeting. That sounded very businesslike. It wasn't a date, it was a meeting. Ray sat in the Jeep for a while, debating what to do. He could run down to Big Jack's and call. How had this day gone so wrong? He headed back to Big Jack's.

Pulling in, he found there were no cars—the busy day was apparently over. Ray and Happy entered. As usual, there was no one around. Ray looked out back and saw Big Jack asleep on his cot, enjoying the warm day. Rather than disturb him, Ray would use the phone and leave—no need to even mention it to Big Jack.

"Hey, what's going on?" It was Tyee.

Ray jumped. "Gave me a little start there—I didn't see you."

"Yeah, Indians are sneaky."

Ray tried to pull himself together. He needed to use the phone but didn't want to discuss why with Tyee. Within a single day Ray had turned into a bumbling moron.

"I was going to do some searching around my cabin in a while to see if I could find anything that might link to the missing woman—care to help?"

"Sure."

"Happy found a woman's shoe that doesn't look that old, so I thought it might make some sense."

"Something wrong, Ray? You seem nervous."

"No nothing. I went by your camp earlier and left a note. So when you get back just ignore the note."

"Come on, Ray, what the hell is going on—you're sounding goofy."

"Oh jeez. For some stupid reason I invited Sue at the café to go searching for dead bodies like it was a date. I don't know, it was like my mind wasn't working. It makes me feel like an idiot. So now I'm going to call her and tell her not to come."

"A date to look for dead bodies—is this some kind of zombie thing?"

"No. It's just some kind of stupid old man thing."

"Indian sensing romance in air."

Ray called information and got the number for the café. It was answered as always by the lady at the register. Ray asked for Sue but was told that she had gone home early with a head-ache. He asked for her number and was told that they couldn't give out employee's private numbers. He hung up. He called information again and asked for the number for Sue Lewis—they said they didn't have a Sue Lewis. He hung up again.

"Come on, Ray, it's not that bad. So you made kind of a silly date—she was the one who said yes. I think you just need to go with the flow here, see how this turns out. What time was she supposed to be there?"

"Either three, if she could get off work early, or five if not."

"Well let's head up to your cabin. You can clean up some and then, if she shows up, we can do some searching and you can go back to normal date mode. If she doesn't show up you and I can search some and see if there's anything obvious in your area, okay?"

"Thanks, Tyee. Don't tell Big Jack about this date fiasco or I'll never hear the end of it."

"Tell Big Jack what?" It was Big Jack, standing at the door.

"This day just gets worse by the minute." Ray realized he had no choice, so he told Big Jack the story. Big Jack laughed in his familiar way for several minutes—putting himself and several display cases in great danger. Ray knew that he would never hear the end of this story.

Tyee and Ray headed toward the cabin. Happy settled into the back of the Jeep and hung his head on Tyee's shoulder. Once at the cabin, Ray began cleaning up. It wasn't real messy, but it didn't quite meet female guest standards. Tyee fixed food for Happy and helped Ray where he could. As Ray was finishing, Tyee and Happy went out onto the porch.

Punctual to a fault, Sue pulled up right at three o'clock. She got out and started toward the cabin. Seeing Tyee sitting on the porch gave her a brief pause, but then she continued with her hand extended.

"You must be Tyee, I'm Sue."

"Hello Sue. Ray's inside cleaning up a little. Have a seat."

"Thanks." Sue sat in one of the rocking chairs and gave Happy a much appreciated ear rub.

"Ready to go look for bodies?" For whatever reason, maybe the way he said it, both Tyee and Sue doubled over in laughter.

"Okay, I know this must be about my stupid invitation. Go ahead and have a good laugh." He had emerged onto the porch with a backpack. He was smiling, but his feelings were hurt just a little.

"Ray, I'm sorry—it was just the way Tyee said we'd 'go look for bodies'—it was just funny. I'm so happy you invited me, and if it had been a problem I would have said no. And by the way, you don't know this but I was a physician's assistant before I became a top-notch waitress at the Lone Post. I'm not squeamish about bodies. And if I don't want to do something, I'm very capable of saying no. So please let me stay and go on the search."

"A physician's assistant waiting tables—how did that happen?" Ray was stunned, pleased and smiling. Sue could take care of herself.

"Long story, Ray. One I would be pleased to tell you later, but let's get this search underway."

Ray agreed. He told Tyee and Sue about the circumstances that made it possible that there would be a body somewhere in the area. He also explained that the area that would eventually need to be searched was large, covering many acres. What he wanted to do today was just let Happy guide them, if he would, and see if there was something obvious. He planned to request that the sheriff's office make a more thorough search the following week to make sure they didn't miss something. He showed them a rough map of the area and the small section he wanted to cover right around the cabin. Once everyone understood the plan, he called Happy over.

Ray was sure that Happy wasn't trained as a search dog, but dogs have an incredible sense of smell and he thought that Happy might be a natural at finding things. He also knew that dogs were disturbed by dead bodies, and for that reason he'd decided it was pretty unlikely that his owner was in the vicinity—Happy would have acted differently if he could still smell her in the area. He let Happy sniff the shoe.

"Okay, boy, find the smell. Go boy, find the scent."

Happy ran off quickly. They spread out, Tyee in the lead, with Ray on one side and Sue on the other, each about an arm's length from Tyee. They followed the dog's path. Happy seemed to be heading in a fairly straight line toward something. It wasn't long before they lost track of him. Tyee seemed to know which way to go, so they just kept walking alongside him. Soon Tyee stopped.

"Ray, call Happy."

Ray called out for Happy and in a moment he appeared. He was obviously tired and seemed distressed.

"Keep him here. I'll be right back."

Tyee headed out. Ray and Sue stood by Happy giving him attention. Tyee was back within a few minutes.

"There's a body over that little rise, an elderly woman. Looks like the body was rolled into a little gully and covered with leaves. There's been some damage done by animals, so the body is in pretty bad shape. I think we should call the sheriff and report it."

"Let me go look. It won't disturb me at all. Part of my duties at one of my stops was forensic—I've seen it all." Saying this, Sue pulled out plastic gloves and put them on. Ray nodded and Tyee and Sue headed back over the little hill. They were back in only a few minutes.

"I didn't want to do much or the sheriff would say we'd contaminated the site, but I do have some things we can discuss."

They agreed that Happy was upset and that they should get him back to the cabin. Ray reached into his backpack and took out police tape, which he gave to Tyee, asking him to tape off the area around the body. He also had a small tarp in the backpack which he gave Tyee to cover the remains, hopefully to prevent any further damage.

Ray petted Happy as they waited for Tyee to come back. Then he pointed him toward the cabin and said, "Home, boy." The dog took off and they followed. They'd come further than they'd thought and it took them some time to get back to the cabin. Happy was on the porch and was very glad to see them. Ray opened the door and let everyone inside. He'd put several bottles of wine in the refrigerator. He opened a white and poured them each a glass. They silently toasted the dead person as they sipped their wine.

Sue described what she'd seen in professional detail. It looked like the woman had been shot, most likely with a large caliber pistol. The wound was in her chest and the damage probably killed her more or less instantly. Sue estimated her age to be in the eighties, probably late eighties. No way to make out facial features due to wildlife predation. Ray asked if it could be someone in their early sixties, but Sue didn't think so. They sipped more wine, and Ray refilled everyone's glass.

"Well, it's someone, but it doesn't seem to fit Ms. Jackson. That lines up with what I was saying before about Happy not going to the body, as I think he would have if it had been his owner. So now the question is, who is it?" Ray was subdued after finding the body, but in a way this might be good news, at least for Ms. Jackson's family.

"Tyee, I'm fixing steaks with a lot more wine, how about you stay and have dinner?"

"Indian must be in teepee after dark."

"Don't give me that Indian bullshit. You're more than welcome to stay for dinner and bunk here."

"Sorry Ray, I already have a date with Big Jack. He promised me beer and a cot if I would join him in a game of chess. For money. Big Jack thinks no Indian knows how to play chess, so it's easy money for me. I'll head out now. It was nice meeting you, Sue—I hope Ray knows how to cook. This is the first time he's ever mentioned that he cooks."

"It was nice meeting you Tyee. I'll keep you posted on Ray's chef skills."

Ray stood up and went to the door. As Tyee approached, Ray gave him the keys to the Jeep and asked if he could come and pick him up the next morning around eleven so they could get ready for the barbeque that day. Tyee accepted the keys and seemed pleased—he'd been prepared to walk to Big Jack's, but driving would be a lot easier. Tyee waved to Sue and left.

Ray had been completely comfortable as long as Tyee'd been there, but now, with just Sue, he was nervous again. "Why don't I get the steaks out and put a few things together?"

"Ray, just a minute." Sue got up, walked up to him, and gave him a kiss. She felt good against him. She leaned back. "Now stop being so nervous, I think we can be great friends—I won't kill you or marry you, so you're safe, okay?" Ray laughed and kissed her back. She went with him into the kitchen and they prepared a wonderful dinner.

Sue stayed over. This was the first woman Ray had been with since his wife had died almost six years before. It was very comfortable and natural. He felt no guilt, only joy. He also woke with a reminder that he might have drunk just a little too much wine the night before.

Ray fixed coffee and toast. She asked if he had grape jelly, and Ray felt a tingle. He told her about the barbeque that afternoon for Deputy Clayton's campaign and she said she'd be there. She didn't linger after breakfast, gathering her belongings and kissing him goodbye.

"I had a great time, Ray. I'm a grown woman and I only do what I want to do—you owe me nothing. But I want you to know that I would enjoy being with you when it's right for you."

"You are something special, Sue. I had a great time too, and I want to see you again."

"How about this afternoon."

"Oh yeah, great, great, I mean yeah."

"You do have a way with words, Ray."

She left and Ray sat down on the porch and just smiled.

# 11

*Sunday*

Tyee picked Ray up at eleven and took him back to Big Jack's. First thing Ray did was call the sheriff's office and report that he'd found a body near his cabin. He told them where and that it was marked with police tape. He didn't know the person he gave the information to, so he kept it to the basics, saying that he'd discovered the body after his dog had brought back a woman's shoe, omitting any mention of Tyee and Sue. He said it looked to him as if the woman had been shot and that she was elderly. He gave the deputy his name and address and also told him he was going to be at Big Jack's today.

The campaign strategy would involve multiple small gatherings, with somewhere around fifty people attending, happening over the next month. They hoped to be able to have twenty or so of these events. For the kickoff barbeque they had decided to try to attract closer to 200 people. This would be their core group. The plan was to get this group excited about Clayton, then have them canvass their neighborhoods. They would also get some of the hosts for the smaller events from this group.

The day before, the flyer team had put out all 300 flyers and talked to a lot of people. Who knew how many would show up, though? Ray was pretty confident that the free food and free beer would be a significant inducement, and he expected to have a large crowd. Big Jack had erected several tents along the side of his store and had a huge smoker working overtime on briskets. For this many people the cost of food and drink would be substantial. It made Ray wonder about Big Jack, exactly who he was and how much money he really had.

The barbeque was to run from one to three, starting after church ended and with an early end time so they would have time to shoo people home—no beer drinking all day on Big Jack's tab. The crew had worked hard all morning and had most everything ready. There were huge quantities of baked beans, potato salad, and Cole slaw prepared and waiting. The beer was iced. At about twelve forty-five the first people began to show. From that point on there was a steady stream. It kept everybody hopping just to keep the food refreshed and handle the large amounts of trash. Ray had taken on the key responsibility of keeping the large tubs of ice stocked with beer. He was impressed with the amount of beer that had already been consumed and hoped they had enough.

Around two, Ray stepped up to the small stage area and tapped on the microphone.

"Ladies and Gentleman, may I have your attention. We're here today in support of Deputy Clayton, who is running for Sierra County sheriff." There was some cheering, largely from the group that had been drinking most of the beer.

Ray told them who he was and why he was endorsing Clayton. He made it very clear that the previous sheriff didn't have his respect and it was time for a change. He didn't mention the current acting sheriff but everyone knew he was connected to the previous sheriff, who'd been selling drugs. Ray made several points, all tied to the key idea that Clayton's goal was fair treatment of everyone by the sheriff's department. He also pointed out that the management of the county jail was the responsibility of the sheriff, and Clayton had a degree in management. He made his points and got several rounds of applause, then introduced Deputy Clayton.

Clayton wasn't as forceful as Ray, but he made a good speech and only made one reference to his opponent—whom he referred to as the mayor's son. The speech emphasized Clayton's background, both his education and his experience as a deputy. He pledged to run the department as a community service and to treat all people equally. He received a standing ovation from the crowd. The heavy beer drinking section was almost in tears.

They had prepared new flyers telling people what they could do to support Clayton, with the number one item being getting people to register and vote. These were passed out to the crowd—which Big Jack estimated at about two hundred people, based on food consumption—right after Clayton's speech. They distributed all of the 250 flyers they'd printed. It was approaching three when Big Jack shut down the free beer—the crowd quickly dispersed.

Once everything was cleaned up, packed away, and stored, they held a debriefing to discuss the event and next steps. Sue was standing with Ray, and they seemed very interested in each other and not so much in the debriefing. Tyee led the analysis, saying that it had been a roaring success. They had over seventy-five cards filled out by people who said they would host an event at their house. He said he would get a list together and distributed it to the team so that each one of those seventy-five could be contacted and they could start making arrangements for the smaller meetings. Tyee was wrapping up when the front door opened and in walked the Mayor and his son, Deputy Martinez.

The Mayor walked up to Ray. "You and I never got along when you were sheriff. Now here you are butting your nose into the business of T or C. Not sure what your problem is, Ray, but you are not welcome here." The Mayor was about five foot eight and nearly spherical. To see him in a huff verged on comical.

"Sorry you feel that way, Mayor—but I don't give a shit what you think."

The Mayor looked around the room and realized he wasn't amongst friends. His face turned red, but he kept his mouth shut.

"Ray, I understand you called in the report of the body on your property this morning—but the body was discovered yesterday. Also we've been up to the crime scene and it's been disturbed by you or others. I believe you are in some serious trouble for interfering with a criminal investigation."

"Deputy, the body was found late yesterday. I marked the area with police tape and covered the body with a tarp to keep the coyotes from damaging it further. I don't have a phone, but first thing this morning I called. If you think that constitutes interfering with a criminal investigation, I guess you better charge me."

All was quiet. The deputy gave Ray some dirty looks, then gave Clayton some dirty looks, then gave Tyee and Big Jack some dirty looks—then apparently got tired and left. The

Mayor waddled after his son.

"He's going to cause you problems, Ray. It's how he works—he'll want to hurt me, but he can't do that directly until the election is over—so he'll go after you or Big Jack or someone. I'm sorry."

"Listen Clayton, I'm supporting you one hundred percent. So are a lot of other people. What we just saw here is one of the reasons you've got that support. What you have to do is win. Then we'll all be winners."

There was some applause after Ray's oration. Everyone shook hands and made arrangements to follow through on the next set of meetings. Ray and Sue were huddled in the corner making their own arrangements.

"My god, this is like a little bitty Chicago. Crime and corruption everywhere you look." Sue was smiling, but Ray could tell the Mayor's entrance had made her nervous.

"Yeah, and there's absolutely no need for this crap. I've known the Mayor for more than ten years. He's always been a jerk. He only represents the people who suck up to him. He's the worst kind of small town politician. Hopefully, after Clayton wins, we can help someone beat that asshole."

"I never would have figured you for an activist."

Ray smiled and realized that he never would have figured himself for one either.

Ray drove by the crime scene on the way to his cabin. There was no one there. The body had been removed along with the police tape. Not much of an investigation by the sheriff's department.

# 12

*Monday*

First thing in the morning, Ray went down to Big Jack's and called Mike Jackson. He told Mike about the discovery of the body and that it wasn't Monica, but an older woman. He asked Mike if Monica had any enemies.

"Well I guess we all have people who don't like us much. But most people found Monica easy to like. There was one exception, a Mrs. Richards, who lives in Albuquerque, was obsessed with the idea that Monica cheated her on a dog she bought. She claimed the dog Monica sold her wasn't a purebred. She sued in small claims court and lost because Monica produced all of the breeding papers. That just seemed to make the woman more upset. She would call Monica and yell at her and also claimed that her husband's recent death was because Monica had cheated them and he'd had a heart attack because he was so upset."

"Sounds like quite a feud. Do you think this woman could have followed Monica when she was on her way to El Paso?"

"It's possible. I know she followed Monica before, and once yelled at her in a pet store. Really embarrassed Monica."

"Did Monica report her to the police?"

"No. She and I talked about it, but Monica thought the

lady was just losing her mind. Mrs. Richards blamed her for everything that had gone wrong in her life for the last year or so, but Monica believed it was because Mrs. Richards was unstable, so she didn't want to cause her any trouble. I know the woman was having mental problems. I called and talked to her son. He was very apologetic about his mother. He said that he had no idea about whether the dog was purebred or not, but that his mother's reaction had to do with her mental health. He said he couldn't deal with her at all and was planning on placing her in a home for Alzheimer's patients. He was worried sick that she would do something to harm herself or someone else."

"How old is she?"

"Not exactly sure, but she's somewhere in her middle or late eighties."

"Monica made some calls from the Hot Springs Inn. One was to you, and there were two calls to the hotel in El Paso where the dog show was being held. My guess is that at least one of those calls was to cancel her reservation for that night since she was staying in T or C. Do you know of anyone who she would have been calling at the hotel?"

"Let's see. She would talk to me about some of the dog show people although I'm sure not every person she knew at the shows. The names I remember are only first names—that might not be much help. There was Betty. She had become great friends with Betty and they often had dinner together since they were both divorced mature ladies, which is the way Monica described them. She sometimes talked about a man named Nate, who, I believe, was one of the competitors that caused Monica to lose. They didn't seem to like each other much. I can't imagine why she would call him. Well, maybe that's all I can remember right now. Oh, wait a minute there was another name. One of the officials of the organization that puts on the dog shows—seems like it was Nathan. She thought he did a good job and had helped her a lot."

"Okay, thanks, Mike. That's very helpful. As soon as I know more I'll give you a call."

"There's something else you need to know. Monica doesn't know this because I just found out yesterday. Our oldest son, Ed Jackson, who lives in Albuquerque, was arrested yesterday for selling forged documents. I went down and tried to bail him out but couldn't get anything done on a Sunday. But I did get to see him. He says he's innocent, that he bought some civil war collectable documents from some guy in Juarez and they turned out to be forgeries. I'm afraid my son has had a lot of problems with drinking, drugs, and money, so I don't know what to believe. But you should know that the dog Monica sold to Mrs. Richards came through my son. He sold three dogs to his mother at a premium price because he had all of the breeding papers. Of course it crossed my mind yesterday that maybe those papers were forged. Monica had said before that she wasn't sure about the dogs because they seem more flawed than you would expect based on their papers. It would be just terrible for Monica if Mrs. Richards had been right all along."

Ray wasn't real sure what to say. The heartache children caused their parents was a constant theme in law enforcement. He felt sorry for Mike having to deal with a deadbeat son.

"Sorry about your son, Mike. Let me know if I can help. When I get more information about Monica, I'll give you a call."

Ray called the Camino Real Hotel next. The first person to answer passed him along to a reservations clerk. Ray identified himself as being with the sheriff's department, looking into a missing person, Monica Jackson. If the sheriff found out about that little misstatement he would have Ray locked up for impersonating a deputy. But it worked. The reservation clerk confirmed that Monica had called Friday and canceled her reservation for that night. She also had a reservation for Saturday, but then didn't show up. He asked the clerk if they'd had someone staying there on Friday named Betty. She told him their system was based on last names, she couldn't search based on first names. Pushing a little more, Ray said that this person was associated with the dog show. Could she identify people who had been booked through the show? There was a pause as she did something with the computer.

"Yes, it looks like I can call up all of the rooms reserved through the dog show association. There are about forty or so. Let me see. Yes, here's a Betty. Betty Adams, she was in room 607. Checked out Sunday."

"How about someone named Nate or Nathan."

"Kind of pushing your luck deputy. Well, let me see. Yes, here is a Nathan Young—he's the President of the Dog Shows of America organization; and here is a Nate. Nate Carter was in room 404. Is that it?"

"Yes, thank you very much." Ray hung up.

Just as he was finishing Tyee walked in.

"Big Jack is bitching and moaning about you being on his phone all of the time."

"Well crap. He's got a point. Guess I should call the phone

company and see what kind of monster charge it would be to get phone service out to my cabin."

"I think mostly Big Jack just likes to blow off steam. Still, having your own phone might be handy."

Ray made a mental note to check out the cost of a phone.

"Any luck on that partial number?"

"No. I need some way to narrow it down. As it is I'm at a standstill."

"Okay. Don't worry about that. How about an organization called Dog Shows of America. Don't know where they're located, but the president's name is Nathan Young."

"See what I can do." Tyee took his seat at the computer and started typing on the keyboard. Soon the familiar screeching sound started that indicated he was connected over the phone line.

"Tying up the line with the modem is pissing Big Jack off, too." Tyee looked up at Ray with a slight grin.

"I'll go talk to him."

Ray went out and found Big Jack restocking his beer cooler. The event yesterday had put a major dent in his beer supplies.

"Big Jack, we need to work some things out."

"Yeah." Big Jack wasn't in a good mood.

"First, about the phone. I'll call in just a minute and find out what it would take to get a line up to my cabin. I don't even know if they would do that, but if the cost's reasonable I'll have that done. I'll also ask them, with your permission, about putting in another line to your store. If that's agreeable to you, I would pay for that line. I can then use that if they won't run one to my cabin and Tyee could use that for his computer stuff.

Is that okay?"

"Ah, fuck, Ray. I'm just in a bad mood. I've got more money than sense—it really isn't a money issue. Don't know. All of this new activity has kind of got me wondering about what I want to do. You know I was just sort of hiding out and had no plans for anything. Then you come along and suddenly I'm involved in things and I guess I miss the action. Maybe I'm just tired of sitting on my fat ass all of the time."

For some reason Ray had thought that Big Jack would be the last person to have mood swings—not so. The guy was human after all.

"Big Jack, I've been thinking about some things myself. I have an idea I'd like to run by you and Tyee. Just a sec, I'll go get Tyee—do you have a minute?"

"Hell, yes. Just got to get this beer cooled down before my afternoon beer break."

Ray asked Tyee to join them out front, then went into his pitch. He wanted to start a private investigation firm. Said it would be a regional company based out of T or C. He wanted Big Jack and Tyee to be equal partners. He thought it might make a little money, and if there were profits they would split them equally. Also, there should be almost no cost to start—just their time.

"How would you get paying clients?" Big Jack didn't seem interested.

"I know every sheriff in New Mexico, most of Arizona and a big chunk of Texas. I would use those contacts to get the firm name out into the law enforcement community. So we would be looking for referrals. Often relatives of victims or even the accused are looking for someone to help them find answers and help communicate with law enforcement people."

"What would each of us do?" Tyee wanted details.

"To some extent whatever's necessary. I would concentrate on field investigation, Tyee you would concentrate on computer research, and Big Jack you would focus on any legal issues we encounter."

"What would we call this company?"

"Not sure."

"First my name can't be on anything. Ray, I have not told you everything about me—let's just say it would be best if I was a silent partner. I like the idea of doing something other than running this store, and I also kind of like the idea of helping people get through the law enforcement bullshit. If I can remain silent, I'm in."

"Big Jack, I would like to know your story—but I don't have to know it—you can be silent, if that's what you want. I value your opinion and think we can make a good team. Tyee what about you?"

"Guess I'm not sure. You know I've cut down on my drinking since we've been doing stuff. I feel better about myself. I don't want to go back to just being a drunk. Also, I think the three of us make a good team. So I guess I'm in too."

"How about *Pacheco and Chino, Private Investigations?*"

"Ray, are you sure you want an Indian name included?"

"Hell yes. You'll be our star attraction. We'll claim you are a long lost tribal Chief who can read minds, track animals or humans over hard rock, predict the future, and other mystical Indian stuff."

Ray didn't even get a chuckle out of Tyee—he thought he might have even offended him.

"Look, I was just kidding. I won't do this without you and Big Jack. If you prefer your name isn't included in the company name that's fine—but I would prefer that it's in there. If you want it to be *Chino and Pacheco Private Investigations*, that's fine too. What do you think?"

Tyee smiled at Ray and Big Jack. "Pacheco and Chino—done." They all shook hands and helped Big Jack stock his beer coolers.

Ray called the phone company and was pleasantly surprised that the price for all the services he wanted was very reasonable. He ordered a phone line to his cabin and an additional two lines to Big Jack's store. He decided that they needed the extra line to allow Tyee to be on the computer while he was on the phone. He asked the person taking his order to bill the phones to his cabin address in the name of *Pacheco and Chino, Private Investigations*. His days of hiding in the woods hadn't lasted long—he was glad.

# 13

*Tuesday*

Around noon, Ray and Happy were headed toward the Lone Post Café. He thought he would have lunch and talk to Sue some and then go by the sheriff's office to see if they had identified the body. The Café was busy as usual. Ray took a seat at the counter and was quickly served sweet iced tea by Sue, along with a wink. Ray was still adjusting to this new relationship.

"How is Mr. Pacheco today?"

"Not so bad, Sue. How's your day going?"

"Busy. Which is both good and bad. I like being busy in that the time goes quicker, but we've been shorthanded today so it's been just a little too hectic."

She took his order and headed in the other direction. Didn't look like they would have much time to chat today.

"I thought I might find you here." It was Deputy Clayton with a conspiratorial grin. Ray was sure he didn't like everybody knowing about his relationship with Sue. He wasn't real sure he wanted to hide it either—mostly it just felt strange.

"Hello, deputy. I was planning on coming by your office in a little bit. Has the body been identified yet?"

"Another good reason I caught you. Might be best to just

avoid the sheriff and the office for a while. Martinez was on the warpath this morning, aimed mostly at you. I actually think part of this is the election and the fact that he might lose—don't believe he thought that was possible until the barbeque."

"Well, I don't really give a damn if he's on the warpath or not."

"Calm down, Ray. I have the info you want. The woman's been identified as a Mrs. Opal Richards, age eighty-six, address is in Albuquerque. Her husband died about a year ago. Her son, who lives in Albuquerque, was notified as next of kin. Does that mean anything to you?"

"Yep. She had a running feud with Ms. Jackson over the sale of a dog. My guess is she's the one who wrote the note and probably was the one who slashed the tires."

"Eighty-six year old lady slashing tires—are you sure?"

"Not one-hundred percent, but I think you can be seventy percent sure she's the one. Once you talk to the son you'll realize that she was suffering some mental problems, probably Alzheimer's disease. She had fixated on Ms. Jackson and was blaming her for everything, including her husband's heart attack. I think the big questions now are where's Monica Jackson and where's Mrs. Richard's car?"

"Do you think Jackson is alive?"

"My first guess was that we would find her body somewhere in the area of my cabin—because of the dog. Now, I'm beginning to think she's alive and there was some kind of confrontation with Mrs. Richards. Looks to me like there are only two possibilities. The first is that Mrs. Richards had a confrontation with Ms. Jackson, which I would guess ended up being a kidnapping by Mrs. Richards. Then something happened and Mrs. Richards was shot. Why, how, by whom—I really don't know. Monica panicked and took off in Mrs. Richards' car, leaving the dog. So where would she go? I would think she'd either head back home to Albuquerque or she'd head to El Paso. I've talked to her husband and if she went back home I think she would have contacted him—and I don't believe she has, so my guess is that she went to El Paso and is hiding. The second option is that there's a third person involved and somehow Mrs. Richards got caught in the middle while she was stalking Ms. Jackson. Once again Mrs. Richards was shot by someone, and this third person took Ms. Jackson and is holding her somewhere for reasons I don't know."

During this discussion Sue had brought Ray his grilled cheese and poured Deputy Clayton a cup of coffee.

"Well, that sure makes sense Ray, based on what we do know. Are you investigating this matter for the ex-husband?"

"He asked me to, but I said no. Not sure our sheriff has any desire to cooperate with my independent investigation. I might still poke around a little, but officially I'm just a casual observer."

"I wish you were investigating. The sheriff isn't going to do anything. He's sent me off to look into a campsite disturbance in the Gila Wilderness. That'll keep me out of his hair for the rest of the day."

"Sorry, deputy. All you can do right now is follow orders. Keep your people out there putting together more meetings and getting people registered. I have a feeling this will work out just fine."

The deputy seemed pleased with the pep talk. He said he'd better get going and left.

Ray finished his lunch and lingered some. Sue came around and they talked. Ray told her about the phone and that he thought it might be working within a couple of weeks. She said that would be nice to be able to phone him. Ray finally decided he couldn't just sit there, so he said goodbye and left. He stopped outside when he realized that he should have asked Sue if she wanted to have dinner or something, once again feeling like he wasn't handling this Sue stuff very well. He had some goodies Sue had given him for Happy, so he opened the back and handed over the treats. As he was turning to get in the Jeep, Sue walked up.

"How about if I come by your place a little later and we have dinner together?"

"That would be great, Sue."

"See you later." She went back into the café. Why was this so easy for her and so hard for him? He had no idea.

Ray headed back toward his cabin, then decided to take a quick trip by Big Jack's and see if Tyee was there. He parked in front and let Happy out. Happy headed around to the dock to find his favorite spot in the sun. Big Jack was helping a customer as Ray walked in—they waved and Ray went into the computer room.

"Hello, Ray. How was lunch at the Lone Post Café?"

"You think you're being wise, but I consider it nosy."

"Oh, a little sensitive today."

"Not really. Lunch was fine. Saw Clayton and he said they identified the body as Mrs. Richards."

Ray filled Tyee in on his speculation about what might have happened. Tyee agreed that the possibilities they'd outlined made sense. He also told Ray that he'd found the Dog

Shows of America. They were located in Phoenix and he had their phone number.

They discussed when Ray wanted to go fishing again and agreed on Thursday morning. Ray was starting to regret agreeing to compete in the tournament. It had seemed like the right thing to do at the time, but now there was just too much going on.

Ray called the number for Dog Shows of America and asked to speak to Nathan Young.

"Hello, this is Nathan Young."

"Mr. Young, my name is Ray Pacheco. I'm working with the sheriff's department looking into the disappearance of Monica Jackson—do you have some time to answer a few questions?"

"Of course. I'm so worried about her. Do you have any idea about what has happened?"

"No, sir. At this point we're just trying to contact as many people as we can and see where it takes us. We really have no solid leads on what might've happened or where she might be. Do you know Ms. Jackson well?"

"Oh, sure. Monica's been a part of our organization for years, both as a breeder and as a dog show participant. We're a full service organization, offering all types of training and certifications for breeders, as well as being a dog show sponsor. Monica's been one of our most enthusiastic participants in many of the programs we put on. I just can't believe that she's missing."

"When was the last time you saw her or talked to her?"

"I would say it was on the phone about two weeks before the El Paso show, so I guess that's more than three weeks ago.

She called to ask me about another member and whether I thought he was going to show his dog in El Paso—they had kind of an intense rivalry going."

"What's his name?"

"Well, I'm sure he has nothing to do with this mess with Monica. They have dogs in the same class and they're usually the one and two finishers. Sometimes he would win and sometimes Monica would. Over the last year or so it had become a little personal and they'd exchanged some unfortunate words at the last show—but it was just the competitive juices flowing—nothing sinister."

"I'm sure that's true, Mr. Young. Still, I'll need to check it out. What's the man's name?"

"Nate Carter."

"Do you know where he lives, and do you have a phone number for him?"

"Sure. He lives in Dallas, I'll have to look up his number."

"That's fine I can get that in a minute. We're also looking for someone connected to the El Paso show named Betty. Does that mean anything to you?"

"Of course. That's Monica's best friend, Betty Adams. She and Monica always spent a lot of time together during the shows."

Ray explained that he would need to know where Betty lived, too, and her phone number if Nate had it. Carter put Ray on hold to get the information. He came back on the line and gave Ray both addresses and phone numbers.

"Thank you very much, Mr. Young. This should help us get some more information. Were Betty and Nate both at the El Paso show?"

"Sure. Nate won again easily since Monica didn't show up. I saw Betty on Saturday morning and then she abruptly checked out and I guess went home. That was after it turned out that Monica wasn't going to be there, so I figured she was upset about that and decided to go home early."

"Were you aware of a problem Ms. Jackson had with a customer of hers named Richards?"

"Yeah, I was. Monica called me several times about the problem with that customer. She even faxed me the breeding papers to look at to see if I could see anything wrong. As I told Monica at the time, they looked okay to me, but forgeries aren't unheard of in the breeding business and I'm not an expert in forged documents. I asked her who she purchased the dogs from, but she never gave me an answer. I think she was really worried that there was something wrong."

"I think that's all I have right now, Mr. Young. Let me give you my private number in case something comes up."

Ray knew it was risky, but he couldn't have Mr. Young thinking of something and calling the sheriff's office, so he gave him Big Jack's number and hoped for the best.

Tyee had stepped out of the storeroom while Ray was on the phone—he came back in with a diet Coke.

"Got some complete names now and addresses."

Ray gave Tyee the information. "Now we should be able to track them down."

"Ray, there was a message for you from Mike Jackson. He sounded very upset and said he wanted you to call him right away. Not sure, but it sounded like some kind of emergency."

Ray took the note with Mike's number and once again got on the phone. He sure hoped they ran that new phone line soon or Big Jack was going to have another fit.

"Hello."

"Mike, this is Ray. Is something wrong?"

"Oh Ray, I'm so glad you called. Everything is wrong. I just can't believe it—it's horrible. What am I going to do?"

"Mike, slow down. What's wrong?"

"My son's dead—my son Ed. The police called this morning. They found him in his car out in the desert—he'd been shot. My god, Ray, what in the hell is happening?"

Ray was stunned. He didn't know Mike's son, but first his ex-wife goes missing and then their son is shot? What *was* going on?

"Mike, did the police tell you anything?"

"They said it looked like a professional hit—whatever in the hell that means. I mean my son was a loser, but he wasn't involved in any sort of gang or the mafia or anything like that. What are they talking about?"

"Mike, I don't know what's going on, but you have to remain calm. I'll help you. I'll drive up tomorrow morning and go see the police—give me any contact information they left with you. Also, you and I can meet once I see the police and talk about this—and about Monica. I have a very uncomfortable feeling that this is all connected. Are you okay to be alone right now?"

"Yeah, I'm okay. My other son, Luke, is coming over in a minute and picking me up. I'm going to go to his house."

Ray took down the contact information for the police and for Luke, as well as Luke's address. He told Mike he would call him sometime the next morning and then they could meet to discuss whatever he'd learned. He hung up.

Ray filled Tyee in on the latest events and asked if he wanted to drive up to Albuquerque in the morning. They agreed that they'd meet at Big Jack's so Tyee could leave his boat at the dock. They set a time and Ray said goodbye. Leaving the store, Ray stepped out onto the dock. Big Jack was petting Happy and getting a lot of dog love in return.

"I think that dog is spoiled."

"Maybe or maybe he's spoiled me." Little chuckle this time, not the huge Big Jack laugh.

"Tyee and I are headed up to Albuquerque in the morning. There's been a development in Ms. Jackson's disappearance."

Big Jack was very attentive as Ray described the latest news.

"I guess you know this forgery business out of Mexico is huge. Had some dealings with some of this in my L.A. days. All we hear about is drugs coming out of Mexico, but forged documents of all kinds amount to millions, hell, maybe billions of dollars. I think it started out as a business supplying illegals with forged papers, but it's branched out into almost anything you can think of. Some of the really big bucks involve forged collectable documents, from sports memorabilia to civil war documents. If the son was involved in this stuff with people in Mexico, you need to be really careful. These are not nice people—just think of them the same way you would drug dealers. They kill to make a point."

Ray noticed a different edge to Big Jack's voice. He still had a lot to learn about his new partner.

"Thanks for the warning. Guess I hadn't thought too much about the forgery business. But the son being executed within a few days of his mother disappearing can't be just a coincidence. I think they're connected, and if Monica's still alive—which is a big *if*—then she's in danger."

Ray told Big Jack about their plans for the next day and left him with various contact numbers in Albuquerque. He also gave Big Jack the personal information he'd need to complete the application form for their PI license. Jack said he'd been working on the legal documents and he hoped to have everything finished sometime that day.

Ray said his goodbyes and headed off with Happy. The drive to the cabin was short and very bumpy. When he arrived, he was thrilled to see Sue's car out front.

# 14

*Wednesday*

Ray and Tyee were on the road to Albuquerque by seven the next morning. Happy was left with Big Jack, which seemed to please both of them. It was about a two hour drive. When they got there they were hoping to be able to see the detective in charge first, then go by and visit with Mike.

Ray had also talked with Big Jack, who had told him that the incorporation papers for *Pacheco and Chino, Private Investigations, Inc.* were done and he'd sent them to the Secretary of State's office. He'd also completed the forms for a PI license for the firm, as well as individual licenses for Ray and Tyee, although getting information out of Tyee had been a challenge. All of this had been accomplished the day before, and very soon they would officially be in business.

"So are you looking forward to being Tyee Chino, PI?"

"I think so Ray. Although this isn't a path I'd ever thought about. Kind of thought I would just do a little fishing and drinking and not much else. I hope I can be useful."

"My god, what's this—a fucking humble Apache? Come on, where are the fuck-you-white-man jabs?"

"Well, maybe I'm mellowing. Finding harmony with my inner self."

"Not sure I can handle this new spiritual Indian. I think I like the fuck-you-white-man guy better."

"Well, in that case: fuck you white man. Maybe it's time Indian get to drive car—why are you always the leader?"

Ray glanced at Tyee to make sure he wasn't serious, but he could never quite tell. He saw a travel center up ahead and took the exit. "Think I need some coffee."

They pulled into the travel center and Ray gave Tyee the keys. He went inside and got two travel cups of coffee, then got back in on the passenger side. "And don't let me hear you complaining about the Indian always being the chauffeur."

New Mexico was a big state and had a lot of variety in terrain. There were mountain ranges on both sides of the I-25 as they headed north to Albuquerque. The mountains on the west side had a lot more trees, as well as huge mesas. Ray wasn't sure what caused these formations, but was always amazed at how flat their tops were—it was as if a mountain had risen up and then someone had come along and sliced off the top. He knew that if you actually climbed a mesa the terrain wasn't as flat as it looked from a distance, but from the highway they looked as if they'd been cut with a knife.

As they got closer to Albuquerque, the traffic started to increase. They hadn't seen many buildings along the road, mostly because much of the land right off the highway was owned by the government, so any developments weren't visible from the road. As they entered the Albuquerque area, it was as if all of a sudden an abundance of civilization had sprung up out of nothing. Coming in from the south the area was fairly barren, and then suddenly it was urban. They quickly came up on the exit that would take them downtown. Tyee seemed to know his way around Albuquerque and didn't make any wrong turns.

They exited onto Central Avenue, then turned onto another street that took them to Roma Avenue NW. Tyee found the headquarters, and they entered the parking garage. They found the elevators, went to the fifth floor, and found themselves in a reception area. The officer behind the counter asked who they were looking for, and Ray gave her the detective's name. She asked them to have a seat.

It wasn't long before Detective Taylor came out and introduced himself, asking what their visit was about. Ray told him, and he escorted them back to his office. Ray could tell that the detective was mostly paying attention to Tyee. Ray had become used to Tyee, but he knew that he was a pretty imposing figure. Plus he had on his Indian-hate-all-white-man face. The detective wasn't going to turn his back on this angry mountain of a man.

"Appreciate you seeing us. As I said, we're here about Ed Jackson. I'm a friend of Mike Jackson, Ed's father. Mike's understandably very upset about his son's murder and asked if I could help him find out more about what happened. And we wanted to let you know that Mike is staying with his other son, Luke, for the moment. I have the address and phone number in case you need to get in touch with him."

"Thanks. I'll tell you what I know, but it's not much more than I told the father when I notified him of his son's death. I know this sort of thing is terrible on the family, but it looks like his son was involved with some pretty bad people. The families always want to believe that their son or daughter was innocent and can't understand how something like this could happen. Obviously there's no question that Ed shouldn't have been killed, but our guess is that this was a direct result of his contact with people engaged in criminal activity."

Something about this detective was rubbing Ray the wrong way. *Hell, all he has to do is tell us what he knows—we don't need a fucking lecture about it being the victim's fault.*

"Well yeah, I think we all know, including his father, that Ed was doing things he shouldn't have been doing. We're just looking for any information you might have to help us better understand what happened."

"Well to tell you the truth, Ed wasn't exactly on our radar. He was picked up because of a request from a task force that was being headed up by the FBI. I think it had something to do with fake documents being sold to illegals or something— anyway this was a task force of several federal agencies. He was arrested at a trade show at the convention center and charged with possession of forged collectable documents—once again not my specialty, so I don't know much about it. What I heard is this was a 'tip of the iceberg' sort of thing and involved millions of dollars. Anyway, he was questioned by the FBI, who no doubt were trying to get him to cooperate with them to find the bigger guys, but he refused. He was bailed out by his father and twelve hours later he's dead. Executed with a small caliber weapon—shot between the eyes. We have no weapon, no evidence at all really, and no suspects—if this gets solved, it'll more than likely be by the FBI."

What a jerk. Their plan was to do nothing because it involved a killing between two bad guys—the world was a better place with one of them dead.

"Sounds like there won't be much done by the Albuquerque Police Department."

"If we have any leads or evidence, we'll follow up. Without that there's not a damn thing we can do."

"Did the FBI share with you anything that Ed did say?"

"Not much. One of the agents mentioned that they thought he might still be high, or maybe just permanently confused. He kept saying something about his mother having all of the facts and once he got out he would fix everything. They had no idea what he was talking about. But you know how the FBI operates—they mostly just ignored us like we smelled bad or something."

Ray got up, said thanks, and walked out. Tyee lingered a bit. The detective just stared. Tyee got up and left.

"Many cops just as bad as people they chase."

"Your Indian wisdom nailed that one. What a waste of time. Just a minute, I need to ask the jerk a question."

Ray stepped back into the detective's office. He was gone only a minute. "Asked him if he could give me the FBI's guy name—he said no. Almost said well, I'll have to send the Indian back in to rough you up some—but decided that was probably an unwise thing to say at police headquarters."

"White man has Indian wisdom."

On their way back to the parking garage Ray stopped and asked a young lady carrying files where the Albuquerque office for the FBI was—she said it was in the building next door—she indicated by pointing—and she thought it was on the fourth floor.

They left the car where it was and walked next door. The building was probably thirty or more stories and there was a lot of activity in the lobby, which also hosted a guard. Ray approached him and asked where the FBI offices were. The police officer had been right—it was on the fourth floor. Exiting the elevator, they arrived at another reception area, this time with an attendant behind glass.

"Hi, my name is Ray Pacheco and I'm assisting the Dona Ana County sheriff's department with a matter that involves a person named Ed Jackson. He was killed here in Albuquerque in the last few days. I have been told by the Albuquerque police that there was an FBI task force that was investigating Mr. Jackson. I was wondering if I could speak to someone who might know about that."

"I'm not sure, Mr. Pacheco. Would you take a seat and let me see what I can find out?" Ray suspected the answer would be no. Even so, he thought the response would at least be polite. They were made to wait longer than Ray had expected, and Tyee was looking like he was ready to call it quits when the woman returned.

"Mr. Pacheco, Special Agent Myers will be with you in a minute."

Ray said thanks and sat back down. Tyee looked unimpressed. It had taken her almost fifteen minutes to come back and ask them to wait some more—no telling how long this was going to take. But in just a matter of minutes a tall, distinguished man in his mid-fifties came out and greeted them.

"Well, well, if it's not Ray Pacheco, famous sheriff. I thought I'd heard you retired."

In that it's-a-small-world sort of coincidence, it turned out that Ray knew Myers, though he'd forgotten. Probably twenty years before, this guy had tried to run roughshod over Ray when he was sheriff. Ray didn't let him get away with it, and they had not been friends. Dona Ana County was under the El Paso FBI office and Ray had had many dealings with them. This guy Myers had come in as a loaner from somewhere and acted like he was the only one who knew anything. He clashed with almost everyone and was soon shipped somewhere else—and Ray had completely forgotten him.

"Agent Myers, long time no see." Ray winced inwardly. *What a stupid thing to say.*

The agent showed Ray and Tyee back into his office—a big office. Apparently he was the person in charge. They took the chairs in front of his desk. The desk was way too large to be functional, so it was a power thing. Ray really hated people who played those games.

"Actually Ray, I know you retired and you're not the sheriff in Dona Ana County anymore, so what's this bullshit about you assisting them in some matter?"

"Just trying to be a good citizen by helping my law enforcement heroes."

"Yeah, you're so full of shit. You'll never change Ray—big fucking ego."

"Who gave you permission to be an asshole?" Oops, that was Tyee.

"Get the fuck out of here big chief, and take your fake sheriff with you."

Okay, sometimes things don't work out. Ray decided—and it was a good decision—that the meeting was over, and left with Tyee. He had a strange premonition that Tyee might cause Agent Dickhead some real damage if things progressed any further.

They got on the elevator and headed down. "Are all law

enforcement people assholes?"

"Well, Tyee, that's a reasonable question. I know some that aren't. But the majority have some kind of control issues. Almost everyone you meet in law enforcement shouldn't be in law enforcement. The people who should be doing it wouldn't take the risk involved for the small rewards. So you end up with very flawed people doing very difficult jobs—that's a bad combination. But you're instincts are right—most of them have serious problems."

So that hadn't been helpful. In short order they had pissed off the local detective and the head of the local FBI office. Pretty good work for only an hour or so. On the other hand, sometimes it's better to stir up the wasps than to ignore them—he knew they hadn't heard the last from either man.

They retrieved the Jeep and headed in the direction of Mike's son's house. Ray drove and Tyee attentively consulted a map, giving Ray directions. Albuquerque isn't a huge town and they were soon in the right neighborhood. After a couple of wrong turns, with corrections from Tyee, they arrived in front of the address Mike had given Ray.

With some reluctance, they approached the house. Mike must have been watching for them—before they could even ring the bell, he opened the door and let them inside. Mike didn't look good. It was hard to tell if his health had declined further or if it was fatigue, but Ray had a bad feeling that Mike was declining fast.

Their meeting didn't take long since there was so little to report. Ray told Mike that they were going to stay in touch with the police and the FBI in case anything new turned up. He also told Mike that both agencies thought this was a result of Ed's own poor choices and that his killer was someone associated with his business activities. Mike listened but didn't seem to take in everything. His son, Luke, was there, but had very little to say. Ray and Tyee left.

"Man this has been one depressing day. Maybe we should go to a bar or something." Tyee wasn't completely kidding, but instead they decided to have a quick lunch at a fast food place, then head back to T or C.

They were back at Big Jack's early in the afternoon and found him and Happy enjoying a cool breeze on the dock. After going over the day's activities with Big Jack, they all concluded that the trip hadn't produced anything positive they could work with and had probably been a waste of time.

Ray decided to call Betty Adams. The contact information he'd gotten from Nathan Young for Betty was an address in Dallas and a phone number with a matching area code. There was no answer, so Ray left a voice mail with his information and the phone number at Big Jack's.

# 15

*Thursday*

Ray had a restless night. Something was bothering him. He knew the scenario involving Monica Jackson, Mrs. Richards, and Ed Jackson was wrong in some way, but he didn't know how. He wasn't sure about his previous theories at this point. What he did know was that there were two people dead and at least one missing, and he was sure it was all connected.

It was a drizzly morning and a little bit cool when Ray and Happy headed out to Big Jack's. He had a feeling Tyee would be pleased with the weather, at least as it related to fishing. Ray had concluded that there was a direct correlation between the lack of comfort for the fisherman and the best chance to catch fish. So the best time to go fishing was when it made you the most miserable. Strange humans find weird things to call pleasure—wow, that sounded very Tyee-like inside Ray's head.

Ray and Happy entered Big Jack's. Happy was completely at home, finding a corner without clutter to lie down in and continue his morning nap.

"Hey Ray, I've got your new phone numbers. They ran the lines yesterday. Tyee has already changed his modem to this one, so I guess the other one's the line you can use as the business number."

"Well, how about that. Something went right."

"Yeah, surprise, surprise. Also one of Clayton's groupies dropped off this list of events they've scheduled. Over the next few weeks they already have ten events, and they wanted you to be at the ones that are checked off. The word from the fishing crowd is that they think Clayton has a good chance of winning—and the only people upset about that are the local business group that thought they ran everything."

"Sounds encouraging doesn't it?"

"Let's just hope Clayton doesn't suddenly become an asshole and start saying negative things about his opponent and his opponent's supporters. If he can run a positive race a lot of those business people will support him after he wins. They're only supporting Martinez because of his dad, and I bet a bunch of them are sick and tired of being controlled by the Mayor and his son."

"Good point, Big Jack. I'll mention that to Clayton—he has to stay positive. I think he's the kind of guy who would do that anyway, but it'll be good to reinforce it."

Ray found Tyee out on the dock getting ready to go. He helped finish loading and they were off. Tyee took them only a short distance from Big Jack's, pulling into a small cove.

Tyee explained that this type of cove would be the best area to fish in, due to the depth and rocky condition of the lake bottom. What he wanted Ray to work on was not getting hung up in the overhanging trees and the junk on the bottom of the lake. Ray listened and then began to practice his casting. Within minutes he was hung up on something close to the shore. After some effort, Tyee cut the line and he started over. Tyee was giving him the you-really-don't-know-how-to-do-this look that Ray had seen many times by now.

They stayed in the same cove for hours. Ray would cast and reel in, then cast again. He began to get a feel for how to get close to the shore but not get caught up in the trees or various things in the lake. Soon he was casting and reeling without any hang-ups. Now Tyee was giving him nods of approval.

Tyee pulled up anchor and moved the boat down several yards to the next cove. While the same basic conditions were present, the details were a little different. Ray now knew what to look for and how to control his casting. He began casting and reeling in without any trouble. Soon he got a strike. He was impressed—it was just as Tyee had said. He'd followed Tyee's instructions on lure and bait and had hit his spot exactly—and presto, he had a bite. Maybe Tyee really was best damn fishing guide in whole damn country.

They moved on to other coves, and Ray continued to have success. It really felt like he was getting the hang of what he was supposed to do. Maybe the fishing tournament wouldn't be a disaster after all. The only problem Ray saw was that Tyee wouldn't be in the boat on the day of the tournament—that worried him.

Tyee said that Ray was now an official graduate of the Chino School of Fishing, and that his degree would be in the mail. Knowing full well Tyee was bullshitting him, Ray still felt a sense of accomplishment. He may not win the tournament, but he now knew he could go out and fish and enjoy himself.

They headed back to Big Jack's dock. Ray helped Tyee unload anything that wasn't going to stay in the boat, and then Ray went into the store. Big Jack was on the phone, but handed Ray a piece of paper. Ray had received a call from a

Jane Adams about her mother, Betty Adams. Ray went into the storeroom—now the computer room, he supposed—and called the number.

"Hello."

"Hi, this is Ray Pacheco and I'm returning your call."

"Oh yes. I'm so glad you called. We're very worried about my mother—she's been missing for days. The police haven't helped at all. It's just horrible. My husband and I don't know what to do. When I was at her house, I checked the messages and heard yours. Do you know anything about where she is?"

"I'm sorry. I didn't know your mother was missing. My call was to ask your mother about a lady she knows through the dog shows who's disappeared. Her name is Monica Jackson. She disappeared from T or C, New Mexico, Saturday a week ago. This is very troubling to learn that your mother's missing too. When did she disappear?"

There was silence on the line. She hadn't hung up. Ray was concerned she might have just walked away from the phone.

"Jane, are you okay?"

"I'm sorry, just a minute." Her voice was shaking and Ray could hear her crying—he waited.

"Jane, do you need to call me back?"

"No. I'm okay now. I'm sorry. Yes, I know who Monica is—she's my mother's friend from the dog shows. I can't believe this—are you saying something has happened to them? Like an accident or something? But you said that Monica disappeared on Saturday. They must not be together because I talked to my mother on Sunday—she was in El Paso. Then on Thursday she left me a message that she was going on a little trip and would call me in a couple of days. I haven't heard from her since. Do you think they're together?"

"Jane, nobody knows right now." Ray went on to relate the circumstances of Monica's disappearance. He told her that he had no idea how any of this was connected, but it seemed likely that it was. He also felt he had to tell her about Monica's son, and understandably she became even more upset. Ray wished they could've had the conversation in person. He hadn't told her about Mrs. Richards, mostly because Ray didn't see how that had anything to do with Betty, but also because he didn't want to add to Jane's worry.

"Jane, when your mother left the message on Thursday, did she say she was still in El Paso?"

"Not in the message, but the phone shows the number of the caller. It was the same El Paso number she'd called from before—I believe it's the hotel number."

"Jane, you have my number. Please call me any time if something comes up or if you have a question. If I learn anything, I'll call you. I know you're worried, but based on what you've told me today I think your mother and Monica may be hiding out because Monica is afraid she's in danger. I'm going to El Paso tomorrow, and if I learn anything I'll call you."

Ray found Tyee and Big Jack and told them what he'd learned.

"So, it looks like a week ago Monica and Betty were still in El Paso at the same hotel as the dog show. They may have just moved to a different room under different names. My guess is that they left the hotel on Thursday—I think that's why Betty called her daughter—and then they went somewhere. Why they did that, or where they went, I don't know. I'm going to go to El Paso tomorrow to the hotel and see if

I can learn anything. I'll also go by the FBI office—anybody want to ride along?"

As it turned out Tyee and Big Jack had other things to handle. Tyee was helping with one of the campaign events the next evening and needed to print off registration forms along with new flyers. Big Jack had Big Jack stuff to do, but he agreed that Happy could hang out at the store. Ray's plan was to be back by early afternoon.

Before Ray left he called Mike and told him the latest news. Mike didn't seem to understand the importance of it, but Ray told him he thought this could mean that Monica was hiding out with Betty and that they were safe. That seemed to cheer Mike some, but even over the phone Ray could sense that he was drifting. He told Mike that as soon as he learned anything for sure, he would call.

Ray attended one of the smaller campaign events and was pleased to see a good crowd. He gave his now refined endorsement speech and received a good round of applause. There was no free beer at this event, so the response was a little calmer, but the crowd was still enthusiastic. It was a surprise to Ray that Sue was there. She said the host was a good customer at the Lone Post, and he and his wife had invited her. Ray's ego thought maybe she was there to see him.

Ray and Sue talked for quite a while before she said that she needed to get home. She gave Ray a peck on the cheek and headed out. Ray and Happy went home, alone.

# 16

*Friday*

Ray dropped Happy off at Big Jack's on his way to El Paso, about a two hour drive with very little traffic. He had made the trip there from Las Cruces many times, so it felt very familiar. As sheriff of Dona Ana County, he'd had many dealings with the FBI and the Border Patrol. Dona Ana County bordered Texas and Mexico. Ray was known for standing his ground regarding jurisdictional issues, but also had a reputation for being cooperative and professional.

Traveling along I-10, Ray crossed over into Texas at Anthony, New Mexico. The border between Texas and New Mexico shifted to the Rio Grande River a little way to the West. The culture in this area was much more Mexican than it was Texan or New Mexican. There were still many families in this part of the country that had grandparents who remembered when the area was part of Mexico, not Texas or New Mexico. There were also many families that resented the U.S. for its expansion into the territory. Ray had been surprised when he moved to the area to find that there was still tension just below the surface arising from the hostility between the two countries, and that people still often took one side or the other.

The downtown exit took Ray into El Paso very quickly.

The Camino Real Hotel was just off of I-10, on South El Paso Street. Originally opened in 1912, it was a very impressive structure and considered a landmark. Extensive renovations had created a first class, impressive building. And it was next to the convention center, so many events used the hotel as their headquarters. Ray had attended numerous law enforcement meetings and events here over the years.

Entering the hotel, Ray was once again impressed by its soaring lobby, and by the Dome Bar with its incredible domed ceiling. He went to the registration desk and asked to speak to a manager. He introduced himself as a past sheriff of Dona Ana County doing some investigative work for the sheriff's department. Of course it was a little white lie, but he knew the new sheriff would support him if something ever came back to bite him.

"What can we do for you, sheriff?" The manager was a very tall, impeccably dressed man in his mid-forties. He seemed to exude confidence and professionalism. Ray wondered if he always said "we" when he meant "I."

"I'm looking into the disappearance of two ladies who were guests here a couple of weeks ago. They were part of the dog show that was being held at the hotel. Monica Jackson and Betty Adams are their names. Not sure if Monica Jackson actually made it to the hotel, in that she seems to have disappeared on her way here when she had made a stop in T or C. However, we do know that Betty Adams was staying here and that she talked to Monica. Looking for any information that might be available about either one of these women."

"Well of course. We are aware of the disappearance of Monica Jackson—several law enforcement agencies, as well as her relatives, have contacted us about that—but we have no information regarding Ms. Jackson. Our records indicated that she phoned and canceled her first night's reservation and then didn't show up for her second night. Regarding Ms. Adams, I wasn't aware that she was considered missing. Are you saying that they're connected somehow?"

"Yes, that's what we currently believe. At this point we don't know that for sure—but we think it's possible that Ms. Adams and Ms. Jackson met here, maybe on Saturday, and either left together or maybe rented another room here and stayed some days longer, more or less in hiding. Is there any way to check your registration for two women staying here on Sunday of that week?"

The super-manager didn't look pleased. "Not sure about that, sheriff. Our guest's privacy is very important to us, and we won't give out information unless you've gone through the proper legal channels."

Could have just said no. Ray and the manager discussed the reasons Ray thought he should by-pass his concerns and provide him with the information. The manager said he appreciated Ray's concern for the ladies' safety, but the answer was still no unless he had a court order. Ray left.

Ray wasn't sure what he'd expected to learn at the hotel. While learning nothing wasn't helpful, at least he knew now that the hotel wasn't a source to pursue. That's what investigations are mostly about, crossing off the things that don't provide you with any information so you can concentrate on the ones that might actually help. Well, that was the theory—it was still very frustrating to continue to plod along gaining very little ground.

The El Paso FBI office was only a few blocks away from the hotel. Ray found the building easily and pulled into the underground parking lot. Once inside, he went to the eighth floor and entered an enclosed reception area. A very attractive young woman sat behind a glass barrier.

"May I help you?"

"Good morning. My name is Ray Pacheco and I'd like to see Agent Sanchez if he's available."

"Do you have an appointment with him?"

"Nope. Just tell him my name and that I used to be the sheriff of Dona Ana County."

She placed a call and had a conversation Ray couldn't hear.

"Mr. Pacheco, Agent Sanchez will be with you in a few minutes."

Ray thanked her and took a seat. He didn't remember Sanchez as the type to play games, so he thought it would probably actually be only a few minutes. Then it turned into fifteen—maybe everybody was playing games.

Agent Sanchez entered the reception area like he was in a hurry. He greeted Ray and immediately showed him to his office.

"Sorry for the wait, Ray. I was on the phone with a buddy of yours. Special Agent Myers in Albuquerque. When I mentioned that you were here, he proceeded to describe you in several ways—none of them nice. What have you done to piss off Myers?"

"I dropped in at his office in Albuquerque and was going to ask him about a man who had been killed. This guy was somehow tied into a task force headed by the FBI. I didn't get to ask him anything, though. He said something to the effect that I was an asshole and our meeting ended."

Agent Sanchez chuckled. "Yeah, he's a real head case. Ray, this is great that you dropped by today. I was going to try and contact you next week to set up a meeting. We have some things we need to discuss."

Ray wasn't sure what that meant and didn't know whether it was good or bad—but at least he didn't toss Ray out of his office. Sanchez asked for someone to bring some coffee to the small conference room, then escorted Ray into what was, literally, a small conference room. He asked Ray to take a seat, saying he would be right back. Once again, waiting.

The very attractive young woman from the front desk brought in a tray with a carafe of coffee and a small tray of pastries and left. Ray was still alone. He poured himself a coffee and was eyeing one of the donuts when Agent Sanchez reentered the room.

"Ray, I'd like to introduce Special Agent Crawford."

Crawford was a big man in his sixties. No question, at that age and still in the FBI, he had to be someone from Washington. They shook hands and everyone took seats.

"Ray, I've heard some very good things about you over the years. The FBI was very sorry when you decided to retire. It's more unusual than we'd like to have a good working relationship with local officials, and we hated losing your expertise." This was said by Crawford without preamble and without any details about who he was or what he was doing here.

"Agent Crawford, I appreciate your kind words. I always felt like the law enforcement community should be a team—however, often that wasn't the case because of overbearing members of Federal agencies. This office always treated everyone with respect, and that led to good cooperation. Some other agencies were more difficult. I'm not sure why you're in here today. Does this have something to do with me?"

"Yes, it does, Ray. I was here to talk to Agent Sanchez about approaching you to assist us. He and I had been discussing the details when you showed up out of the blue. We were surprised, but we thought why not take the opportunity to discuss with you what we had in mind. I'm sorry if I seem abrupt—maybe that's a problem all Federal people share—we need to learn to be more open. It's not in our nature, so it'll take some practice."

Ray liked Crawford. He seemed like a no-nonsense kind of person who focused on results and not egos—just Ray's kind of guy.

"Look Agent Crawford, maybe I'm the one being abrupt, but what do you mean by assisting you?"

"Ray, we at the FBI are putting together a new approach, hiring outside people to help us with some internal matters along with certain investigations. Some of this is being driven by budgets, with more money being allocated for private contractors as opposed to employees. Mostly, though, this is about results. We want to experiment with hiring special contractors such as yourself with unique experience in certain parts of the country to provide our people with a better understanding of that local environment. I think Agent Sanchez, as you pointed out, is doing an excellent job in El Paso, but we have areas where our agents do run roughshod over the local officials and are creating barriers to getting the job done. Agent Sanchez was going to contact you and set up a meeting next week to discuss this, but what the hell, you're here now so I thought let's take advantage of the coincidence and tell you what we were thinking."

"Hire me as a contractor to the FBI?"

"Yes. There would obviously be restrictions on what you could do and how you could conduct yourself. But in essence you would be providing us with investigative services outside of our normal channels. We also would be looking for you to provide us with insight on how our people are handling themselves. Your association with the FBI would only be known by a select group—your contact agent—in this case Agent Sanchez—and select people in Washington, including myself."

"Well, that's the last thing I expected when I walked in here."

"Yeah, I bet that's true. When you retired we'd planned on talking to you about this idea. But you moved to T or C pretty fast and seemed settled into retirement, so we dropped it. Recently, you've been looking into this missing woman, and we were notified that you'd applied for a PI license, so we thought maybe you'd decided that retirement was boring. We thought we'd approach you and see if you were interested. What are your thoughts?"

"Well, the part about retirement being boring's correct. I thought I wanted to just be left alone. Then after a few months, I needed something to do. Settled on fishing, which as it turns out I do like, but what really got me to thinking I wanted to be more involved was this thing with the missing woman. I've been more alive and happier since I've had something to do and to think about. How'd you know I applied for a license?"

"Ray, we're nosy. Part of it's our job and part of it's just our nature. As I said, we thought we might be hiring you once you'd retired, so your name was entered into a tracking system that monitors public information about that person. So when you filed your application, it sent a red flag to Agent Sanchez. I hope you don't think that's sinister. Much of what we do is about compiling data, most of which we never use. Anyway, when we saw that you'd applied for a PI license, we knew we should talk to you. I'm in the process of putting together a proposal for you that would include a monthly retainer we would pay, plus hourly rates for you or your firm's services. If you decide to do this, anyone in your firm who'd have access to FBI information would have to pass an extensive background check. I'd hope to have the final proposal to you by mid-week next week."

Background check. Ray wondered about Tyee. And most assuredly he was concerned about Big Jack—or whatever his name was.

"Agent Crawford, I believe I'm interested in discussing this further. My plan is to start this investigation business with a recent acquaintance of mine, Tyee Chino. I'll need to talk to him and see if this is something he'd be interested in pursuing. Can we leave this open until after I get your proposal? We could talk about specifics then."

"That's just fine. Please give Agent Sanchez your contact information and we'll be in touch." Agent Crawford stood and shook Ray's hand before leaving the conference room.

"Sorry, Ray, if that felt like an ambush—I had no idea you were going to be here today and Crawford didn't want to pass up the opportunity to talk to you himself. I hope you decide to do this—I think you could help us with a lot of things we're working on right now. And your insights into this part of the world would be greatly appreciated."

"Thanks. I'm going to think about this real hard. The reason I dropped in was to ask you if you had any information about the missing woman from T or C, or the murder of her son in Albuquerque. Sounds like you know something about my involvement with the missing woman, which only started because of her dog."

Ray related the whole story about the dog showing up, how he eventually met the ex-husband, and the call from the ex-husband saying his son had been killed. Also, the information from the local police that it had something to do with a joint task force headed by the FBI and Ray's short, ugly meeting with Agent Myers in Albuquerque.

"Yeah, Myers called me. He says you're a loose cannon. He's always been difficult and I have no idea how he landed the job in Albuquerque. Listen Ray, this is just between us girls, I happen to know that there have been a lot of complaints about his performance in Albuquerque and he's getting some pretty close scrutiny right now. He's not only angry at you, but everyone else too. So rest assured his opinion about you has no impact on anything. As far as information about the missing woman or the murder of the son, I have none. I know it has something to do with forged documents coming out of central L.A."

"Central L.A.? I'd heard the documents were being made in Mexico."

"Don't believe that to be the case, Ray. Most of this activity is being driven by the Mexican Mafia—but their base is L.A. not Mexico."

They talked some more, but Ray didn't learn anything

new. He had a bunch to think about. Sanchez had his new contact phone number, so he said his goodbyes and headed out.

Once back on I-10, Ray put it on auto-pilot and thought about everything that had happened. He couldn't be more surprised by the offer to work as a contractor for the FBI. His ego was pleased, but there was a part of his brain saying he should be cautious.

After a few hours, Ray took the T or C exit toward Main Street and the Lone Post Café. It was Friday night, and Ray was going to ask Sue to join him for dinner at his cabin. He parked in front and went in. There were no customers and only the lady at the cashier. Ray asked if Sue was still there, but was told she just left. He'd learned that Sue lived only a short distance off of Main, and that she didn't have a phone. While he was reluctant to just drop in, without a phone he had no choice if he wanted to see her.

Within a few blocks of the café, Ray pulled up to a small, plain house that was in need of some repairs. Out front was Sue's car. He sat for a while, and was about to get out when the front door opened and out walked Sue.

"Hi. Were you just going to sit out here until I came out?"

"Maybe."

Sue laughed. "For some reason I thought you'd come by the Café today. I was real disappointed when you didn't."

"Yeah, I went to El Paso. I did come by, but it was just after you left, the lady said. By the way, who is that lady and why does she dislike me?"

"Ray, you really are something. She doesn't dislike you—she just thinks you're too old for me. And I believe she has a crush on you."

"Oh, I didn't know that. Sue would you have dinner with me?"

"I'd be most pleased to have dinner with you, Ray Pacheco. Would you like for me to bring anything?"

"Don't think so. I have an old grill I use sometimes, so I was thinking maybe some grilled chicken with pasta and a salad. That okay?"

"My goodness, Ray, you really are a cook aren't you?"

"I'm trying to impress you."

"I thought it was the woman who was supposed to cook to impress the man."

"Yeah, guess I got that confused."

"I'll see you in about two hours. And you stay away from the Café cashier lady, okay. For the time being you are mine."

Ray smiled. He knew she was teasing him and he liked it.

# 17

*Saturday*

Ray had two Clayton campaign events scheduled for the day. He also hoped to talk to Tyee and Big Jack about the FBI offer. He still didn't know what to think about the idea. Obviously it would give them an immediate boost in business, but somehow working with the FBI felt a little odd to him.

Sue had left before he was up. She'd fixed coffee and left Ray a note saying she was working this morning and had left very early. He felt bad that he hadn't remembered that she worked the Saturday early shift. Once again it proved to Ray that he was a lot more self-absorbed than he thought. Deciding he needed to do a better job of seeing the world from other people's perspective, especially Sue's, he started getting ready for the day.

As Ray and Happy stepped out onto the porch, he noticed large trucks in the distance and men milling about. A better look told him it was the telephone company. How about that. It looked like they were working on getting phone service to his property. While Ray's instinctive impulse to hide from the world during his retirement still held a warm spot in his heart, being involved with Sue and the new business had given him a renewed sense of purpose in life that felt good. The phone would be a tangible sign that he wasn't hiding any longer.

Ray found Big Jack on his dock dealing with a customer. The customer seemed irritated with Big Jack about something. As Ray approached he heard some of the conversation.

"Listen, fat man. Just because you own this pile of shit store gives you no right to tell me what I can do on this goddamn lake—got it?"

Ray could see immediately that the customer was very drunk—and it was barely eight in the morning. He had a buddy in the boat who looked like he was passed out.

"Hey, pal. I'm not telling you what to do—I'm telling you I won't sell you anymore beer. Now get the fuck off of my dock."

Not the thing you say to a big drunk guy so early in the morning. The big customer took a step toward Big Jack. In a move that completely surprised Ray, Big Jack moved unexpectedly fast, with impressive power and skill, and quickly had the man flat on the dock. By all appearances, Big Jack had dislocated the drunk's shoulder. Ray ran up and helped Big Jack subdue the man, who was yelling his shoulder was broken. Ray finally got the man's attention and told him to shut up.

Big Jack headed back into the store where Ray hoped he was calling the sheriff and an ambulance. T or C only had a small clinic for emergencies, so the guy would probably have to be transported to Las Cruces—but this guy was going to need some immediate help.

As Ray tried to make the man comfortable, he could see that he was going into shock from the pain. He found an old tarp and tried to cover the man to keep him warm.

"Dumb, drunk bastard. Found him trying to steal beer out of the store room. Then he wanted to buy beer, and I told him he'd drunk enough. He starts yelling at me. Sure didn't mean to hurt him that much—you think he'll be okay?" There was genuine concern in Big Jack's voice.

"He'll need medical help quick or it could be serious."

"I called the sheriff's office and they said they'd dispatch the ambulance. Should be here pretty soon."

Ray would never have guessed that a man as large as Big Jack could have moved that fast and with that much power. He could easily see the years of training that had to be behind the coordinated moves. He also had the feeling that if Big Jack had wanted it, the man could easily be dead now rather than just injured.

They heard the siren as the ambulance neared the store. The paramedics moved in quickly and took charge of the injured man, speaking on the radio with someone as they examined him. In one of those moves that's probably best not to watch, one of the paramedics skillfully relocated the man's shoulder. With a deep groan the drunk patient passed out.

"He's going to be fine. Don't see anything else wrong with him other than the shoulder. We're going to take him to the clinic and let the doc look at him. Might keep him there or take him to Las Cruces. Will the sheriff be involved in this?"

Big Jack said he wasn't going to press charges so he didn't know, but that a deputy would be there soon and Big Jack would let him know where they were taking the guy.

"How about his buddy over there?"

"I think he's just passed out. I'll let the deputy handle that one."

The paramedics put the man onto a gurney and took him to the ambulance. As they were pulling out, a deputy's car pulled in. After a discussion with Big Jack, the deputy roused the other morning drunk and got him out of the boat and into the deputy's car.

"Life in the big city, right Big Jack?"

"Well, there're morons everywhere." Big Jack was headed to the store to make some more coffee. It was obvious he was a little pumped up, and it would take him some time to calm down.

Happy, who had observed all of this from his customary spot on the dock, decided it was all over and it was time for his fifth morning nap. Ray followed Big Jack into the store.

"Big Jack, there's something I need to talk to you about. You know yesterday I was in El Paso. I dropped in the hotel and went to the FBI office. I was just poking around looking for anything that might give me some ideas on where Monica might be, and something very surprising happened."

Ray went on to relate what had happened in the FBI office. He gave Big Jack the details, as far as he understood them, regarding the FBI offer. Ray said he thought it was something they should consider but that there were problems.

"The biggest issue I see at this point is the background checks. I only want to do this new business if you and Tyee are involved, and I understood your reluctance to have your identity compromised. I guess I'm not real sure of Tyee's background as far as an FBI check."

About that time, Tyee entered the store from the dock. "What's this? The FBI wants to check my background?"

Ray explained everything that had happened to Tyee.

"Let me say I think we have some flexibility here with the FBI. Of course I don't know what they might find, but my gut says they'll overlook some things to get us onboard with this new program of theirs."

"Ray, what you're saying is they might overlook some minor things in my past, or Tyee's, to get you to work for them. I'm not sure they want us at all."

"You can read it anyway you want. I'm telling you that if this doesn't work for either one of you, I won't do it. This isn't just being loyal—it's reality. I can't do everything I once could. I'm not dead yet, but I'm also not getting any younger. Whatever we're going to do with this business, I'll only do with you and Tyee as partners—end of story."

"Ray, my story is fairly simple," Tyee said. "I don't have a criminal background, just a lot of stupid personal decisions. After a messy and very emotionally trying divorce, I dropped out of life. My family had turned against me when I married a white woman I'd met in college, so I couldn't ask them for help. The woman was the love of my life, and when she left me for another man I fell completely apart. When I graduated from college I'd been hired by a software company in Denver and I was on a path to financial success like nothing I'd ever dreamed about. But due to my depression and drinking, I was fired. Everything got very bad. I spent a lot of years just barely getting by and avoiding all responsibility. Looking for a place to hide, I ended up on this lake. Then you came along and things started to change for me. This company and our friendships mean a great deal to me—I'll do whatever we agree is the right thing to do."

Ray was touched by Tyee's honesty and trust. He knew that trusting people after a personal trauma like that was the hardest human skill to regain. They all stood there quietly for a while as they absorbed their friend's difficult past.

"Well, fellas. My story isn't so simple." That was Big Jack. "There may be some criminal charges, and there are definitely some less than desirable associations. On the good side is that there are no convictions."

Big Jack wasn't going to be as casually forthcoming as Tyee. It was going to take a while to get the whole story. Ray was concerned that Big Jack wouldn't see the benefit to him of letting someone delving into his past. Why risk whatever threat his past held for him by becoming visible again? But then Big Jack continued.

"Fuck it—what the hell. First off, my real name's Philip Duncan. I'm a graduate of the Stanford Law School. I was practicing law in L.A. and was a very successful criminal defense attorney working for the largest firm in California. I was making big bucks. Life couldn't have been better. One day I was contacted by a member of the Mexican Mafia—you may think this doesn't exist, but let me tell you, it does. He wanted me to represent him. Most of my clients were criminals, obviously, but this guy was a real kingpin. I should've stayed away. I knew this guy was the lowest of the low, but greed got in the way."

Big Jack paused for a moment, then continued. "Almost from the beginning, things went wrong. I'd quoted him a huge figure as a retainer. The next day several large boxes showed up at my house, and inside was the retainer in cash. Should have stopped right there and called the cops. Instead I counted it. More cash than I'd ever seen. I put the boxes in the garage. Went to work and was in court all day on another case. Got a call from the police that my house was on fire. When I arrived it had burned almost to the ground, including the garage. So this asshole calls me at the office the next day and says that it's really tough about my house—he hopes I put his retainer in a safe place."

"No question in my mind, some of his goons stole the cash back and then burned down the house. After a couple of days of worrying about this mess I called him and said I wasn't going to represent him. He said sure that was okay. Just give him back the retainer. I told him I didn't have it—it had been in the house and burned up with everything else. He said I had two choices, represent him or return the retainer. So I represented him for nothing. The partners in the law firm came unglued. Not only were they not going to associate with these assholes, they weren't going to associate with me—I was fired. I told the client I'd been fired and couldn't represent him anymore. He said fuck that—I was still an attorney, and I would represent him until I returned the retainer or I was fired by him. One day I'm on top of the world, making more money than I can spend, and the next day I'm a legal slave to the lowest scum on the planet."

"It actually got worse. I wasn't being paid and now he had me representing one scum bag after another who worked for him. I was being chauffeured around in a big black SUV by an armed thug and being watched at the apartment I rented by an around-the-clock team of thugs. I confronted him. They broke my leg. I was in the hospital for a week. When I got out, they were there. Now, I'd lost all contact with any friends or associates. Everyone had decided that I'd gone to the dark side. I had two ex-wives who were receiving substantial alimony payments, but over the next few months of living on my savings and going to court defending these useless indefensible creeps, I missed two months of payments. I was served a summons by both ex-wives to appear in court. One night I'm sitting around drowning my sorrows, and the FBI shows up at the door. In full site of the babysitting thugs, they drop in to ask me to testify against my so-called clients. I told them that any information I had was protected by privilege. They said they didn't give a big fuck, they wanted me to become a confidential informant and they'd put me into the witness protection program. They said I had two days to join their side or they would drop a big rock on me.

"The next day during a court recess I took a taxi to the bus station and left town. Left everything behind and told no one. Except that morning I'd cashed out my savings and had it in a duffle bag. Went to Portland first, bought an old car and started driving. Lived in the car for a week or so before I began to relax. My savings had been depleted over the last few months, but it was still substantial and it was in the trunk. I expected at any moment to be stopped for some violation of something and never see freedom again. Somehow or another I made it to Las Cruces via Phoenix. Was hanging out there in an incredibly cheap motel when I decided to head north. Wandering had become my practice, so I would often take exits and see where they headed—that's how I ended up here at Elephant Butte. Most of the story you've heard about me buying Big Jack's is true—it was just a fluke and an impulsive decision. I thought I could hide here forever and none of the people who wanted me dead or in jail would be able to find me."

"My god, Big Jack, what a story." Ray was stunned that his friend, whom he considered an honorable man, had such a past.

Tyee shook his head. "Wow, Ray, you've got two fucked up partners." Big Jack looked like he might laugh at Tyee's comment, but didn't.

"Do we still call you Big Jack or Philip?"

"I never liked the name Philip—you could shorten my new name to just Jack if you like." Why that was funny Ray didn't know, but suddenly he was laughing, and soon all of them were laughing.

"Jack, I don't know this for a fact but I have a feeling you were a pretty good lawyer. What would you do right now if you were your own client?"

"Interesting question."

"Fuck white man before white man can fuck you." Tyee's wisdom *sounded* right on target, but nobody actually understood what he was saying.

"What in the hell does that mean, Tyee?"

"You've got to give them what they want and in return they give you what you want. Tell the FBI—that Washington guy—your story, and say you'll provide confidential information about what you know concerning the Mexican Mafia but won't testify in court. In return they give you a new identity and clear you to work with Pacheco and Chino."

"I suppose that could work—probably depends on what they think I know. Plus, it's been a few years and the whole landscape of the L.A. scene has changed several times, I'm sure. Might be they don't give a shit about what I know because all those thugs are dead and have been replaced by new thugs."

"Jack, let me act as go-between. I can call the Washington agent and tell him your story without mentioning your real name and see if he's interested in discussing this or not."

"Why not, Ray."

They agreed to talk later. Ray headed out to the first campaign event. It was being held at a small campsite just off of the lake. They were expecting fifty or so people, but when Ray got there it looked to be twice that amount. Ray greeted people, some of whom he had met before. He gave his usual stump speech and then answered some questions.

"Ray, are you going to help Clayton if he's elected?"

"Well, I will if Deputy Clayton feels he needs help, but he has a lot of years of experience in the department and I don't believe he'll need any assistance from me. The area he may find the most difficult is the political side of things—but I have great confidence in Deputy Clayton. He knows law enforcement and he knows people—he'll do just fine."

"We have all kinds of problems around the lake that the sheriff has completely ignored for years. How is the new sheriff going help us?"

"Mr. Ramos, right? Well, he's said he's going to try and keep one patrol car in the lake area on most days to cut down on response time. Also, he wants to organize a monthly meeting where he can answer questions about what the department's doing to support the lake community. Let's be candid: Deputy Clayton's relying on your support to elect him—when he wins, he isn't going to forget that."

"I talked to the Mayor and he says that he can cut the department's budget. If Clayton wins that's exactly what he'll do."

"The Mayor and his son have said some things that are very self-serving. So what's the Mayor saying? Vote for my son or you won't have any services around the lake. Well, he can say that but the Mayor's one vote on the commission, and he's losing support because of these kinds of threats. Deputy Clayton wants to provide the best policing services for the entire county—not just T or C. I think the Mayor's comments and attitude are the best reasons to vote for Deputy Clayton. Thanks everybody for coming today. Make sure that you and your neighbors are registered and remember to vote. Thanks."

Ray stayed around for a little while, shaking hands and answering a few more questions, and then he left. The next event was only about a mile away, so he headed that way.

The second event only had about twenty-five people. But, all in all, Ray was impressed that people were showing up and seemed very interested.

Ray gave the same speech. Some of the questions were more or less the same, except one.

"You just moved up here a couple of months ago and now you think you can run Sierra County like you ran Dona Ana. I, for one, think it's a bunch of crap to have you interfere in this race. You don't know anything about this county. You and your crazy Indian and that old fat fart who owns the store, are not part of the community. The Mayor and his son have lived here their entire lives and it's wrong for you to try and take their jobs away."

There was a smattering of boos. Ray raised his hand for quiet.

"Don't know you, sir—but I'm not trying to run any county. I'm supporting Deputy Clayton because I think he's the best professional law enforcement officer in this county. Nobody's taking anyone's job—this is an election where the residents decide who best can serve their needs. If you think that's Sheriff Martinez, then by all means you should vote for him. The Mayor isn't up for election yet. And I take offense to your characterization of my friends. So why don't you watch your mouth?"

This got a brief round of applause. The loudmouth left in a huff, mumbling things under his breath, while Ray shook hands. As far as he could see, the moron's comments had done more than anything he could have said to firm up the support for Clayton.

# 18

*Some Days in the Past—Monica's Story*

Monica loved driving her little Subaru—especially with Bruce asleep in the back. It felt cozy and safe. She'd had so much on her mind lately that she could never seem to fully relax—her mind was so preoccupied with her many worries that it was impossible to just think about nothing. It was one of the reasons she'd looked forward to this weekend in El Paso.

While she loved her car, it didn't go far on a tank of gas. She had mapped out her trip and knew she was going to stop in T or C to get gas. And it was also a good place to eat. She'd been there before and seemed to remember a local café that would meet her needs. Monica hated the fast food places that made every town look—and taste—the same. When she'd been young each town had had its own character. They were unique, the stores were unique, the restaurants were unique. One of the joys of traveling was stopping at different restaurants that looked nothing like the restaurants in your town. Now every exit had a McDonalds and a Subway—the same in California as in Texas as in Florida—and she hated it.

Bruce was the Icelandic Sheepdog she was showing at the El Paso dog show. He was a champion, and if it hadn't been for dishonest judges he would've been named overall champ.

Monica could get real pissed when she thought about the show judges and how they made sure their friends' dogs won.

She pulled off at the T or C exit, found Main Street, and parked in front of the Lone Post Café. The food was delicious and the quantity was generous, enough for both her and Bruce. The experience was wonderful until she returned to her car. She was confronted with a threatening note and two slashed tires.

Monica only had one real enemy that she knew of, an eighty-something-year-old woman named Mrs. Richards who thought that Monica had cheated her on a dog Mrs. Richards had bought from her. The woman was relentless. Monica would have given her the money back just to have it done with, but that didn't seem to be what she wanted—she wanted Monica to be punished for hurting her and her husband.

When this had first come up, Monica had talked to her about the fact that the dog seemed to be a bit flawed, although all of his papers were in order. Mrs. Richards insisted that Monica had to pay triple damages to make up for her suffering. The one time Monica had talked to Mr. Richards on the phone, he'd been more reasonable. He'd explained that his wife was having some mental issues, and he hoped to have her in a controlled environment in a few weeks—a nursing home. He had told Monica that trying to take care of her had just about worn him out. Monica thought the best thing she could do was just wait until everything quieted down and then try and give the refund to the husband. Unfortunately, it didn't go that way. The husband had a heart attack and died—and everything got worse.

Mrs. Richards started calling Monica every day. She

insisted that Monica pay for all of the things that had happened to her and for killing her husband. Monica reported her threatening phone calls to the police, who told her that they'd spoken with Richards's son, who said he was trying to get his mother into an Alzheimer's facility in Albuquerque. They advised Monica to ignore the threats and said time would take care of the problem.

After reading this terrible note, Monica knew it had to be from Mrs. Richards. But slashing the tires—that seem pretty far-fetched for an eighty year old woman. Then again, who knew? She sure was angry, and Monica had decided she was also crazy.

Monica talked to the deputy about the note and the tires. He seemed concerned, but she couldn't bring herself to mention Mrs. Richards. She didn't want to cause her any trouble— and maybe she was wrong, maybe it was just some random vandalism and had nothing to do with Monica's only known enemy.

After she checked into the Hot Springs Inn, Monica tried to relax and enjoy the break. She was still very energetic for her age, but the last few months had been trying. She knew her ex-husband's health was declining rapidly. She still cared for him and didn't want to think about him dying. They had three grown children— two of them more or less leading normal lives. The third, the oldest, was still a problem child, even at almost forty. He seemed to bring a new heartache into their lives every day.

Monica called the hotel in El Paso and canceled her reservation for that night, but confirmed she would be there the next night. She called back to the hotel and asked for Betty's room. Once again getting voice mail, she left a message that she would not be at the hotel tonight, explaining her problem with the car. She left her hotel's number and her extension. Then she called Mike, her ex-husband.

"Hello."

"Hello, Mike. It's me. How're you doing?"

"I'm okay. Where are you now?"

"Well, I had some car trouble, flat tires. I'm going to be spending the night in T or C. They didn't have the right size tire, so they've ordered the right ones from El Paso. They'll be here in the morning. Anyway, big pain in the butt. I'm safe, though, and maybe a good night's sleep will help everything."

"Sorry you've had trouble, but glad you're safe."

Monica gave Mike the hotel number and her room extension.

"Mike, something kind of strange happened. Someone left me a threatening note on my car while I was in the restaurant here. Maybe it had nothing to do with me and was some local prankster, but I'm concerned that it might be Mrs. Richards. She's the only person who hates me, which is what the note said. Could you find Ed and have him give me a call. I'm very worried that the papers he gave me for that dog weren't real and I really did cheat her, even if I didn't know it."

"Look, Monica, you've tried to refund the money. What're you going to do, give her three times the money? You and I have discussed this, she's nuts—there's no way to deal with her. Maybe Ed did cheat you, and you cheated her, but you didn't intend to. Plus, that was a good dog. She wasn't going to show him anyway, she just has a screw loose."

"Well thanks for the support Mike. That makes me feel

a little better. I still want to talk to Ed, though. I'm so worried about him. I can't imagine how desperate he must be if he thought he needed to cheat me out of money with this dog nonsense. Could you find him and give him my number here at the hotel?"

Mike agreed that he would try. He gave Monica a new phone number he'd just gotten for Ed so she could call him the next day if Mike couldn't reach him. He told her he'd tried to call him just a little while before, but he hadn't been home. He thought Ed was doing some kind of show at the convention center, so he'd try to contact him later. He reminded her to be careful and hung up.

As soon as Monica hung up, the phone rang.

"Hello."

"Monica, it's Betty. What's going on with your car?"

Monica related the whole story to Betty, who knew all about Mrs. Richards from talking to Monica about it several times.

"I just can't believe that she would slash my tires—can you see that old lady slashing tires?"

"Well hell, Monica. Who knows what she's capable of? I think you need to take the advice of the deputy sheriff and give him all of the information you have about Mrs. Richards. If she's following you, I think the sheriff's office should get involved."

"Yeah. Maybe. I'm reluctant to push this any further. Her son says that within a week or so she's going into an assisted living facility where she'll be locked in. I sure don't want to punish her because she's lost her mind."

"Okay. Maybe you're right. What time do you think you'll

be here tomorrow?"

"Most likely before noon. The car is supposed to be ready by nine in the morning but you know that won't work out. So I'm going to miss the first round of the dog show. I think I won't even enter, I'll just hang out with you and watch the others. Maybe I can boo Nate as he wins the championship."

"Sounds like someone's in a bad mood." They shared a little laughter. Betty always made Monica feel better. They agreed they would see each other the next day and hung up.

Monica decided she needed a good soak to ease some of the tension. After her bath she put on pajamas and got into bed with the book she was reading at the moment. Finally, feeling less tired after such a trying day, she almost smiled. Then the phone rang.

"Hello."

"Mom, is that you?"

She immediately suspected he was on something. His voice was too quick and a bit too high. Shit. She absolutely hated dealing with his problems. Maybe she was just a bad mother, but she was tired of hearing about everyone else's screwups.

"Yes, Ed. Where are you?"

"Mom. Some bad stuff's happening. I've got to let you know something. This is hard and it'll make you angry with me, but you need to know."

"Just tell me what it is, Ed—we'll work it out."

"The papers I gave you on those dogs were forged. I'm sorry, I thought it wouldn't hurt anyone, but then that old lady started to harass you. I'm really sorry. There's something else. I've been doing other things with some very bad people. Selling all sorts of forged documents, mostly collectables at shows like the one I'm at today. They were selling me stuff on credit and I was selling the crap for cash. Well, I used a bunch of the cash on drugs and other things we don't want to talk about. So when they came to collect I didn't have it all. They roughed me up some and when they thought I was unconscious, they talked about their boss. I'm not going to tell you what they said because I think it will be dangerous—but they also asked me about you. They wanted to know if you were involved in selling the documents. Listen, Mom, I have no idea where they came up with such a stupid idea. But I think they for some reason think you may have some of the money. I told them that they were crazy, which didn't help much—they hurt me some more and left."

"My god. What the hell are you talking about? You've mixed me up in your fucked up mess of a life? My god, Ed. Are you crazy? Call the police, do something. They think I have their money—Ed that's so stupid. I'm an ex-school teacher. I don't have some gangster's money!"

Monica started to cry. She couldn't help it. She was crying for herself and also for Ed. She felt like she was going to throw up. My god, what was she going to do? The note, the slashed tires—was this from the crazy people Ed was associated with, or that nut case Mrs. Richards?

"Mother, I'm so sorry. I can't call the police—the top guy has connections everywhere. It wouldn't do any good. I have to run. I know this is the worst thing I've ever done in a life full of bad things, but I can't fix it. I have to leave tonight. You should go to the police and tell them everything you know. Maybe do that in El Paso and ask for protection. I'm so sorry. I know you must hate me—and you and Dad have every right to curse the day I was born. I don't know what's wrong with me, but I can't deal with this anymore." He hung up.

Monica fell over onto the bed and cried until she went to sleep. Bruce lay as close to the bed as he could.

Monica woke early in the morning. Even though she'd slept, she didn't feel rested. If she'd had her car she would have left right then. Suddenly she felt like nothing was the same— everything was a threat. She got up and dressed. She sat on the bed trying to calm herself. What should she do? She remembered the card the deputy had given her. She decided she would stay in the room until it was light and then she'd call the deputy and tell him she needed protection. She was just going to sit here until someone came to help her. Bruce sensed her anxiety and put his head in her lap to comfort her. It did.

Bruce started making his usual soft noises, indicating it was time to visit the out of doors. Monica was anxious and just wanted to stay in the room, but she couldn't ignore Bruce's needs. Hell, a dog needs to be walked. She was probably being paranoid to think that just a quick walk outside would put her in danger. She would do that now while it was still dark, get back to the room, and lock herself in. She got Bruce's leash and went out the sliding glass doors. She found a pathway that went out a short distance and then came back around by the parking lot. She thought it looked protected from the street and headed out along the path.

As she was walking with Bruce, she caught movement out of the corner of her eye—oh no, someone is out here— she almost screamed. When she looked closer she could see someone carrying tools and pushing a cart with bags of soil. It must be the gardener. He waved and she returned the greeting with a sigh of relief. She couldn't believe how jumpy she was. Now she just wanted Bruce to finish so they could get back to the room. Bruce found a suitable spot at last. Monica always picked up after her dogs, but she didn't have a bag today. Nature would just have to deal with the dog poop. She turned and headed rapidly back to the hotel.

As she got closer to the parking lot, she once again thought she saw movement. Her nerves were on edge. She rounded a corner and there were two men standing in her path. Bruce growled.

"Better not release that dog lady, or I'll shoot him and you."

Shit. What the hell was happening? Monica felt faint and frozen—she couldn't move. One of the men had pulled out a gun and was aiming it in Monica's general direction. She wanted to scream, which probably would have been stupid, but it didn't matter because for some reason she couldn't make a sound. The other man walked over and grabbed her arm.

"I think we need to have a little talk. If you don't make any noise and do what you're told everything's going to be fine. If you don't, it's going to be very bad. Now, start walking with me, slowly."

They moved toward a van parked in the rear of the lot. The other man followed. When they reached the van, one of the men opened the sliding door. He was about to push Monica into the back.

"Don't move you assholes."

It was Mrs. Richards and she was holding a gun that looked to be the largest handgun ever made. She was small and feeble, but her aim and grip seemed very steady on a gun that was huge in her tiny hand.

"I don't know who you two assholes are, but if you make any sudden moves you'll be dead."

Monica was impressed. She wasn't real sure that Mrs. Richards had the strength to pull the trigger, but she sure wasn't going to test that theory.

"Mrs. Richards these men are very..."

The man who'd been leading her held his gun to his side, grabbed Monica's arm roughly, and whispered for her to shut the fuck up. She did.

The other man had moved away from the van and out of Mrs. Richards's vision.

"Listen old lady, I don't know what you think you're doing but if you point that gun at me, I'm going to kill you."

Mrs. Richards seemed to blink. Maybe the way the thug said that had penetrated her addled brain. She was pausing. At that moment the other man grabbed her gun hand and pulled the gun away. With absolutely no effort, he tossed poor Mrs. Richards into the van, then pushed Monica and Bruce in with the old lady.

One of the goons looked into the back and demanded Mrs. Richards to tell him which car was hers. She didn't say anything. The other one said he thought it must be the little white Toyota because he hadn't seen it earlier. One of the men went over to the car.

"The keys are in it—it's hers. I'm going to handcuff both of them to the frame in the back, then I'll follow you in her car. You remember where you're going, right?"

"Yeah. I have the map. What's the chief going to think

about this other woman?"

"Jeez, watch your mouth."

One of the thugs roughly handcuffed Monica and Mrs. Richards to an exposed portion of the frame in the rear of the van. They drove off. Mrs. Richards didn't seem to be responding to anything. Monica worried she might have had a heart attack or a stroke—but said nothing. Instead she stayed quiet, wondering if she was going to die soon.

They raced away from T or C and very quickly were in complete darkness. After ten or fifteen minutes they pulled the van and car over to the side of the road. Releasing the two women from the handcuffs, they pushed them outside. Once Monica got out of the van she unleashed Bruce. "Run boy," she yelled. He took off. The men cursed and one slapped Monica so hard it knocked her to the ground.

"Goddamn dog."

"Forget him. That fuckin' show dog won't last a day out here."

One of the men reached down to pull Monica to her feet, when all of a sudden Mrs. Richards pulled out another gun. This one was smaller and had apparently been in her purse—always search old ladies for an extra gun or two. She took aim and shot the man holding Monica. The bullet knocked him to the ground. Mrs. Richards took off running. The other man pulled out Mrs. Richards's own gun and took a shot at her.

Monica was scared to death. She was trembling so hard she could barely stand up. With more clarity than she thought possible, she realized she had to get to Mrs. Richard's car and hope they'd left the keys in the ignition, otherwise she was dead.

Mrs. Richards was hidden behind a tree and still armed. The man who had shot at her and missed followed her down the road.

Monica could see the guy on the ground was still alive but maybe not conscious. She took off for the car. Once she got there she could see the keys inside. Could she just leave Mrs. Richards without trying to help her? She was standing there wondering what kind of person she was when Mrs. Richards stepped out from behind the tree and started walking toward the man with the gun. She aimed at him, but before she pulled the trigger he shot her. Monica was terrified. Mrs. Richards was hit in the chest and propelled backwards more than five feet. She landed on the ground, definitely dead.

Monica stopped thinking. She jumped into the car, started it, and hit the gas. Just as she peeled out, the man jumped out into the road, aimed Mrs. Richard's old gun, and pulled the trigger. A rusty old gun like that might have jammed, but it didn't. Monica's erratic driving saved her life, the bullet hitting just to the right of her head, leaving a large hole in the windshield. Without thinking, or really making a decision to do so, Monica ran straight into the man with a sickening thud. He flew off into the trees and Monica floored it. She was travelling dangerously fast and she knew it, but the thought didn't stop her. She was going to get out of there as fast as the car would go.

The sun was coming up and Monica was able to navigate her way back to the main road without too much of difficulty. When she reached it she had to guess which way to go, but she didn't hesitate. She knew one man was hurt when she hit him with the car and the other man had been shot, but either one or both might still be alive, and she was still terrified that they would follow her and catch her. She wasn't going to stop for anything.

Before she realized it, she was at the entrance to I-25. Once on the highway, she slowed down to a pace closer to the speed limit. She didn't want to get stopped and have to explain the bullet hole in the windshield. Her son had said she shouldn't trust the cops. She started to cry, but kept driving.

It was a couple of tearful hours later that Monica reached the El Paso downtown exit. When she pulled off, she could see the hotel in the distance. She found an area not far from it that looked to be less than well kept. She parked Mrs. Richards' car and left the keys in it, hoping that it wouldn't be there for long. She was very upset about Mrs. Richards—she'd never seen someone killed before. And she was frightened about what would happen to Bruce. She wondered if he could survive. She walked slowly to the hotel, entered by a side door, and headed toward the ladies room. She cleaned herself up some, found the house phone, and dialed Betty's room.

Betty didn't answer. Monica left a voice mail telling her she was at the hotel and would wait in the lobby area. She found a quiet corner of the huge lobby and waited. It was almost an hour before Betty appeared.

"Monica, why didn't you come into the show and get me. Oh my, what's wrong?"

"I think it would be best if we went to your room."

They left immediately for Betty's room. Before they could get into the room, Monica started to tremble and cry.

# 19

*Monica's Story, Part II*

After Monica calmed down, she told Betty everything that had happened. Betty was in disbelief. Monica was exhausted by the incredible events and the rush of adrenaline. She meant to rest for just a minute or two, but quickly fell asleep.

Betty wasn't sure if she was also at risk from the people who'd attacked Monica. Would they know who Monica's friends were? All of a sudden everything seemed sinister. Betty decided she was making herself crazy. She wrote a note to Monica saying she had gone back to the show to let her sleep. She'd be back in a couple of hours and Monica should stay in the room. She left the note next to Monica on the bed, then went down to the main ballroom where the dog show was still in progress.

Betty wasn't showing a dog at this show. She was there just to enjoy the event, to see Monica, and support Monica's dog, Bruce. With that thought she realized that Monica hadn't said anything about Bruce, and the thought made her shudder. Several people asked Betty about Monica, but she said Monica was still having car problems and it was looking like she might have to go back to Albuquerque and miss the show. Everyone was very sympathetic—except Nate, Monica's chief rival. He just smiled.

It hadn't been two hours, but Betty decided she would go back to the room anyway. She hated for Monica to wake up alone. Once inside, she heard Monica in the shower. Betty sat down and just stared into space. Monica was out in a few minutes. She only had on a towel, so Betty found her a robe.

"What should we do now?"

"Not sure, Betty. I'm sorry to get you involved in this—I just didn't know what to do. Thought about calling Mike, but I don't know what he can do. At this point I just want to hide for a while until I'm sure who I can ask for help."

"Well, the people at the hotel in T or C are going to know you're missing. And the place with your car will know you didn't show up—so they're going to contact the police, which means there'll be some kind of investigation, right?"

"Yeah. It's the sheriff's department in T or C. But they'll know I'm gone and that I wouldn't just leave without my stuff and my car, so they have to assume there was foul play, right? Do you think they'll find bodies in the woods? Mrs. Richards, and maybe at least one of those goons?"

"Well, if they find bodies, will they figure out that you escaped with her car? If they think you got away, they might figure you headed to El Paso, and that could lead them right to this hotel. But that could lead the bad guys here, too. Maybe staying here isn't a good idea."

"Betty, the first thing is you need to go home. You aren't connected with this and you need to stay away from me."

"No way am I leaving you alone. Look, I can go to the bank down the street and cash a check. We can make a reservation for two under assumed names right here in the hotel. We pay cash and just stay more or less in our room for a few days. I think that's safer than trying to figure out some place else to be."

"Oh Betty, I don't know. I'm so worried I just can't think straight."

"Look, nobody in this hotel will pay any attention to us. Tomorrow, after all of the dog show people leave, we'll just blend in—nobody will bother us. After a few days we can decide what to do next, okay?"

"I guess so." Monica smiled a weak smile and began to cry again. She felt like such a baby.

They put their plan into action and everything went smoothly. They had a new room on the tenth floor and just stayed in the room watching TV and reading. They talked a lot about their lives and about how things hadn't gone as they'd planned. Betty called her daughter and told her she was staying an extra couple of days in El Paso to do some shopping and sightseeing. She hoped her daughter didn't hear the fear in her voice.

Monica called Mike, but got his voice mail and decided not to leave a message. Maybe it was best if she was missing. She hated that her family wouldn't know what had happened to her, but she was too scared to call anyone. They fell into a routine over the next couple of days and it started to feel normal, the hiding.

They went out one day and Monica bought some clothes and personal items. Being away from the hotel made them anxious—it felt like everyone was watching them—but nothing bad happened. No one seemed to pay them any attention at all, but that didn't lessen the overpowering fear—it never seemed to stop.

"I think we need to leave. Don't ask me why. We have to get out of here, now." It might have been claustrophobia talking, or some blind instinct, but the feeling was real.

Betty agreed, but she wanted to call her daughter and let her know she was okay and Monica agreed that she should. Betty would tell her she was taking a little trip and not to worry. She would call her during the day and more than likely wouldn't get her—she'd just leave a message. She was afraid that if they talked she might start crying. They'd been crying a lot.

They debated about what to do afterward. Betty thought they should contact the local police, or maybe even the FBI. Monica said she wanted to talk to her son first before she contacted anyone. She suggested that they drive back into New Mexico. She knew a place in Cloudcroft, outside of Alamogordo in the Sacramento Mountains, called The Lodge.

"This place is beautiful. I was there once for a wedding. The best part is it's remote, and not a common destination. It's probably about two hours from here and completely isolated. We can take a direct route from El Paso to Alamogordo without getting on any interstates or main highways. I can't imagine anyone finding us there. We'll need to get some more cash, and then call to make reservations—maybe get traveler's checks. Do they still have those? We can use our own first names and say we are sisters having a retreat. Pick a last name like Smith. I know that sounds stupid, but Smith is a common name. So we would be Betty and Monica Smith, sisters from Houston having a family retreat."

"Okay. Let's get going before we change our minds."

"Great. First, I'm going to the bank downtown and get some cash or traveler's checks. We don't want to use a credit card, since they—whoever in the hell *they* is—might be able to track us. I'll be back in an hour or so. You get us packed."

Monica left and quickly walked the few blocks to one of the large banks in downtown El Paso. She wrote a check for about everything she had in her checking account. Luckily, when she had left the room in T or C she had grabbed her wallet so she would have her ID, and she had some emergency checks in the wallet. They verified her identification and called her bank to verify her balance. She thought that might leave a trail, but it would only point to El Paso. She requested some in cash and the majority in traveler's checks—which were still available, and didn't seem to be an unusual request, at least at this bank. She thought it might have something to do with being close to the border.

Monica headed back to the hotel. Feeling a little like a thief with all the money in her purse, she chuckled at the thought that she was stealing her own money. Back in the room, Betty had everything packed. Monica got a cart and loaded the luggage, mostly Betty's. They exited the hotel into the parking garage and found Betty's car, a fairly new Honda minivan. Betty wanted Monica to drive since she wasn't familiar with El Paso and didn't know how to find the road to Cloudcroft.

They didn't check out of the hotel—didn't need to since they'd paid in advance. In fact they had another day paid for, but thought it was best to just forget the money and leave. Fear was driving all of their decisions. Mostly they wanted to get on the road and feel safe again.

Betty found a map of the area in the glove compartment. She told Monica the road they were looking for was Highway 54. They had gotten onto I-10 at the downtown on-ramp, and almost as soon as Betty mentioned the highway they needed they saw a sign for their exit. In a matter of minutes they were on the right road, headed north to Alamogordo.

As they proceeded on Highway 54, they began to relax and smile a little. Each mile away from El Paso made them feel safer. In a strange way, it started to feel like an adventure. The drive to Alamogordo was faster than they'd anticipated. They drove straight through town, stopping only to refuel. Their next objective was Highway 82, which would take them up the mountain to Cloudcroft, and they found the turnoff easily.

If it had been a direct shot up the mountain it probably wouldn't have taken long, but with all of the turns and switchbacks it took some time to reach the top. Once they arrived, they found a small village with a few shops and restaurants and a prominent sign pointing the way to The Lodge. Their climb had taken them up to about 9,000 feet elevation. There were large pine trees and the air was cool. They were in the mountains—safe.

When they pulled up to The Lodge it seemed even more impressive than Monica had remembered. It was a large Victorian structure with many windows, reminiscent of a ski lodge but with more refinement. Obviously a historical structure, it had beautiful landscaping, lots of large trees, and a golf course behind the main building. The main lodge had smaller outbuildings scattered around it. Both women felt immediately comfortable with their choice.

The interior was inviting, too. There was an old world charm that made them feel welcome and, more importantly, safe. They checked in using their new identities, and several staff members commented that they had been able to tell immediately that they were sisters. This amused Monica and Betty, making them laugh and feel very welcome. They had requested only one room—sisters needed to be close—and were surprised at the attention to detail they found inside. There were two beds and a small sitting area. The furnishings appeared to be period pieces, either very good reproductions or actual antiques. It was all so charming. They unpacked and went downstairs to have something to eat. There were several areas where food was served: a bar, the main dining room, and a less formal lunch area. They went to the lunch area, mostly because of the large windows and streaming sunshine. The view was of the area behind the lodge, which included a portion of the golf course—it was beautiful.

Monica ordered a chicken salad sandwich and Betty had a grilled cheese with ham. While they hadn't starved, this was the first day since Monica had arrived at Betty's hotel room in a frenzy that either of them had felt hungry. Maybe it was the mountain air. Their lunch was delicious and they ordered coffee and lingered at their table.

"What's the plan now?" Betty broached the subject first, but this was in a different tone then when they'd last discussed their plans—if anyone had been listening, it could have been mistaken for vacation planning. Much of the tension of the last few days was gone.

"I think we just wait a few days. I need to talk to Ed, and also to Mike, then make a decision about who I can trust to help. But for the time being, I think it makes us safer to just wait. Plus this is such a lovely place I'm not anxious to disturb the good feelings."

"I agree."

That night the ladies went down to the bar for a couple of drinks before dinner. Betty wasn't much of a drinker and was talking a little too loud, although Monica didn't notice much since she was feeling no pain. The next morning they slept in—until almost noon.

The days started to run together. They'd developed the habit of walking most of the golf course in the morning. Neither played, but the views were impressive. And they'd fallen into the habit of having a few drinks before dinner—although not as much as that first night—and being very open with the friendly staff. They started being treated as regulars and receiving special service. They had never felt so important.

On the fourth or fifth night they finally had the "are we lesbians" conversation. This was necessarily preceded by several nightcaps after dinner, which helped inspire an "oh fuck it" attitude. They knew they cared about each other as much as two people could. If there'd been any doubt it had been dispelled by the way Betty had taken care of Monica during her crisis. After a little crying and a little hugging, they realized that they didn't want to confuse their friendship and love with something romantic. Both women confessed that they would still like to be with a man. This brought many giggles and an occasional all out laugh. It also seemed to lift an unspoken tension that they'd been feeling ever since this aspect of their friendship had first been rumored by the dog show morons. They were the best of friends and knew they could always rely on each other.

The next morning was another sleep-in morning. Betty remarked "a person could get use to this lifestyle pretty quick."

That day, to break out of their rut, they drove over the mountains to Ruidoso to look around—there were lots of small shops full of useless stuff to look at. They enjoyed the day, but felt somewhat exposed and were happy to return to their hideout.

They'd been at the Lodge for well over a week now. All of the staff knew their names and treated them in a solicitous way. If the money could have never run out they might have just stayed there forever. Of course that couldn't be. Each of them had family to be concerned about. They each had their dogs to care for and, in Monica's case, she had to decide how to keep from getting killed. It was time to make some more plans and start dealing with reality.

"You know when I was in T or C right after the tires were slashed, I met a deputy sheriff who seemed very nice. He also was very concerned about my safety. I ignored him because of my concern about who might be involved—but he gave me his card. I'm thinking that maybe a small town sheriff might be the best option to find someone who could give me advice about how to protect myself. What do you think about my calling him?"

"Monica, I don't know anything about this stuff. What I do know is that you're going to have to trust someone. We can't hide out here forever, although it's a nice thought—the rest of the world won't let us do that. I'm sure there's already all kinds of concern about where we are and whether we're alive or dead—we can't let our families live with this much longer."

"Yeah, we've kind of stretched this beyond a reasonable time. I think that's what frightened people do—I believe it's called acting irrationally. Well, it's time to end this."

They smiled at each other. They'd done what they thought was right, and now it was time to move on to the next step. While they were talking, Monica had been digging around in her stuff.

"You know what. That card was in my purse. When I went out to walk Bruce that morning, I grabbed my billfold and put it in my pocket but I'd left my purse in the room. Shit, I don't remember his name—other than Deputy."

"Well, you know its T or C sheriff's office. Just call the main number and describe the guy. Can you describe him?"

"Yeah. He was very handsome. I remember him in some detail." Monica was grinning.

"Good gracious, Monica. I know there're nasty old men—are there nasty old women, too?" They had a good laugh.

Monica called information and got the number for the T or C sheriff's department.

"Sheriff's department. This is Cindy. How may I help you?"

"Cindy, a few weeks ago a young deputy helped me after I had some car trouble. He gave me his card, but I've misplaced it. I'd like to talk to him. He was very handsome, about six-one, with light brown hair cut pretty short and he had blue eyes. Do you know who that would be?"

There was a pause. Monica wasn't sure if something was wrong with the phone or not.

"Yes, I know who that is. Is there any chance that you are Ms. Jackson?"

Now it was Monica's turn to pause. She hadn't thought anyone would even remember her, but in a small town somebody disappearing would still be news. Monica had made a mistake. She hung up.

"What is it?"

"The girl asked me if I was Ms. Jackson."

"What are we going to do now?"

"I don't know."

# 20

*Monday*

Ray and Happy were on their way to Big Jack's to meet with Tyee and discuss strategy for the next weekend's fishing tournament. Ray was anxious to get the competition behind him—he still wasn't sure he wanted to have people monitoring his fishing skills.

They had planned to meet in the computer room, but Tyee wasn't there. The message light was blinking on the new answering machine. Ray hadn't retrieved messages from the machine before, but he thought he might as well give it a try.

"Ray, this is Clayton. Had a strange message from Cindy, that someone called and described me. Said they wanted to talk to me. The caller had recently talked to me when she had problems with her car. For some reason Cindy thought that it might be Ms. Jackson. She asked her if that was her name and the person hung up. Cindy got the number—it's for the Lodge up in Cloudcroft. Ray, I wanted to talk to you before I did anything about this—give me a call."

Ray called immediately. Cindy told Ray that Deputy Clayton was in the building and she would get him on the line, pronto.

"Guess you got my message."

"Yeah. What do you think—could that have been Ms. Jackson?"

"I think so. We don't have too many stranded women in town, and then there's the way she acted with Cindy. It was like she had lost my card and needed to talk to me, but then she hung up. I think I should call the Lodge and ask for Monica Jackson and see what happens. What do you think?"

"Well, sure. Maybe just use her first name. Say you're returning a call from a guest and all you have is a first name. When people hide and use assumed names, often they'll keep their first name so they don't get caught not responding when someone addresses them by name. Anyway, I think you should call and see."

"I'll do that and call you back."

Ray went out to the dock area and found Tyee. Happy had beaten Ray out and was already giving Tyee some high energy attention. Ray told Tyee about Clayton's message.

"You figured out how to use the message machine?"

"You don't have to act so surprised. I can type too."

"Do you really think it could be her?"

"Well sure. It could be. There's even some logic to it. The best place to hide is often right in your own area. Cloudcroft is a long way from Albuquerque, but she would blend into the background in a place like that. I'd thought, if the two women were together, they might take off for Mexico, since they were in El Paso. But that could be hard because they probably know nothing about Mexico and they'd stick out like a sore thumb. So it makes sense. Why she called I can only guess—but I'm sure Clayton made a good impression and now she's looking for help."

They started to discuss fishing and Tyee demonstrated how to use a depth finder. He also had the latest lake map and marked areas he thought would be the best for Ray to try on the first day. Tyee told Ray his goal should be to catch the biggest fish. There were two categories you could win, one was most fish, but the other one, for the largest fish, was the top prize. He explained that you could almost never do both—catch the biggest fish and the most fish—so what Ray should do was catch a fish and release it unless it might be the biggest one. Tyee had a theory about this. If you were in an area and you started pulling out as many fish as you could, the fish sense this and move on—especially the big ones. If you released the fish you caught then the others didn't feel threatened and would stay around. Then you could catch the big one.

"You gotta be shittin' me—you really believe that?"

"Yes. I can't explain it, but yes, I really believe it."

There were days when Ray thought Tyee might be a genius and then there were days when he thought he was an idiot. While Ray thought most of what Tyee was saying sounded stupid, he was going to follow his friend's advice to the letter. Tyee might be stupid, but Ray wasn't and he was going to do exactly what Tyee said. Indian knows fishing.

They continued to discuss strategy, including the fact that it was important for Ray to avoid attracting the other fishermen to his area. Tyee had several methods for concealing the fact that you were getting good results from the other competitors. Several times Ray wondered how grown men could get so involved in the silliest things.

Ray noticed someone coming toward them. Shielding his eyes from the sun, he saw that it was Deputy Clayton.

"Hey, Deputy. I was expecting you to call back not drive out."

"Well, I wanted to talk to you about this in person."

"Sure, pull up a bucket and have a seat."

Clayton found one of the old fishing buckets, turned it over, and sat down.

"Well, it's her. Ms. Jackson is alive and in Cloudcroft—has been for over a week. Betty Adams is with her. She's very nervous that someone's trying to kill her because they think she has her son's money. Mostly Ray, she wants someone to tell her what to do next. I think this gets out of my league pretty quick. Plus, if Martinez finds out I have no idea what he might do. So I told her about you. Told her you had talked to her husband and knew a lot more about the whole thing than I did. I hope you're okay with this, but I told her you could be there tomorrow and talk to her. Can you do that?"

"I can. That's great news she's alive. There have been several times that I thought the only likely outcome was that she was dead. Tomorrow will work—I've got some things to take care of today and I'll head out first thing in the morning."

"Also Ray, I want to thank you, Tyee, and Big Jack. I actually think I have a chance of winning and it's all because of you guys."

"Well, Deputy Dan Clayton, you have more to do with this than we do. We're just helping. The people are responding to you and to what they sense about how you'll run the department. You should never forget that this is a tough job. Right after you're elected one of the people who voted for you will ask for a favor and you'll say no. That guy will think you are an ungrateful jerk, but how you run this department after you are elected will determine if you are elected again—it's all on you."

"Man, you're a hard guy to thank."

Ray smiled and shook the deputy's hand. "I know. We're glad that you appreciate the things we've done—but we're doing this because we live here and you'll make it a better place to live."

Ray said he had some calls to make and disappeared back into the store. Tyee looked at Clayton and grinned. "You better win Dan, or Ray will be real pissed." Clayton nodded his head—he knew.

Ray called Agent Crawford in Washington D.C. The number Crawford had given him went right through to his direct line. He left a message saying that he needed to talk about some issues related to Crawford's offer. He left his new phone number.

While Ray was sitting there thinking about what to do next, the phone rang.

"Hello, this is Ray Pacheco."

"Ray, this is Agent Ben Crawford, what can I do for you?"

Ray told Crawford the entire story, leaving nothing out. He'd told Big Jack that maybe he could find something out without giving the FBI his actual name and information, but he'd rethought that approach, deciding that if they were going to work together they needed to be honest. And if they weren't going to work together, Ray still wanted the contact with the FBI. So he revealed everything he knew about Big Jack, aka Philip Duncan, and about Tyee Chino.

"I don't want you to take this the wrong way Agent Crawford, but I've decided I can't enter into an agreement with the FBI without these people on my team. For one thing, we work well together and have diverse skills, and beyond that I need their energy and support to be able to do what I think you'll want from us. So even though I've only known them both a short time, they've become important to me and necessary for this venture to have a chance at success."

"Ray, I understand. You have to have people around you that you can trust. Sounds like there'll be no issues with Tyee. Not sure about Big Jack. Let me do some preliminary checking and I'll see what we can do. No matter what happens with the contractor deal, I'll try and help Big Jack with regard to the problems in L.A. Give me a couple of days and I'll give you a call."

"Thanks, Agent Crawford. That sounds more than fair."

"Ray, unless we're in a meeting with other FBI types, why don't you call me Ben."

"I'll do that, Ben. And I'll wait for your call."

Ray thought that if there was any way to make this work, Ben Crawford was the guy to make it happen. If it didn't work out with the FBI, they could pursue other work. Ray was convinced that he could spend a few weeks on the phone and place the name *Pacheco and Chino, Private Investigations* in front of a lot of law enforcement people. They'd start getting referrals pretty quickly—he wasn't worried.

Ray went back out on the dock. Tyee was still going over some lake data he'd found by accessing a government database. Clayton had left.

"Interested in riding along over to Cloudcroft tomorrow morning?"

"Sure. Don't think I might spook the ladies?"

"Well, I guess it would depend on how you act. Are you

going to be in your Indian getup with war paint?"

"You know, I could be offended by such backward comments."

"Yes, you could. You can bunk over in the guest room if you want."

"Okay, apology accepted."

# 21

*Tuesday, Cloudcroft*

A straight shot from T or C to Alamogordo would be about eighty miles, but that wasn't possible. There were no direct roads because of the White Sands Missile Range. Even if you had a plane you couldn't fly directly, because it was restricted airspace. The fastest option was to go to Las Cruces and then cross White Sands. This involved going south to Cruces and then northeast to Alamogordo, a trip of about 150 miles. From Alamogordo to Cloudcroft wasn't far—it was just all uphill, going up the mountain. And just to complicate things further, when the military was firing missiles the road across the white sands area was closed, creating hour-long delays. Ray, Tyee, and Happy got an early start, but even so it would be late morning before they arrived.

Ray and Tyee chatted about fishing and the upcoming tournament. They both felt that Ray was ready, although Ray was less sure than Tyee was. They also talked about the business and what might happen in the future, and on that front Ray was more confident about the future success of the business than Tyee.

Soon they found themselves in Alamogordo. They located the turnoff to Cloudcroft. There was a noticeable change in the trees as they climbed the mountain, and the temperature cooled. They rolled down the windows and took advantage of the refreshing air. Happy was most pleased and hung his head out the window to maximize his pleasure.

When they approached the Lodge, they were both impressed by the beautiful building and the lush landscaping. Ray had been to the Lodge on several occasions to attend law enforcement gatherings and had always found it beautiful.

They parked, then let Happy run about for a while before they entered the hotel. They went to the desk and asked if the staff would let Monica Smith know that Ray Pacheco was there to see her. Monica had shared her alias with Clayton. The woman at the desk dialed the room and told the person who answered that Ray Pacheco was downstairs. Ray and Tyee walked into the lobby area and took a seat. Very shortly they were joined by two women in their sixties.

"Mr. Pacheco, I'm Monica Jackson. Oh my goodness, it's Bruce."

Happy, also known as Bruce, hurried excitedly over to greet Monica. She hugged the dog and began to cry. After a while she laughed.

"I thought I'd never see him again. How was he found? This is so wonderful!"

"Actually, Ms. Jackson, he's the reason I got involved. You see, I live in the area where Mrs. Richards' body was found, and that evening your dog turned up on my porch. He's been with me ever since. I call him Happy."

"Oh that's is so wonderful. I just knew he had died out there. He looks wonderful—thank you so much for taking care of him." Monica continued to rub and pet the dog, and Bruce wagged his tail as fast as it would go.

After a while Monica and Bruce settled down.

"I appreciate you seeing me," Ray said. "I know it may be a little confusing that Deputy Clayton isn't here, but I'll explain. First, I'd like to introduce you to my associate and business partner, Tyee Chino."

Tyee was pleased with the introduction and stepped forward to shake Monica's hand.

"Nice to meet you Mr. Chino. This is my friend, Betty Adams." Everyone exchanged greetings and they took seats in the casual dining area. A waitress came by to take drink orders.

"First, I should explain why Deputy Clayton isn't here. While there's no question that a crime took place in Sierra County, and that would mean that the sheriff's office has jurisdiction, there are some reasons that we thought it might be best if I met with you before the officers stepped in officially. One consideration is that I've met with your ex-husband and he asked me to try to find you.

"Another element in the decision is that Deputy Clayton has made a judgment regarding the current sheriff. They're both running for the sheriff's job, with the election in just a few days. Deputy Clayton was concerned that the current sheriff might not be too diligent about pursuing this matter at this time. There's no evidence linking you to the discovery of Mrs. Richards' body, so as of right now you're a missing person. Since you're an adult, being missing isn't a crime. There are a lot of unanswered questions regarding what happened, how you were involved, why you left your belongings behind, including your car, and why you haven't contacted anyone until now. I believe Deputy Clayton thought we might be able to get some answers quicker if we didn't officially involve the sheriff's department just yet."

Ray paused to collect his thoughts. Everyone was listening but Ms. Jackson hadn't offered any comments.

"Ms. Jackson, you may not be aware that Mike is staying with Luke. I don't know if you've been trying to call him or not, but I know he wants to talk to you."

"Has his health gotten worse—why is he staying with Luke?"

"Ms. Jackson, I'm deeply sorry to have to tell you this. Your son Ed was killed. He was shot about a week ago in Albuquerque. The police there can only say that it appears to be a professional hit, and they have few if any clues. That's why Mike is with Luke."

Monica sat stunned and said nothing. Soon she started to cry. Betty came over and held her for a moment. Bruce put his head in Monica's lap.

"I'm so sorry Ms. Jackson. If you'd like to wait for a while, we can talk later."

Monica shook her head. "Let me go to the ladies room. I'll be back in a little bit." She and Betty left.

Ray and Tyee sipped their coffee and waited.

The women returned and Monica seemed more composed.

"I'm not completely surprised, Mr. Pacheco. I talked to my son before the incident with Mrs. Richards and he had told me he was in danger. He also told me that I was in danger."

Monica related everything that had happened from the time she checked into the Hot Springs Inn until the meeting with Ray and Tyee. Ray had some clarifying questions which she answered as completely as she could. When she was done, she seemed to slump and she looked very tired.

"Monica, I know you probably need to rest a little before we talk about what to do next, but there's something you need to do—you need to call Mike. I know he's incredibly worried and I haven't told him that we had heard from you. I wanted to talk to you first and see what was going on. Could you call him now?"

"Yes. You're right. Could we meet here in about an hour?"

They agreed on a spot to meet and then Monica and Betty went upstairs accompanied by Bruce. Ray and Tyee had lunch before taking a walk along the path by the golf course.

"Do you believe everything she said?" Tyee asked after a while.

"I do. It all rings true and it lines up with the facts we already have. I suppose she could have been involved in the bad stuff with her son, but that doesn't make a lot of sense. That would almost have to include her ex-husband and I'm a hundred percent sure that he's not involved in anything."

"How about the reference to 'Chief'. Do you think that's someone in Albuquerque?"

"Don't know. They were obviously working for someone, and my guess is it was someone local. Of course, that person could've been taking orders from L.A. No way of knowing."

Tyee added his own thoughts.

"Ed Jackson's suggested to his mother that he knew who was in charge—that sounds like maybe it's not just some goons. His actions and his reluctance to tell his mother because it would put her at risk suggest something—I'm just not sure what. But he had to know something if they were going to take such drastic measures to shut him up."

"You're right, Tyee. If he'd just failed to pay them then it would've made more sense to hurt him some and then make him pay the money back by fronting for them with no cut. Or use him in some way that involved a risk in visibility they could not take. Now they have to find a new front man."

They both thought about the implications and realized they were getting ready to step into a big dark hole with no idea what might happen.

They returned to the lunch area and ordered iced tea as they waited for Monica and Betty.

When the women returned, Monica looked worse. Betty helped her walk into the room and take a seat, with Bruce following behind.

"I talked to Mike. He seems to be in a bad way—I think I need to be there and help him. He said I could trust you completely. He was very complimentary about you, Ray. I'm thankful that you've helped him the way you have. He also said that Bruce should stay with you until we get things sorted out—he said he thinks the dog has adopted you. I agreed that made sense if you would agree. Other than that, just tell me what to do and I'll do it."

The trauma of dealing with the loss of a child must be one of the most horrible things a parent could experience, and Ray could see the toll it was taking on Monica.

"Monica, I think you should go and be with Mike. Betty, I think you should go home to your daughter. This isn't over by a long shot, and there'll be more that each of you will have to deal with, but for now you should be with your families. And Monica, you'll have to have protection. I know you have no reason to trust law enforcement people right now, but I recommend that you let me contact some people I know in the FBI. I'll fill them in on what's happened and what we think may be going on—if that's okay?"

"I'll do whatever you say." Monica seemed defeated, wanting only that Ray would tell her what to do. Betty nodded, looking very sad. Reality had found them and their adventure was over.

"Regarding Happy, I know he's your dog. I'll be pleased to keep him until things quiet down, but then he can go with you—that's his home."

They formulated a plan. Ray suggested that Betty call her daughter to let her know she was okay and that she'd be coming home. Monica would go with Ray and Tyee back to T or C. Then, the next day, Monica and Tyee would go to Albuquerque and see Mike. Tyee would stay in Albuquerque until Ray could make other arrangements regarding security.

"One last question Monica. When we talked to the police in Albuquerque they said that Ed had said something to the FBI about you having the facts, and that once he got them he would fix everything. Does that mean anything to you?"

"Not at all. He told me he couldn't tell me anything because then I'd be in worse danger. What do you think it means?"

"Not sure. Maybe nothing—he might not have even said exactly that. I think it's time we get moving."

The women departed, leaving Happy with Ray. They needed to make calls, pack, and check out of their room. Betty called her daughter, who was ecstatic to hear from her mother and said she would fly to El Paso to get Betty and drive back to Dallas with her. Betty called and made a reservation near the

El Paso airport for herself and her daughter. Betty and Monica took some time saying goodbye, and it was apparent they were each worried about the other.

After checking out and saying goodbye to nearly every staff member at the hotel, they loaded the cars and left.

Monica sat in the back, petting Bruce and talking sweetly to him. Soon they were both asleep.

"Hope I didn't step out of line saying you'd stay with Monica for security—security was never part of our discussions about this business. I can understand it if that might make you a little nervous." Ray was speaking softly in order not to disturb Monica.

"It's okay, Ray. Figured all along it would come up some time. I don't have your training solving crimes, but I was a boxing champion on the reservation and I'm a black belt in karate. Plus, I'm loaded with charm. So if the bad guys show up, I can beat 'em up or try and talk them into being nice."

That got a chuckle out of Ray.

They arrived back at Ray's cabin in the late evening. Monica had slept most of the way. They unloaded everything and got Monica settled into the guest bedroom.

Tyee said he would return in the morning, but needed to head home and check on some things.

Ray fixed a small dinner for himself and Monica. They enjoyed the quiet surroundings and let the tension ease a little. Finally, Monica couldn't keep her eyes open any longer. She expressed her gratitude for everything Ray was doing and then she headed off to bed. Ray stayed up trying to decide what to do next. He knew this could be dangerous; for everyone.

# 22

*Wednesday*

When Ray let Happy out for his morning rounds, there was Tyee sitting on the porch.

"Come in, just put the coffee on."

"Thanks."

They discussed their plans for the day. Ray said he'd found a note on the door indicating that the new phone line would be installed that day, so Ray wouldn't have to run down to Big Jack's to use the phone anymore. As soon as Ray got the new number, he would let everyone know. They also talked about Tyee's trip to Albuquerque that day and how long Tyee should stay.

"My plan is to talk to Agent Sanchez or Crawford today and fill them in on what's happened. Not sure how quickly they'll be able to provide security for Monica, but one way or another there'll be some backup for you by tomorrow."

Either there would be some support from the Feds or Ray would be there himself. Ray said he would let Big Jack know about any developments in case he couldn't get ahold of Tyee.

"Sounds good. Don't worry about me. I'll be fine."

Monica entered with a smile and a friendly greeting, although she still seemed very subdued. Ray got her a cup of coffee and told her the basic idea of the plan for the day. He said she and Tyee should leave in the next thirty minutes or so and that he would call Mike and let him know they were on their way. One question was what to do about the cars. Monica's Subaru was still at the Firestone store. He thought it might be best to get her car and take that to Albuquerque, but pointed out that he wasn't sure if the sheriff had placed a hold on the car or not.

They agreed that it made everything easier if they could get Monica's car, leaving Ray with his Jeep. They got everything ready and everyone into the Jeep, heading out toward T or C. Mr. Lopez was thrilled to see Monica. He told her that he'd heard she'd disappeared and had been very worried. She assured him that much of what happened had just been a misunderstanding, downplaying any drama. She settled her bill using some travelers checks she still had and retrieved her car. She agreed to let Tyee drive, and they transferred her belongings and some things for Tyee from the Jeep to the Subaru.

They talked about the personal things she had left at the Hot Springs Inn. Ray said he believed they'd had been taken by the sheriff's department and he thought it would be a major delay to try and get the stuff. She said she didn't want to deal with anyone right now, so she would retrieve her things some other time. Ray agreed that that was best. He didn't know what Martinez might do—he might even hold Monica as a material witness to murder. Ray didn't want to deal with Martinez right now. Since there weren't any charges or anyone looking for Monica, Ray would just plead ignorance if something came up later.

After Monica and Tyee left for Albuquerque, Ray and

Happy went to Big Jack's. Going around back, Ray found Big Jack on the dock helping a customer fuel up his boat. Ray waved and went into the computer room to call Mike. Mike was pleased that Monica would be there that day and thanked Ray for everything he was doing.

Then Ray checked the messages on the phone. There was one from Crawford, asking him to call any time. Ray returned the call.

"Agent Crawford."

"Ben, this is Ray in T or C. How are you today?"

"Good Ray, thanks for calling me back. Just wanted to touch base with you regarding the missing woman. I've received some information that makes me question some of the things about her son's death. You need to be careful, and make sure if you find her that she's protected—my instincts say she's at risk. Also, you should know that Agent Myers, who heads the Albuquerque office, had some pretty harsh things to say about you—he says you've overstepped your authority. Matter of fact, if it was left up to him he might arrest you for obstruction of justice."

"Well, I know he doesn't like me—that goes back to many years ago when I think I embarrassed him. But as far as obstruction, I have no idea what he's talking about. I went into his office a few days ago to ask if he knew anything he could share with the family regarding Ed Jackson's death. He basically threw me out. Acted like I'd asked him something out of line—he didn't seem to be completely rational."

"Ray, I'm going to look into this. Maybe you should avoid Agent Myers for a while."

"No issues there. I'd been told that he was heading a multiagency task force and that he gave the order for Ed Jackson to be arrested by the Albuquerque Police. All I wanted was some insight into what might have happened to Ed—he seemed to be mad before I even walked in."

"Probably just stress of the job stuff. Don't have anything definitive on Big Jack yet, but I'll call as soon as I hear."

"Ben, regarding the missing woman. Monica Jackson's been found. She was a witness to a woman being shot by some thugs, probably associated in some way with her son. They had kidnapped Monica and another woman who just happened to be there and got caught up in this mess. It was the other woman who was shot. Monica managed to get into one of the cars and take off. She's been hiding ever since. Right now she's headed to Albuquerque with my associate Tyee. I was wondering if there was any way you could arrange for some security for her."

"Well that is interesting news. Not sure about the security, but let me see what I can do. I'm glad she's alive."

They said their goodbyes and hung up.

Ray decided he was going to Albuquerque. He didn't completely understand what Crawford had been hinting at during their phone call, but it was clear that Monica was still at risk. He went out into the store, found Big Jack, and told him that he'd decided to go to Albuquerque immediately. He related the tone of his conversation with Crawford and said it made him concerned for Monica and Tyee. He said he'd call Big Jack once he got to Monica's son's house.

Ray went back to the cabin, gathered some things, and tossed them in the Jeep. He got Happy some food and water for the trip, and with Happy in the back of the Jeep they headed out.

Once Ray got to Albuquerque he stopped at a convenience store and called Luke Jackson, Monica's son. He explained to Luke who he was and asked him for directions to the house. Luke asked Ray where he was and then said it would take Ray about fifteen minutes to get to his place and provided clear directions. Ray hung up and headed out. When he found Luke's house, he was alarmed to see a police car out front.

Ray and Happy went to the front door and rang the bell. Tyee answered the door and stepped out onto the porch.

"Hey, did they call the police on you?"

"White man thinks he's funny, Indian knows better."

"Yep, you're a wise Indian. Everything okay here?"

"Think so, Ray. The police officer just showed up about an hour ago. Said he was here to provide security for Ms. Jackson. I asked who sent him and he said it was Detective Taylor, our good buddy from the other day. Not sure what that's about— thought maybe you had something to do with it."

"Not directly. I talked to Crawford and asked if he could arrange something—maybe this is it. If it is, then I don't know how he knew where she was. I told him she'd been found and was headed to Albuquerque with you. Everything about this makes me nervous, because we don't know who's involved. How's Monica?"

"She seems mostly worried about Mike. He doesn't seem to be doing well. She and her son were talking about admitting him to a hospital. She'll be pleased to see her dog again. I went with her to her house to see about the other dogs. That was quite a scene—there are a lot of them. If Mike goes to the hospital, I'm sure she'll want to go home so she can take care of the animals."

"Yeah, I'm sure she would, and maybe that's okay, but I have an uneasy feeling that this thing isn't over."

Ray and Tyee talked some more about what they might do to provide security and whether the police would provide extended protection for Monica when she went home since she lived outside the Albuquerque jurisdiction. As they were talking, Monica appeared at the door.

She greeted Ray, then began hugging and rubbing Happy, who was very excited to see her, and bouncing around like a windup toy. Happy's excitement made everyone smile, despite the circumstances.

"Ray, I'm glad you're here. I know you think there's still some risk to me, but I need to go home and take care of my dogs. My neighbor's been helping, but he's elderly and he just can't manage anymore. Just feeding and watering them once a day is wearing him out. Plus, my son and I think Mike should be in a hospital. He seems to be declining. In the last twelve hours he's gotten noticeably worse. I'm sorry to be a bother to you and Tyee; I just need to take care of things."

"Monica, you do what you think is right. You're not a bother. We'll adjust—that's what we were talking about. Tyee was filling me in on the fact that you needed to be at your house to take care of the dogs. I'm going to make some calls and see if we can get some other security, but what I want you to do is what you think is right—we won't go away until we're sure you're safe."

Monica started to cry. Ray hated that—he never knew what he should do when someone cried. Monica solved the problem by reaching out and giving him a hug.

They went inside. Ray introduced himself to the police officer, a very nice young man who was taking his responsibilities very seriously. Ray immediately liked him. Then he saw Mike and was shocked at how much the man had gone downhill in such a short time. He talked to Monica about it, but she didn't know what was causing it. It seemed like he'd just given up and was ready to die. Monica was very emotional—she wasn't as bad as Mike was, but she seemed to have aged noticeably in just a few days. The whole atmosphere made Ray want to go fishing and then spend the night with Sue—he didn't want to deal with death.

Monica called an ambulance for Mike, who would be taken to St. Anthony's Hospital downtown. Monica and Luke agreed on a schedule of who would go to the hospital and when.

Ray called the State of New Mexico Attorney's General office and asked to speak to Tony Garcia. Tony was the AG. He and Ray went back many years—and he owed Ray.

"Ray, it's great to hear from you. Are you in Santa Fe? Can you come by? It would be great to see you."

It was good to hear such a friendly voice. Tony and Ray's friendship went back to the time when Tony was the Attorney for Dona Ana County and Ray was the sheriff. They had formed one of the best working relationships Ray had ever experienced. He greatly respected Tony and the work he'd done to make life better for everyone in the county. Ray had also helped him out of a couple of spots that would have been embarrassing. They were good friends.

"I wish I was able to see you—I'd like that. Right now I'm in Albuquerque working on a matter for some friends."

Ray gave Tony the short version of what had happened over the last few weeks. He left out most of the parts involving the FBI because he was still unsure who was who when it came to the Feds. He didn't want to get Tony involved in anything that might put him in a bad place with the "fire-breathing" Feds.

"Ray, I knew you couldn't retire and just go fishing. You're the best law enforcement person I've ever met, and you can't just sit in a rocking chair when there are people in need. I think it's great that you're working again."

"Well thanks, Tony. Not sure what it's going to be in the future, but I did form a company with a couple of partners to take on some investigative business, so we'll see how it works out."

"You need some protection in Bosque Farms," Tony said. "That's Bernalillo County, so that would be Sheriff Romero. You may not know him Ray—he was just elected a few months ago and he's fairly new to law enforcement. He's a good man, though, and he's trying to clean up a bunch of messes he inherited. I've worked closely with him over the last month or so. I've even talked about you and about our working relationship in Dona Ana, how that was great for both of us in terms of getting things done. Let me give him a call and tell him briefly what's going on. I'll tell him that you'll be calling sometime today—does that work?"

"That's great, Tony. I owe you one on this."

"Well, I think I owe you more than one, so don't worry about it. When you get a chance in a few weeks, give me a call and let's get together and talk about what you're doing now."

They agreed. Ray got the number for the Bernalillo sheriff's office and hung up. The sheriff might not want to contribute any manpower to this deal, but Ray had a feeling getting a call from Tony would be persuasive. He was also sure that it would be only for a few days. Something was going to happen—one way or another—he could feel it.

Monica had left right after the ambulance had gone. She was going to the hospital to get Mike checked in, then to her house to take care of her dogs. The plan was that Ray and Tyee would be at her house more or less by the time she arrived. Ray informed the police officer that Monica was leaving to go to the hospital and that they no longer needed security. The officer didn't seem pleased, but he said he'd let Detective Taylor know and he left.

Ray and Tyee, along with Happy, got into the Jeep and headed out.

"How about lunch—Indians do eat fast food, right?"

"You're treading close to offensive, Mr. Sheriff."

Ray was partial to What-a-Burger's green chili cheese burger. It was appropriate food for a teenager—probably life-threatening food for an old codger like him. But all this talk about declining health had the opposite effect on Ray to what might be expected—he wanted to have a cheese burger, just like back when he was only middle-aged.

After consuming a whole day's worth of calories, they headed south toward Monica's house. They got back on I-25 and went about ten miles south of Albuquerque, then took the Bosque exit. This was an area with many small farms. It had a rural feel, with a slow pace that felt very different from the urban Albuquerque they had just left. Following Monica's directions, they had no trouble finding her place.

It was a small house with a couple of outbuildings, one of which was obviously a large kennel. There was a large fenced-in area where the dogs could go outside, and many of them were out there watching as Ray and Tyee pulled into the yard. When they opened the doors, Happy jumped out and the dogs went nuts. Maybe they were greeting their returning king or something, but whatever it was it created a great deal of excitement for Happy and the other dogs. Happy ran up and down the fence line with the other dogs, barking and jumping.

Before Ray or Tyee could figure out how to get into the fenced yard, Monica drove up. She smiled at the obvious delight of the dogs. She unlocked a gate and let Happy join the others.

"They haven't seen their leader in a while–they're very excited. I'll come out in a minute and feed and water them. For now just let them play. Please, come inside and I'll get us something to drink."

Monica was looking beat again. Dealing with the death of her son, the threat to her life, and Mike in the hospital, all while taking care of her dogs, was exacting a major toll. She fixed tea.

Ray asked to use the phone and called the Bernalillo sheriff. He talked to Sheriff Romero and found him ready to provide whatever they needed. Ray said he would like to have a presence at the house. If a deputy could park out front for a couple of days, that would take care of it. If the threat extended beyond two days, Ray would make other arrangements. The sheriff said a deputy would be there within the hour. They agreed that they needed to meet one another and that they would make an effort for that to happen within a few weeks.

Ray discussed the new arrangement with Monica and

Tyee. Monica seemed to be verging on disinterest, and he could see that to her the threat was becoming less real as time passed. She couldn't deal with everything going on and also deal with the threat, and Ray understood. The threat wasn't specific—the guy next door with a gun—that's real. Some mysterious bad guys were just not real enough to keep you afraid. Of course, the bad guys knew this—just wait a few weeks and all the defenses will have come down.

Monica said she was going to clean up a little before taking care of the dogs. Ray and Tyee went outside to talk.

"Ray, do you think all of this is because of the L.A. Mexican Mafia trying to get back the drug or fake document money they think Monica has?"

"You know, I think that's the issue—I don't believe it's the Mexican Mafia. We know there are bad people who call themselves the Mexican Mafia—Big Jack can attest to the fact that they are real—but to be in New Mexico and be expending so much energy to recover, what? Thousands of dollars? It can't be millions with someone like Ed. That would be absurd. So why would L.A. thugs go to that much effort to recover what would have to be an insignificant amount to them? Ed was a small time crook, mostly supporting his personal drug and drinking habits. There's no way, based on what we know, that he was handling big deals. It was all small time stuff, so why kill him? And go after his mother? Something is missing."

"There's something more sinister going on here," Tyee said, and Ray was sure he was right—this felt almost personal.

# 23

## *Thursday*

"Ray, thank god I finally tracked you down. We've got a big problem. Clayton was arrested by the FBI and is in jail in Cruces. They're looking for you, too." Big Jack had spent several hours trying to find out where Ray and Tyee were. He'd called the last place he knew, which was Luke Jackson's house, and had left a message, but no one had returned the call. Monica Jackson's number was unlisted, and Big Jack didn't have it. But while searching in Tyee's notes, he'd found Betty Adams' number. He'd explained that he was a friend of Ray's and he thought Ray might be at Monica's. Betty was concerned at first about giving out Monica's number, but Big Jack convinced her it was the right thing to do.

"What! Arrested him for what?"

"Cindy told me it was for obstruction of justice—they claim he was interfering with an ongoing FBI-DEA investigation. She also said that they asked where you lived and said you'd be charged with the same thing. Nobody came by here, so I don't know if they went to your cabin or not. Cindy said the guy in charge was an Agent Myers who acted like a complete asshole—yelling at everybody and treating Sheriff Martinez like he was a moron—of course, why shouldn't he?

Anyway she said she's not a hundred percent sure, but for some reason she thinks they took him to the jail in Las Cruces. She heard Martinez say he didn't want him locked up in T or C. What the hell's happening Ray?"

"Well I'd say this is the shit hitting the fan. The problem is, I don't know why. Look, Jack, I'm going to call an attorney I know in Las Cruces—his name is Jeff Young. I'm going to ask him to find out what happened with Clayton—where he is and what he's been charged with. I'm going to leave your number with Jeff. If something comes up and he can't get a hold of me, I'll have him call you. I may head back to T or C later today or tomorrow. Still have some things that are not settled here, but I'll let you know."

Ray hung up and went to find Tyee to let him know what had happened. They had stayed the night at Monica's and a Bernalillo County sheriff's deputy had been stationed out front since yesterday. This morning a new deputy was in place. The deputy and Tyee were leaning against the patrol unit, chatting. Ray waved Tyee over to the front porch.

"Think that deputy knows what he's doing?"

"Seems so Ray. He said his boss, the sheriff, made it clear he was on special duty and not to screw up. Seems like you have friends in high places."

"Yeah, more like a friend of a friend. Just talked to Big Jack and there's some bad news back home."

Ray filled Tyee in on the latest developments. Tyee was beside himself.

"Do you think that Martinez had anything to do with this?"

"Seems odd that he could get the FBI to arrest a man just

because he was losing an election. So, once again we have a situation that doesn't make sense. I'm going to call an attorney in Las Cruces and let him see what he can find out. Also I'm going to call the sheriff in Dona Ana County and talk to him. Then I'm going to call Crawford. This whole thing with the FBI smells real bad. He may not tell me what's going on, but if he doesn't, then we sure the hell aren't going to work for them."

Tyee could tell Ray was about as pissed as he had ever seen him. Tyee was beginning to understand that it took a lot to make Ray angry, but once you did there was going to be hell to pay. Tyee was just fine being on his good side. Ray hurried inside to make his calls.

"Ray, good to hear from you. Are you in Las Cruces?"

"No, Jeff, I'm in Albuquerque. Something has happened in Cruces that I need your help with—and this will be on my account, so send me the bill. Yesterday, according to my sources, a deputy sheriff was arrested by the FBI on obstruction charges and he's in the county jail in Las Cruces. I haven't called the sheriff yet to confirm this, but I believe it to be true. The person arrested is a friend of my named Dan Clayton. He's running for the sheriff's job in Sierra County. I can't believe the current acting sheriff up there has enough clout with the FBI to get his opponent arrested, but this is a strange coincidence since we're so close to the election. I need you to find out what's happening and how we can get Clayton released."

Ray and Jeff talked further. Ray added more details and then gave Jeff the number at his current location, the number to his business line, and the main line to Big Jack's. Jeff said he would get started immediately.

Ray's next call was to the new sheriff in Dona Ana County, Sam Diaz. Sam had been a deputy when Ray was sheriff and was a very competent man. Ray was pleased when he won the election after Ray retired. Diaz wasn't available, so Ray left a voice mail asking Sam to call him at one of several numbers.

Then Ray called Crawford. Expecting to leave a message, Ray was surprised when Ben Crawford answered.

"What the hell is going on Ben? The FBI has arrested a deputy in T or C on charges of obstruction and interfering in a FBI investigation, and they parked him in Las Cruces. This is a friend of mine who's running for the sheriff's position there, with the election in just a few weeks. What the hell's the FBI doing?"

"Ray, I don't know anything about this. This isn't Sanchez is it?"

"No my understanding is that it's Myers—and he was directing the current T or C sheriff like he owned him. Also, I've been told he was looking for me so he could arrest me at the same time. Is this guy on some kind of vendetta?"

"Give me some time. How can I reach you?"

Ray recited his list of contact numbers and they hung up. Ray couldn't have been angrier. The phone rang, and without thinking Ray answered—immediately realizing this wasn't his phone.

"Jackson residence."

"Is this Ray Pacheco?"

"Sam, thanks for calling back so quickly. A friend of mine, a deputy from T or C, was arrested by the FBI and I was told you are holding him—his name is Clayton—is that true?"

"It is Ray. I've already talked to Jeff. Look, I have no idea what is going on, but Clayton is in his own cell and won't have any contact with any other prisoners. He's safe. My hands are tied as far as releasing him since this is a federal order to hold him. Jeff left here and headed to a federal judge in El Paso to force some kind of release—he was saying the documents they gave me to hold Clayton aren't valid without a judge's signature. Also I won't release Clayton to anyone until I've heard from Jeff about the judge. If the FBI asshole who brought him in doesn't like it, tough shit. Matter of fact, if that guy comes back here and acts the way he did when they brought Clayton in, I'll throw his ass in jail and wait for orders from Washington or God."

Ray's kind of guy.

Ray found Tyee hanging out on the front porch and filled him in on what he'd found out.

"Think we should head back to T or C. I'm going to call the Bernalillo sheriff and make sure they can cover Monica for a few more days."

"Fine with me, Ray—whatever's needed."

Ray found Monica in the yard working with one of her dogs. Not far away, Happy was lying on the ground watching intently.

"Looks like we'll be headed back to T or C in a little while. I'm going to make sure the deputies stay around a few more days."

"Ray, I don't think I need any protection. Those people, whoever they are, can't be so stupid as to think I have drug money or whatever it is—I think they just made a mistake and once they realized it, they went back to L.A. or Mexico or wherever."

Ray knew that this wasn't a rational response, but he'd

seen this kind of wishful thinking before. She wanted the ordeal to be over right now and just go back to her normal life. If everyone would just leave her alone, she'd be fine. Of course, Ray knew that made no sense and was just Monica's need for peace and quiet overriding her good sense.

"You know Monica you may be right, but let's be on the safe side for a little while longer. The deputies will be out front for a couple more days and then we can decide what, if anything, needs to be done after that."

"Of course, Ray. You remember, anytime you're in my area, you and Tyee are always welcome guests in my house. I can't tell you how much you've meant to Mike and me—we owe you a lot."

Ray said she didn't owe him anything. Then he changed the subject, asking her what she was doing with the dogs. She started talking about how she trained the dogs, and she was immediately more relaxed and happier than Ray had seen her. The dogs gave her meaning and purpose.

Sheriff Romero said he could leave a deputy out there for a couple more days. Ray could tell that he didn't want to commit to anything beyond that, and he understood. There wasn't a sheriff's department anywhere that had extra men just sitting around. Ray thanked him and assured him he wouldn't ask for anything further.

Ray and Tyee, along with Happy, headed back to T or C. Ray wasn't sure about Happy. Monica had insisted that he go with Ray, but Ray was beginning to wonder if he wouldn't be better off with Monica and all the other dogs. But for now, he decided not to argue with Monica about it—he knew it was her way of saying thank you.

"Tyee, there's no question we've made an enemy of Sheriff Martinez. I was thinking about stopping in his office and talking to him face to face about what's going on with Clayton—what do you think?"

"Indian may stay in car with dog."

That was good for several miles of laughter. "No, really. What do you think?"

"Ray, Martinez is a bully. Everyone knows if you challenge a bully, he either backs down or pulls his revolver. The problem is you never know which he might do."

"Good input. I think you're right. If I back him into a corner, he could be dangerous. But I don't see a good alternative. Something has to give here. We need to know how much of this is being caused by the stupid sheriff and how much is related to Monica and the killings. I think I'm going in with the attitude that if the dumb son-of-a-bitch pulls his gun, I'm shooting him. But I'm not going to let that happen. I don't think he'll pull his gun, and I think he'll tell me something I need to know."

"So let me see. You are going in armed to confront an armed, stupid sheriff about a possible criminal act the sheriff did—all because you are a good citizen."

"Pretty much."

"Looks like stupid is pretty common in the sheriff business."

More miles of laughter. Ray thought Tyee was very funny—it was just that sometimes he couldn't tell if he intended to be funny.

By the time they got to the T or C exit they'd regained their composure and were ready for business when they arrived at the sheriff's office.

"Sheriff Pacheco, hello." Cindy was very nervous.

"Hello, Cindy. Is Sheriff Martinez in?"

"Uh, I believe so. Just a minute." Cindy dialed a number and said something and then hung up.

On impulse Ray went through the door into the back of the building. The sheriff was just leaving his office through his private back door.

"Hey, sheriff. We need to talk."

"The FBI is looking for you asshole—now get the fuck out of this building."

Ray had continued to walk towards Martinez as he made his little man speech. Now he reached up, grabbed his arm, and swung him around, pushing him into the wall. At the same time he removed his service revolver.

"What the hell are you doing? You stupid son-of-a-bitch you'll go to jail—you just accosted a sheriff. Are you an idiot?"

Ray pushed him into the empty room next door and slammed the door.

"Shut up, Martinez. I'm working for the Attorney General of New Mexico, Tony Garcia, and it's under his authority that I'm arresting you for abusing your office and for just being really goddamned annoying."

Martinez was stunned. He wasn't sure what to do or say. He was afraid of Ray, and now Ray seemed to have a legal right to do what he was doing. Martinez started to shake.

Ray stayed in the room with Martinez for some time. When he left, Martinez was handcuffed to the window frame.

"Cindy, I want you to call Sheriff Diaz of Dona Ana County and tell him that I've just arrested Sheriff Martinez for unspecified crimes on the authority of Attorney General Tony Garcia, and I'll be bringing him to Las Cruces within the next hour or so."

Cindy just stared. She didn't seem able to move.

"Now, Cindy. Please call now."

That got her going. She dialed the phone.

Ray went over and talked to Tyee. Tyee went into the back, brought Martinez out, and walked him to the Jeep. Tyee secured Martinez in the back and got in beside him. Happy moved to the front seat.

They drove to Las Cruces. At the sheriff's office, they were met by Sheriff Diaz.

"Ray, do you know what you're doing?"

Ray had handed Martinez over to one of the deputies standing next to Diaz, and Diaz directed the deputy to put him in an interrogation room.

"Sam, I'm not sure this is the right thing to do but there was too much going on, I had to take some action before someone else got hurt. My authority to do this is pretty weak, but I assure you that Martinez has been involved in several things that could put him in prison for life or get him the death penalty."

"Ray, you know I want to believe you—do you have any proof?"

"He signed this confession about an hour ago." Ray handed Sam the paper.

"I'll need to talk to Martinez—without you in the room."

Ray and Tyee went over and sat on a bench.

"Sure the hell hope you know what you're doing Ray."

Ray kind of grinned. It wasn't a confident look—it was an

expression that said "I sure the hell hope so too."

"Ray, Martinez says you threatened him and that's why he signed the confession."

"Sam, I didn't write the confession, he did. I didn't tell him what to write, he just wrote it. My threats amounted to saying that he was in trouble and could go to jail—which is true."

"He said you hit him."

"I took his gun away from him. When doing that I grabbed his arm and pushed him into a wall. I never hit him."

"What is this bullshit about the Attorney General?"

"Well, it's not complete bullshit. I know he wants all citizens to take an active role in fighting crime."

"Ray, I should lock you up for just saying that out loud. What I'm going to do is hold Martinez until we can figure out what's going on with Clayton. But if you made all this shit up just to get back at Martinez because he was involved in Clayton's arrest—even though there is no one I have more respect for, I'll arrest you."

"Fair enough Sam. You should hold them both until you hear officially from the FBI, but it needs to be the FBI out of Washington D.C., a man named Crawford. You do what you think is right. And if you need to arrest me, call me and I'll turn myself in, or you can find me in T or C."

Ray turned around and left. Tyee followed.

"Ray that seemed kind of crazy to me. The whole thing with Martinez, was that planned or did you just go nuts?"

"I think you have wonderful insight into human beings Tyee, and I will always trust your judgment. What I did was nuts—but it was nuts because otherwise some people were going to get hurt. I didn't know if that was going to be Monica, or me, or you, or Clayton—or maybe even Big Jack—but someone was going to get hurt. The problem we had was that we didn't know why. What was the crime at the source—the thing that these people were committing new crimes to cover up? It all looked like a mixed up mess with no meaning. Well, I scared the crap out of the weakest link and now I know."

"You know what all of this is about?"

"Think so."

# 24

*Friday*

It seemed like it had been a long time since Ray had slept in his cabin. He really enjoyed where he lived. It made him wonder why he was out looking for trouble—and finding it—when he could just stay here in complete calm and occasionally go fishing. But he knew the answer: he would be bored silly. Plus, he enjoyed the sense of accomplishment of a job well done.

As of this morning, though, he wasn't feeling any sense of accomplishment. It felt a lot more like he'd stirred up one big pile of shit. He knew Martinez was worthless, but what Ray was doing better work out or he'd probably be looking for a new home, somewhere far away.

Ray was fixing coffee when there was a knock on the door. Normally Ray would have just opened it, but today he was on edge. He found his service revolver and eased up to the door.

"Who is it?"

"Man, that's not very friendly. How many people even come up to this place?"

Ray pulled the door open and gave Sue a big hug.

She noticed the gun. "What's going on Ray? There's some kind of crazy story going on that you arrested Martinez because he arrested Clayton. Can you still arrest people?"

Ray laughed. He quickly realized how much he had missed her in the last few days.

"Well, actually, I think that's being debated as we speak. I'm very happy to see you. Don't you work the morning shift—didn't get fired did you?"

"No, they let me take some time off if I'd come back and tell them what's going on."

"Ah, I see—you're spying."

The phone rang and they both jumped.

"Hey, you have a phone—when did that happen?"

"This morning. I didn't think anyone had the number yet."

Ray went over and answered. He listened.

"Okay, thanks, I'll call her."

"You're calling girlfriends now?"

"Not exactly. That was Tyee, he's down at Big Jack's. There was a message from Monica Jackson. She seemed pretty upset about a package she received. I'm sorry, Sue—do you mind if I return her call?"

"No that's fine, I understand. But I think I'm going to miss the time when this place didn't have a phone." She got up and stepped out onto the porch with Happy.

"Monica, this is Ray—what's going on?"

"Ray, this is unbelievable. I was just looking through my mail. It'd been stacking up for some time and I hadn't really been paying attention. In the pile there was an envelope addressed to me and it was Ed's handwriting. It gave me a chill. When I opened it there were several pages of information about the gang, or whatever you want to call them—the people Ed was dealing with. Plus there are some names of people who

Ed knew were behind the whole thing. He signed a confession detailing the whole operation as far as he knew it, naming names. There are also photos of various people. I recognized one of the creeps who took me, and who shot Mrs. Richards. What should I do, Ray?"

Maybe this was what they'd been looking for all along. They knew Ed had put together a "get out of jail free" package, but they killed him anyway. Or maybe they only found out after he was killed and didn't know where it was. It started to make sense to Ray on why the goons seemed so eager to use the amount of force they had with Monica.

"Monica, can you leave right now—would the dogs be okay?"

"I guess so. The deputies are still here. Do you think I'm at risk?"

"I need you and the information to be safe. What I'd like is for you to get in your car and drive to my cabin. I can make sure you're safe. We can review the information and decide what to do. I think it's very important for everybody that we're together for the next couple of days."

Ray debated with himself about what to do. He could go there or Tyee could go. Or he could have Monica go to the Bernalillo sheriff and give him the information, but he was hesitant to have anyone else see the information until he knew exactly what it was and what it meant. He knew he was becoming paranoid. Of all of the options, the one he liked the most was for Monica to leave immediately and drive to his place. He knew he only had one more day before the deputies stopped watching her, at which point something would have to be done. He was probably burning his bridges to both the

Bernalillo sheriff and his friend the Attorney General, though, because of what he did yesterday with Martinez. He decided time was short and it was necessary for Monica to drive to him—for her safety and his.

"Ray, if that's what you want me to do, that's what I'll do. I think it'll take me a couple of hours to get ready and to make arrangements for the dogs. I'll do that and then drive to your cabin. I'm not sure I remember where your cabin is, though."

"Go to T or C and go to the Lone Post Café. I'll wait there for you. If you leave in two hours you'll be here in four. You need to stay on that schedule, otherwise I won't know what's going on. Are you okay with this?"

"I think so. You're scaring me a little bit, but I'll be there on time." They hung up.

Ray went out onto the porch and told Sue what was going on. He didn't give her all of the details, but enough for her to realize there were people in danger. He went back inside and called Tyee. Ray told him what was happening and asked Tyee if he could stay at the cabin for a few days until the situation was resolved. They agreed on a good spot to hide the key in case Ray left.

Ray went back out and sat next to Sue on the porch. Happy was lying next to her so she could rub him occasionally.

"Seems like your world is changing. You came up here to retire and now you're fighting the bad guys just like before, only without all of the support troops. Is this really what you want to do?"

Ray noticed the implied criticism. It didn't bother or surprise him. He'd been in law enforcement for most of his life, and every person he ever got close to eventually thought the risk was too high for the reward. It was hard to explain why you did it, but there was nothing else that could give you the same feeling. No doubt it was the power and the adrenaline when things happened, but there was also a sense of accomplishment—you mattered.

"I know it doesn't make a lot of sense, Sue. I just know that this is what I want to do. It makes me feel useful, and maybe even important. It's probably wrong, and I'm too old to be running around punching young sheriffs, but I sure feel alive."

"You punched the sheriff?"

"That's a slight exaggeration. I shoved him into the wall."

Sue leaned over and gave him a kiss. He mentioned that he had a few hours open before he had to meet his next woman. Sue gave him a pretty good slug to the shoulder, then took him inside. They felt completely comfortable with each other.

Sue told Ray that she thought she should stay at the cabin while he went to town to meet Monica. It was clear that Sue was going to stay put as long as Monica was around. Ray knew this, didn't completely understand it—but at the same time, found it pleasing. Happy decided to stay with Sue as Ray headed to the Jeep.

He drove into town alternately thinking about Sue and wondering what was in the package Monica was bringing. He entered the Lone Post Café and immediately realized he should have told Monica to meet him at the Firestone store or Smith's grocery or something. This place was packed with living, breathing gossip machines.

Ray sat at the small lunch counter and ordered coffee.

"Hey, Ray. Sue's not here today. Actually, we thought she

was with you."

Ray hated this small town nonsense.

"She's at my cabin—I'm meeting my cousin, who's visiting. She doesn't know the way to the cabin. So, going to meet her here and Sue is waiting for us at the cabin."

Ray sipped his coffee. Thirty minutes after the agreed time, Ray started to worry. If something happened to Monica because he'd asked her to drive here, Ray would never forgive himself. He should have just called the Bernalillo sheriff and had them escort Monica to their office with the documents. Ray should have driven up there. That seemed to make more sense to him now than what he'd asked her to do—he was really worried. He got up and was going to the payphone, when Monica walked in.

"Monica, I was so worried that something had happened." His concern was all over his face.

"It's okay, Ray. I'm sorry I worried you. It took me a little longer than I thought to put together all of the arrangements. My neighbor is just too old to handle the dogs. I asked the man down the street if he could if I paid him. So then we had to work out a price and I took him around and introduced him to the dogs—well, it just took longer. But here I am."

Ray realized his behavior didn't fit with his story of greeting a cousin, but couldn't do anything about it. He hurried Monica out the door and back to her car. He told her in a general way where they were going and said that she should just follow him. Once they got outside of town, Monica followed very close—as if Ray might try to get away. He drove slower than usual, so it took a little longer than normal to get to the cabin. Pulling up to the cabin, he could see Tyee and Sue sitting in the chairs on the porch. Monica pulled in behind him.

Ray introduced Monica to Sue, but they said they already knew one another. Monica remembered how nice Sue had been to her when her tires had been slashed. They greeted each other like sisters. It was amazing to Ray how easy women were with each other and how hard it was to even get a man to smile.

They all went into the cabin. Monica immediately gave Ray the package. Ray sat down and started going through the material. It was explosive stuff—no wonder people had been killed. After Ray had finished, he addressed the group.

"There's no question in my mind that this implicates some important people in some serious crimes and has put us all at risk. You need to know that being here puts you in danger. Sue in particular, you need to be aware that your safest recourse right now is to leave."

"Not sure what's going on, but I'm not leaving. If this is going to be some kind of Wild West shootout, all I ask is that you give me a gun."

"White man's woman got guts."

Sue and Monica looked at Tyee like he had just said the strangest thing possible. Only Ray knew this was his way of easing tension.

"Tyee in his vast Indian wisdom hit the nail on the head. Sue and, also you, Monica are very brave. I don't believe there will be a shootout. But we'll need to be extra careful. I'm going to make some calls and see if we can get some assistance."

Ray went to make the calls. Sue looked at Tyee like she wasn't sure who he was—and he winked at her. She began to laugh and soon all of them, even Monica, were laughing.

Ray had called Sheriff Diaz in Las Cruces and told him that he had corroborating evidence of some serious crimes involving Martinez. The sheriff reported that Martinez was still in jail, but that he'd released Clayton. Jeff Young had gotten an El Paso federal judge to sign for the release. Ray thanked the sheriff and told him he was contacting the FBI and hoped that Sam would have all of the information shortly.

Ray then called the T or C sheriff's office.

"Hello, sheriff's office."

"Cindy, is Deputy Clayton there?"

"Yes, he is. He's been trying to find you—he was just headed out to Big Jack's. Just a minute, I'll get him."

"Ray, where are you?"

"Dan, it's good to hear your voice. I'm at my cabin. The new phone line was just put in. I need some protection, deputy. I have a long story to tell you. The bottom line is that there are some very dangerous people looking for the information I have in my hands. Could you send someone out to my cabin to help secure this area?"

"I'll be there is just a few minutes."

Ray then called Crawford in Washington, but got his voice mail. He left a message saying that he needed to talk and gave his new phone number. Ray then called Agent Sanchez in El Paso. He was told that Sanchez was out and was put through to his voice mail. Ray left the same message and again gave the new number.

Shortly, Deputy Clayton showed up with another patrol car.

"Ray, I've got no idea what happened between you and Martinez, but I'm sorry you've been dragged into this ugly mess."

"Dan, you've no idea how ugly this mess is, and it may be the other way around—that you were dragged into an ugly mess because of me."

They went inside and Ray went over the material they had and its implications. As they were beginning to discuss what it might mean, one of the deputies outside came to the door and told Clayton that there were FBI officials on the road and they wanted to see Ray.

# 25

*Friday*

Walking out the door toward the road, Ray could see Crawford and Sanchez waiting patiently. Ray showed them into the cabin. Everyone cleared the room, going outside to give Ray and his visitors some privacy.

"Ray, looks like you're getting ready for a battle."

"No, not really. I think there's a bunch of shit you haven't told me and because of that you've put a lot of people at risk. I know about Myers and Martinez, and I can guess at a bunch of others who are involved. This isn't the Mexican Mafia—this looks like a rogue FBI operation."

"I'm afraid you've stumbled into the middle of one of the biggest mistakes the FBI ever made. We've been gathering evidence on Myers for months. We thought we had everything covered so that he couldn't do any more harm while we monitored his communications and put our case together. But we screwed up. His order of the hit job on Ed Jackson caught us flat-footed. We arrested the two men involved in the killing and also charged them with the murder of Mrs. Richards. We were planning on arresting Myers today or tomorrow. We just haven't been sure up until now that we had enough evidence."

"How long have you know about this?"

"Ray, I'm not going to tell you everything about this. It's just too embarrassing for the FBI, so this whole story is going to be buried. Let me just say that we've known of a problem since the arrest of the Sierra County sheriff for drug trafficking."

"You mean the sheriff was involved with Myers?"

"At first the sheriff stayed quiet. A few weeks ago there were some incidents during one of his stays in a Texas county jail. He was admitted to a hospital and at that point he said he wanted to make a deal. He's ready to testify against Myers, claiming he was the person running the whole operation. We didn't believe him at first, but it didn't take long to start fitting the pieces together. We were planning on moving on Myers this week but then things got out of hand."

"Not a good outcome—two people dead while you were watching."

"No—it's a piece of shit. We'll owe you big time Ray if we can keep this quiet. I have to tell you that the offer to use you and your new firm on a consulting basis was a way for us to watch you while we were still in the middle of this mess. But you can go ahead and agree to that plan and you'll have the bureau beholden to you. I personally apologize for this whole mess—it's not the way I like to do things."

"Maybe there's something you can do for me."

"No doubt you're talking about your partners—Big Jack in particular. Let me tell you we'll fix everything so that the background checks won't be a problem. I've already put a process in place to clean up any history on Philip Duncan—he just won't exist anymore. We'll process new paperwork and create a new identity for someone called Jack Parker, including a new license to practice law in New Mexico. You might be surprised that we can do that, but we have our ways. We'll provide Jack Parker with a complete new background—all we want from him is a couple of briefing sessions where he explains what he knows about the inner workings of the L.A. Mexican Mafia."

"Well, yeah—that's what I wanted. If you can make that happen then we're ready to do work with the FBI. I won't discuss what I know about how Myers was mishandled. The Jacksons won't know—not sure it would matter to them anyway. It'll be kept quiet, except that I'll let my partners know."

"Ray, I think we have the basis for a mutually beneficial agreement. We'll immediately implement our plan regarding Myers. He'll just be gone and the new agent in charge in Albuquerque will be Sanchez. Agent Sanchez will contact you and let you know that everything's been handled. Thanks, Ray. I look forward to working with you."

Ray sat and thought. He wasn't sure who was more to blame for Ed's and Mrs. Richards' death, Myers or the reluctance of the FBI to move quickly on one of their own. Of course Ed had created many of his own problems and Mrs. Richards had been armed and stalking Monica. No telling what might have happened even without the goons getting involved. So they had their share of the blame as well.

"I guess we all try to cover ourselves, but I have to tell you I'm disappointed. Both of you guys seem like good people. But there are two people dead, a mother who's lost her son and been frightened almost to death, along with a whole host of other people affected in negative ways because you wouldn't move on one of your own without perfect evidence. This will take some time to heal."

Crawford promised that they would keep Ray informed and that he had men watching Myers and didn't believe there was any current danger. Ray made sure Crawford and Sanchez had his new phone number. He showed them to the door and watched them walk to their car.

Ray told the others he was going down to see Big Jack for just a minute and would be back soon to tell everyone what was happening. He also told them that he had been assured by the FBI that the danger was over. Ray drove to Big Jack's and went out to the dock area. Big Jack was finishing up with the customer.

"Got some information for you, Big Jack. Got a minute?"

Ray filled Big Jack in on the situation with Monica and related his conversation with Agent Crawford. Big Jack listened and didn't interrupt.

"So they fucked up, and two people are dead—and we get FBI business and I get a new identity and a law license. Somehow that doesn't seem right."

"No, it doesn't. The alternative could be us raising hell with anybody who would listen, including the media, and seeing how much shit we could stir up. No doubt ending any chance of working with any law enforcement agencies and putting a target on your head for the Mexicans to aim at."

"Yeah, that doesn't sound too good, does it?"

"I don't like it, but my feeling is that it's in our best interest to keep our mouths shut and take the deal."

"Jack Parker says Fucking A."

Ray left Big Jack's, went back to the cabin, and explained to everyone what he'd learned from the FBI, but he left out some of the sensitive parts.

"So it looks like the coast is clear. The FBI will be arresting the bad guys, including one of their own, and I think we can all feel secure. Monica, they were after you for the information your son had on them—mostly on Myers, the FBI guy in Albuquerque. Myers was the main guy running the operation, and Martinez was involved along with the previous sheriff. As far as we know there wasn't anyone else directly involved with what happened to you except the two goons, and they've been picked up and charged with murder. Martinez is in the Dona Ana County jail and will be charged with a long list of crimes and may be charged with accessory to murder related to Mrs. Richards. Myers will be arrested today, or may already have been arrested. He'll be charged with various crimes, and with some special federal crimes because he used his FBI position to commit the other crimes."

"Can I go home, Ray?"

"Yes, Monica. You can leave whenever you want or you can stay as long as you want."

"I think I'd like to go home now."

Ray said he understood perfectly. Sue and Monica went off to gather her things and get Monica ready to leave. Ray told Clayton that he could leave too, along with his deputies, since everything seemed to be wrapped up. He told Clayton that he should assume the acting sheriff's position immediately to keep the department running. Ray explained that he would contact some of the council members and county commissioners and make sure they understood all of the things that had happened over the last few days. Clayton and his deputies hurriedly left.

Tyee sat down at the table, saying that just to be on the

safe side he thought he'd stay the night at the cabin. Ray said he was sure welcome to, but he really didn't think it was necessary. He told Tyee about the FBI screwup and the fact that they'd known about Myers for some time but taken their time, probably to try to cover their own asses before they moved. That delay likely cost two lives. He also told Tyee about the agreement he'd made and how it impacted Big Jack.

Finally, Ray told Tyee he should go home and get some rest. Everything was fine now.

# 26

*Saturday*

The new phone in Ray's cabin rang early. Ray finally found it after fumbling a bit.

"Hello."

"Ray, this is Crawford. We had a foul up—Myers got away."

Ray wasn't sure he could say anything without screaming.

"What the hell do you mean he got away? You told me you had him under surveillance. How the hell did he get away?"

"Ray, we fucked up bad. Looks like he guessed we were onto him. I know it's dumb but he's an agent—he knows what we do. He managed to leave the building and just disappeared. I have fifty agents working on nothing else—we'll get him."

"Shit, that's so bad it's almost unbelievable. You have no idea where he's gone?"

"Look, yell at me if you want—we lost him, it's our fault—we'll fix it. There is no way Monica Jackson is in any danger. He never cared about her. It was the information her son had that he was looking for and we already have that—he won't bother her. Plus, I've stationed a team of people to watch her—she'll be safe. Ray, it's you I'm worried about. He hated you already from the old days, and I can imagine he's blaming you for all of this coming out. I want to send some men to stay with you until we get him, okay?"

"No way in hell. I'm better off without your help. Once you get him, you let me know." He hung up.

Ray thought about the fact that Myers and Emerson had been managing a major drug-running operation right under his nose when he was sheriff. This irritated him to no end. He couldn't believe that there hadn't been any leaks, or even hints, that the Sierra County sheriff and one of the richest men in New Mexico had been drug dealers—but to involve the FBI's top agent in Albuquerque was almost beyond belief. And Ray was embarrassed. He was yelling at Crawford, but what he felt was humiliation that such an operation could have run out of his jurisdiction.

Sue came into the room. She looked worried. Ray realized that much of his conversation with Crawford had involved him yelling—no doubt she'd heard most of it.

"What's going on Ray?"

"The bad guy got away. Stupid FBI couldn't even arrest their own crooked agent. He was in his Albuquerque office and they let him slip out. Just unbelievable."

"What does that mean to us?"

"Mostly it means you need to go home and go to work and not worry about this stuff. The FBI has really looked bad on this, but they'll get their shit together and find this guy and get him off the street. So just get going or you're going to be late."

"You sure this is okay?"

"Of course."

Ray wasn't sure of anything at the moment. He needed

Sue to go home, or go to work, so he could think about this and decide what he needed to do.

After Sue left, Ray and Happy went to Big Jack's. By now Happy was right at home at Big Jack's and immediately found a corner he could curl up in to take one of his many dog naps. Ray found Big Jack and Tyee drinking coffee and reading the El Paso morning paper.

Ray gave them a heads up on what he'd just learned about the FBI bungling Myers's arrest.

"I think we need to consider this a threat, but a mild one. I can't imagine this guy would consider coming after me, or any of us, a major priority. No doubt he's focused on getting out of the country and has little interest in revenge, but I wanted you to be aware of the situation. Martinez is still in jail, and based on the charges they're bringing he'll more than likely not be able get bail. I'm sure that once the full weight of his crimes are revealed he'll start to talk. All of the charges against Clayton have been dropped. I don't know if Clayton would want to sue somebody, but I'd think he would have a good case against the government for bringing those charges in the first place."

"Mild threat or not, Ray. I think we need to talk about security."

"I agree, Tyee. I was wondering if we could fix up an area in the storage shed that would be suitable for you to stay in for a few days. I know it wouldn't exactly be luxurious accommodations, but just for a short while it might be a good idea."

"That's fine—I'll move some things in today."

"No need to do it today—maybe tomorrow we can move some things around and make the place a little more livable for you. Also, I think this just demonstrates that maybe we need to consider getting weapons for both of you. I know we mostly talked about this new PI business as being about research rather than anything else, but based on what we've just gone through I think it'd be prudent to be ready for emergencies. What do you think?"

"Well, Ray. The truth is I'm fairly well armed." Big Jack reached under the counter and pulled out a Smith & Wesson 38 Special.

"Do you have a permit for that?"

"No."

"Well, there's no question you have adequate fire power—now we just need to make you legal. I think Clayton can help us out."

"I'm not sure I'm comfortable with handguns," Tyee said, "or any kind of gun for that matter. My weapon of choice is the computer."

"Tyee—I understand. I just want you to know that some of this work, as we're seeing, can lead to danger. On the other hand, I do believe the majority of the cases we'll get are going to be based more on research and investigation than combat."

"Ray, on another note—we had a call just before you walked in. The Mayor has resigned. Told the local paper he couldn't continue as Mayor because of the problems his son was experiencing. He apparently told them he had no idea any of this was going on and was completely caught by surprise."

"You know I think that's probably the truth. The Mayor's a pompous ass, but it just doesn't fit that he was involved with Sheriff Hermes—for one thing, I don't think Hermes would have trusted him."

"Also, I heard the local politicos are discussing calling a

special election for the mayor's position. Some people were saying this morning that maybe you should run, what do you think, Ray?"

"No way in hell, Big Jack. If anyone around here should run it should be you. You're prime Mayor material if I've ever seen it."

"Large white man would seem to be requirement for the position. What do you say, Mr. Mayor?"

"Big Jack say fuck you Indian."

"Mayor going to have to clean up language before he make many speeches."

Ray felt good with the banter in the room, but there were still issues to discuss.

"Something else we need to go over. The FBI is going to be paying us a retainer—actually a rather large monthly retainer. At this point there's no way they'll back out of that, so it's up to us if we want to continue with it. I say yes. Anyone else have thoughts?"

"Seems to me it's perfect for us. I have no idea what they are going to ask us to do but until we know more, I say we continue with the plan." Tyee looked to Big Jack for his thoughts.

"I agree, Tyee. Obviously I have a vested interest with this new identity, but it would also seem to be a good opportunity for us to get started and have some money to spend on things like security."

"Good then. We're in agreement about our deal with the feds. I have no idea if they'll start to give us work soon or never, but I'll make sure the retainer checks are showing up. With that in mind I'd like to suggest two more things, both of which are going to sound like I'm padding my own nest, so just speak up if these don't sound logical to you."

Ray paused. He'd been thinking about a plan to improve their operational facilities and their ability to handle communication—but it was still a work in progress.

"Much of what we're going to be doing will involve communications—phones, computers, faxes—every way that people are communicating, we need to be able to handle. I've been thinking about making some improvements to the main outbuilding at the cabin. We could turn one area of the building into living quarters—say, two bedrooms, a bathroom, and a small kitchen. Then Tyee could stay on a more permanent basis, if you wanted to, or at least have pleasant temporary accommodations. Also, we could upgrade the larger space into offices and move all of the computers into that building. That would require more phone lines and some furniture, along with some remodeling."

"What, you don't like my storeroom anymore?" Big Jack said this with a smile.

"Was that all of you featherbedding projects or just one?" Tyee was paying attention.

"That's one. The second one we won't refer to as featherbedding for obvious reasons. I want to hire Sue. I want her to work in the office helping with communications, I'd like her to be available to provide some forensics, and I'd like for her to help Jack with the store so that he can be more involved in the investigation business—and I know Jack, that we haven't talked about this—so just say no if this is me butting into your store business."

"Well, not sure what to say—that's out of the blue." Big Jack looked thoughtful.

"I think it's a great idea," Tyee said. "Aside from the fact that Ray gets a live-in girlfriend, which doesn't seem quite fair, I think she'd add a lot to what we're trying to do. The phones are already becoming a problem. Just with this Jackson case we had several times where we had problems with communications because we didn't have a central person keeping in touch with everyone. As far as helping Jack out, the only person who should object to that would be Sue. I vote yes."

They all agreed. Big Jack still wasn't completely sure about having Sue in the store. It was a "manly" domain, and he was going to take some time to get used to the idea.

The conversation turned to fishing and the upcoming tournament.

Ray and Happy returned to the cabin. Ray was expecting Sue to be back for dinner. He found some small steaks and put them out to thaw. It looked like it was going to be a pleasant evening, so he thought he would fire up his small charcoal grill. He also decided to take a nap.

Sue arrived straight from work and went in to take a shower. Ray started the grill. She came out looking refreshed and he poured them each a glass of wine.

"Sue, how would you like to work for the PI business and also part-time at Jacks?"

"Well, hello to you too. What's that about?"

"Maybe I should have eased into the conversation. It's about me needing help. If this business is going to be successful, we need to improve how we communicate and keep in touch. Also, I'd like to see Jack participate more, which he can't if he can't leave the store. I'm talking about remodeling the storage building into offices and bringing in more phone lines—also putting in some living accommodations for Tyee."

"My goodness, those sound like big plans—how are you going to pay for all of that?"

"Not completely sure. We're going to have ongoing money from our retainer with the FBI. As far as the initial cost, I guess I hadn't thought about it much."

"No question, Ray. You could use my help—in a lot of ways. Are you suggesting that I move in with you?"

Now the conversation was getting out of hand. Ray *was* suggesting that, but he didn't want to say it. He could talk to men all day long, but ten minutes into a conversation with a woman he was all confused.

"Sue, I guess I was. I haven't said this the way I should have. Maybe we should just drop it."

"Don't get embarrassed and crawl back into your shell. You can talk to me. I won't faint or scream or bite you, unless of course you wanted me to—just tell me what you're thinking."

"You would be a great benefit to the business. You'd be paid. It has nothing to do with our relationship. You don't have to move in here for it to make sense for you to participate in this business venture. You'd make us a real business in so many ways—plus, your skills in forensics would be really valuable. We're going to be getting referrals from the FBI, and I think we're going to be very busy. That's only part of what I was saying so poorly. I'd like it very much if you would move in with me. I know I'm too old for you, and you're probably ready to move on and use your skills in a big city somewhere—I guess, I'm not real sure what I'm asking."

"Oh, sure you are. You and I are very good together. The business part I'll have to think about, but I would move in with you." She smiled.

They talked more as Ray started the steaks. Sue said she wasn't staying the night because she had to take the early shift tomorrow due to one of the girls being ill, and she was tired and wanted to get a good night's sleep.

They ate their steaks and salad with more wine and enjoyed the evening. Ray felt pleased that Sue would want to move in with him and also very nervous about what that might mean. He seemed to be progressing toward something that he hadn't completely thought through. In a totally mistimed thought, he wondered what advice his wife would give him. He had relied on her so much in his life when there were difficult decisions to be made. The thought was quickly gone, but it still embarrassed him.

Sue and Ray cuddled a bit as she said goodbye, then she got in her car and left. He knew they were entering a new phase of their relationship and it held many unknowns. He didn't like not knowing what was going to happen. He finished his wine and went to bed.

# 27

*Sunday*

Ray woke abruptly. He looked at the clock—it was only about five. He'd heard something, but now he wasn't sure what it was. He could see Happy standing by the bed, and he appeared to be on alert. Ray got up and put on his some clothes and shoes, then found his old service revolver. He knew that most likely it was some wild animal sniffing around outside, but he was still extra alert.

He went out the front door onto the porch, Happy coming just behind him. The dog stood still a minute, then took off toward the outbuilding. Ray realized his mistake—he should've held onto the dog. He started to yell but shut himself up. He headed in the same direction as the dog.

As he got closer to the building he could see the front door was still shut and appeared to be undamaged. He couldn't see Happy. More than likely it was a wild animal and Happy was having his early morning exercise chasing whatever it was. He turned to head back to the cabin when he was struck in the head and fell forward. Ray was still conscience, but only barely. He heard Happy barking and then the dog yelped in pain. Ray was blearily furious that someone would hurt his dog.

The next thing Ray knew, he was becoming aware of his

surroundings, and he realized that he must have been unconscious. He had no idea how long he'd been out, but based on
the sunlight it had been some time. He opened his eyes, but it
was hard to see. He was probably inside the storage building.
He was bound with some kind of rope or cord. So it was worse
than a wild animal—it was a human animal. Ray thought it
could be Myers, or maybe someone else just trying to rob him.
No matter who it was, he was in trouble.

Ray tried to rise up off of the floor, but quickly realized
that he was too dizzy. He lay back down and tried to listen. He
heard noises out behind the building. It sounded like someone was digging—not a good sign. Ray remembered what he'd
heard before, Happy yelping. He didn't see or hear Happy—
another bad sign. There didn't appear to be any good signs. He
tried to sit up again and did a little better this time.

The front door was pushed opened and Agent Myers
came in wearing a smirk and carrying a large metal case.

"Well hello, Ray Pacheco, world famous asshole. How's
your head doing?" Myers actually smiled—it was worse than
the smirk.

"What happened to the dog?"

"Guess what, you dumb fuck, you don't get to ask questions."

Ray didn't say anything. He was trying to figure what he
could do to protect himself, but so far he hadn't come up with
anything.

Myers set the case down on the table with a thud. It was
obviously very heavy, maybe fifty pounds or so.

"You know what's in that case dumbass?"

"No."

"Well of course you don't. It's about two million dollars in hundred dollar bills—my escape money. Hidden behind your storage building. What a dumb shit you are for buying this old cabin. This was the key location for all of the drug smuggling business—right here in your backyard. You know Ray, I wouldn't have wasted my time trying to find you and kill you—but here you are living on top of my escape money. So guess what—you're dead."

Son-of-a-bitch. Ray really was a dumbass. Myers was no idiot, so of course he would have a hidden stash. Ray had forgotten this was once used by Sheriff Hermes as the staging point for the drug shipments. That's why the goons were headed up here with Monica and Mrs. Richards. Not by accident. They knew where they were going.

Myers was busy manhandling the case out the door, no doubt putting it into whatever vehicle he'd used to get there. He was gone for a while, but returned with his sneer still in place.

"You know you're going to get caught—why don't you lessen the pain and give up."

Myers let out a genuine laugh.

"Oh, I suppose I should surrender to you. I wonder, should I untie you first? That's a good one, Ray. Who's going to catch me? The FBI? Maybe you've forgotten Ray, I used to work for those morons. I've been working this gig for years—they've promoted me twice while I've been doing my moonlighting job. The FBI does nothing but file reports. They're useless. Right now, I'm sure they're looking everywhere for me, but not here. They're busy monitoring the airlines and checking the borders. I'll go up in the mountains in Colorado to a little place nobody knows about and assume one of my identities—this one's a reclusive writer. All of the area people know me and know I don't like company. I could stay up there forever and the stupid FBI would never find me. But you know what, I don't want to live in a remote cabin like you and waste my life fishing. In a few months I'll go across the border to Canada, get on an airplane, and from there I'll ship out to someplace you've never heard of. A few days later I'll be living like a king."

Ray realized Myers had finished his story. He needed to keep him talking.

"Myers, I know you're going to kill me so what does it matter—what did you do to my dog?"

"What the hell do you care what I did to that stupid dog. I hit him with the same two-by-four I hit you with—but the damn dog just yelped and headed out somewhere. Probably dead by now, just like you're about to be."

End of story. Ray felt a calmness that surprised him. He knew there was nothing he could do to stop Myers, and some place deep inside himself he felt okay with what was going to happen. At least no one else had gotten hurt on his account. He sure hoped Happy was all right.

Myers took aim. Suddenly there was a loud explosion and a large part of Myers had disappeared as if he'd been shot with a cannon. There was no doubt Agent Myers was dead—very, very dead—but Ray wasn't sure how it had happened. Just then Happy came running in and began enthusiastically licking Ray's face.

"Next time you need help, send a fucking car will you—not the dog. My god, how does Tyee climb up here so fast? Seemed like it took me hours." Big Jack had just killed a man and yet he was as calm as he could be. He began undoing the knots to release Ray.

"My god, Big Jack. How'd you know to come?"

"Your trusty dog came and got me. Also he's hurt a little—looks like he was hit on his side. He came to the double-wide and made one hell of a racket until I finally got up and came outside. I thought dogs only did that sort of thing in movies, but it was obvious he wanted me to go with him. Got my trusty pistol and here we are."

"Big Jack, you'd be surprised at some of the things I've seen animals do over the years when their owners were in trouble. Like those stories you see in the paper about a dog dragging someone to safety or a cat howling to wake people up when the house is on fire. Now help me up to the cabin so we can give Happy some attention and make some phone calls."

As they made their way to the cabin, Ray could see that Big Jack would need some attention too. His face and arms were scratched up pretty bad, with some long gashes in several places. No doubt from following the direct path set by the dog. Plus, he could see Big Jack was close to exhaustion.

Ray helped Big Jack into a chair and got him a glass of water. Ray then looked at Happy. He thought that one leg might be broken, but there was no bleeding. He got Happy his water bowl and the dog laid down and went to sleep.

Ray called Clayton and told him that Myers had been killed at his cabin. Clayton said he was on his way. Then Ray called Crawford. There was no answer. He left a message with the same information. Then he called Sanchez at the number in Albuquerque. Sanchez answered. Ray told him what had happened. Sanchez said he was on his way.

Ray got himself a glass of water and sat down. He'd never been that close to death. He felt a little chilled and faint. He looked over at Big Jack and was shocked to see he had gone to sleep.

Soon people started arriving. Clayton and his men were first, and they taped off the site. Not long after that, the FBI arrived via helicopter. The helicopter landed in a clearing about a quarter mile from Ray's cabin. Agent Sanchez stepped in and immediately took command, of course. And the New Mexico state patrol showed up—Ray wasn't sure why. The one and only T or C ambulance arrived.

Ray's new phone rang. It was Sue wondering what was going on. He told her he was fine and that Big Jack was the hero. He said she should probably stay away for a few hours, but that he definitely wanted to see her later today.

Tyee arrived and went at once to see about Big Jack, who was awake and answering questions from the FBI. Tyee suggested that they pause for a minute and let Big Jack get some medical attention. The FBI guy gave Tyee the evil eye, but that didn't faze Tyee, who helped Big Jack up and took him into the extra bedroom so he could rest.

"Ray, do you know what was in that case?" Agent Sanchez was looking a little shop worn.

"Yeah, or least I know what he told me. Myers said it was his escape money, about two million dollars. That's why he was here—he was going to kill me just because I was here, where the money was hidden."

Ray's phone rang again, but he decided not to answer. One of Clayton's deputies did it for him.

"Mr. Pacheco, it's Agent Crawford, he'd like to talk to

you."

"Hello."

"Ray, are you alright?"

"I suppose so Agent Crawford. Thanks to my dog and my good friend Big Jack—otherwise, I'd be dead."

"I never thought he'd come after you Ray. If I had I'd have sent men whether you wanted it or not. I'm sorry."

"Look, Ben. We have all screwed this one up, probably nobody more than me. He wasn't after me, he was after his escape money. The outbuilding to this cabin I bought was used by the drug running business he was doing with the sheriff up here. Apparently at some point he buried two million dollars here just in case he needed emergency cash. Finding me here was just a bonus for him. He was a bad guy, Ben, I don't blame the FBI for anything, so you can stop apologizing."

"Well, I'm very glad you're okay. Tell Sanchez that I'm flying into Albuquerque this evening and I'll see him tonight or tomorrow morning. Glad that asshole didn't kill you, Ray."

"Me too. Thanks Ben."

A coroner's vehicle had arrived from Las Cruces and removed the body, and they had a crew with them whose job was to clean up after shootings and other messy crimes. After a few hours of heavy activity, everyone began to drift away. Sanchez and his team left in their helicopter. The ambulance people wanted to take Big Jack to the clinic and have him checked, but he declined so they left. Clayton had stationed one deputy at the end of the road to discourage anyone from showing up just to gawk.

"I'm going to take Happy down to the vet. I've already called one and he's waiting. He seems okay, but I think his front leg is injured. You guys can stay here until I get back."

Tyee helped Ray move Happy to the Jeep. No question he wasn't eager to put weight on one of his front legs. Once in, they headed to town. Ray believed there was only one human doctor in town, but there were four vets. The population of animals in the area far exceeded that of humans.

Once there, the vet helped Ray get Happy inside. After a short examination, the vet said he didn't believe the leg was broken, but that Happy had suffered the equivalent of a human having a shoulder separation. He said it was amazing that he'd continued to walk on that leg—it had to be terribly painful. The vet gave Happy a shot to relieve the pain and put his leg back in place. He also created a sling apparatus that would help Happy get around more easily, but it would be several weeks before he was completely healed. The vet gave Ray some pills that would ease the swelling and another set for pain. He gave Ray all the instructions and told him to bring Happy back in about a week for a follow up.

No doubt due to the pain shot, Happy hopped into the front seat of the Jeep when they were ready to leave. The vet told Ray to keep him off the leg as much as possible. Ray lifted Happy into the back of the Jeep and headed home. He waved at the deputy as he turned into his yard. Ray lifted Happy out and placed him on the porch. That wasn't what Happy wanted, though, and he managed to hop down the stairs, then went a little ways away and took care of his needs. Ray had no idea how he was supposed to keep Happy off of the injured leg. Tyee came out and helped Ray get Happy into the cabin. Happy had some food and water, then curled up and went into a very deep sleep.

"How's Big Jack?"

"He seems okay. He's still asleep. I think what got to him was the climb. I'm sure the adrenaline rush added to the exhaustion, but it's not an easy climb up here even for me. For Jack, at his size, it could have been deadly."

"Yeah, I know. That dog on three legs and in great pain, Big Jack risking his life getting here, and once he got here, saving my life. Big Jack is an amazing person and Happy is an equally amazing dog."

Ray decided it was time for a beer. As soon as he opened one, Big Jack appeared at the bedroom door.

"Just because I'm asleep is no reason not to offer me a beer."

Big Jack sat at the table and sipped his beer. He seemed much better.

The phone rang. Ray rolled his eyes—he was definitely tired of the phone already.

"Hello."

Ray listened for some time.

"Thanks. That will help a lot." Ray hung up.

Ray sat back down and took a sip of beer. Tyee and Big Jack were waiting to hear what the call had been about, but Ray just smiled.

"Okay, Ray. Are we going to have to ask?"

"That was Sanchez. He just talked to Crawford. There are establishing a ten percent reward on the money recovered today. That's two hundred thousand dollars to us. How about that—we now have the money to do those improvements for the business. What do you say? Especially you, Big Jack—by all rights that money is yours. What do you want to do with it?"

"I say we put it all into the business as an equal contribution from all of us, and we get on with making this a viable business. On one condition."

"What's the condition?"

"Sue has to agree."

Maybe Big Jack's life and death experience had showed him that he needed some help, or maybe that was just Big Jack taking care of Sue and Ray. Who could say?

Tyee took Ray's Jeep and gave Big Jack a ride back to his store, and said he would sleep in the store just in case Big Jack needed anything.

Soon after they left, Sue arrived and paid special attention to Happy. Even so, Happy wasn't very peppy and it began to dawn on Sue what a huge sacrifice it had been for Happy to do what he'd done. He had almost killed himself to help Ray. For reasons that would have been difficult to explain, Sue started to cry and found it hard to stop. Ray helped her into the bedroom, and they both took a nap. He knew this was where she belonged.

# 28

*Monday*

Sue had stayed over. Happy seemed better, but still was moving very slowly. Ray had never felt better. Maybe almost being killed was all it took to make him recognize the joy in the world. He was on the porch drinking coffee and humming. Sue walked out.

"Well, someone sure is in a good mood after almost being killed yesterday."

"Actually, that's why I'm in a good mood. I wasn't killed. Today is a wonderful day."

Sue laughed in a way that made Ray want to hug her—so he did. Sue started to cry again.

"What's the matter, Sue? Did I do something wrong?"

"No. Of course not. I don't know. I'm just having some trouble dealing with you almost being killed. Then I start to think, you're going to be doing this all of the time—what happens next time?"

"First, Sue, let's just hope there never is a next time. I was in law enforcement for almost thirty years and yesterday was the first time I thought I was going to die. It was just a fluke. How crazy is it that I lived in the same place where the bad guy hid his money? Really, how often would that happen?

I understand being scared and thinking this is some kind of western shoot-out, but it's not. Most of what we'll be doing is gathering information. We aren't hiring on as a SWAT team. I'm sorry this has worried you, but I won't risk the rest of my life for a few bucks—if it was always this dangerous, I'd just continue to fish."

Sue gave him a hug.

The ringing phone interrupted their moment. Ray was still annoyed by the phone, but at least today he wasn't cursing every time it rang. He answered it and listened.

"Okay, I'll be there on Wednesday."

"What was that?"

"The Attorney General wants to see me in person in Santa Fe. No doubt to chew on my ass. When I arrested Martinez, I told the sheriff's staff that I had the authority to do that because of the AG. I just made that up so I could get Martinez off of the streets. Apparently, he's heard about it and wants to dress me down in person."

"Is it serious?"

"No, I don't think so. I know the guy, Tony Garcia. We used to work together in Las Cruces. I didn't commit a crime. He probably just wants to make sure I don't use his good name again."

Ray told Sue about what Big Jack said regarding the reward money.

"You asked me where the money was coming from—now we know. Have you thought about what you want to do?"

"Yes. I might as well just say this and get it over with. Ray, I love you."

Ray stood there knowing he should say something. He

was ready to talk about Sue being in the business and how they could work things out—but this was unexpected. Sort of.

"Sue, I love you."

There, take that. He was no coward. They both just stood there looking at each other. Finally they embraced.

"All the rest of it's fine, although I don't believe I heard what the pay was."

Ray told her what he was thinking and how to handle the different pay from Big Jack's and the PI business. She said it seemed very reasonable and they hugged again. Ray was enjoying this kind of negotiation.

"Ray, I just want to be important to you. I still don't want to be your wife—I just want to know that I matter."

"You do." Ray got another hug. Maybe he was being trained for something.

Sue said she was already hours late for work—it was a good thing she was going to quit before they fired her. She needed to go anyway, though, or the other girls wouldn't be able to handle the rush. She gathered her stuff and gave Ray a kiss on her way out.

Ray went back into the cabin and called a couple of contractors he knew. He was looking for bids on the upgrades to the new office building. One said they could be there that afternoon, the other tomorrow morning. Ray also called the phone company and ordered two more lines to be run to the new office. He thought about pulling the cabin line out, but decided he would adjust.

With a little time on his hands, Ray decided to go check on how Big Jack was doing. Then he remembered that Tyee had the Jeep. At that moment, Tyee pulled into the yard.

"Thought you might need your wheels."

"I was just thinking about heading down to see how you and Big Jack were doing—remembered you had the Jeep. How is he?"

"He took a tumble and it looks like he sprained his ankle. I took him to the clinic. They put a wrap on his ankle and said it would be sore for a few days. He's on crutches, so not moving very fast. Other than that he seems to be in good spirits. While we were at the clinic, several people asked if he was going to run for Mayor. I think he's thinking about it."

"Sprained ankle. Will he be able to run the store?"

"I don't think so. When I asked him about it, he said I should butt out. He just can't move enough to deal with the dock customers. I called my cousin who lives up toward Ruidoso and asked if he needed a part-time job. He said he could use some money—common situation for both poor white people and poor Indians. I convinced Jack to hire him on a trial basis. I know we were talking about Sue doing that, but it might be best to see if this works out. My cousin, his name is Chester Chino—don't even ask how he got the name Chester—knows a lot about fishing—equipment, baits, lures, plus he's absolutely honest. I'm the black sheep of my family, Chester's the saint. Anyway he's supposed to be here this afternoon. I'm going back now to watch the store until Chester arrives."

"I'll go with you. Help me get Happy into the back of the Jeep and we'll hang out at the store. I'd like to meet Chester."

Ray lifted Happy into the back and let Tyee drive them to the store. Once he lowered Happy to the ground, the dog seemed fine to hop into the store. Ray let him in, and naturally he found a good warm spot to sleep. Big Jack was at the register, holding his crutches.

"Good Morning, Mr. Mayor."

"First I save your damn life and now you're trying to make mine miserable as payback—how does that make any sense?"

"You're right, it doesn't. Good Morning, Big Jack. Thank you for saving my life. How's your ankle."

"Hurts like shit. I'm just too fat. Can't even see my feet when I walk. Stepped in a hole or something. Got me thinking about a diet. But then I got depressed so I decided to have a beer." Big Jack held up his bottle to make the point.

"Hear you have some help coming."

"Yeah. Tyee's cousin Chester. What kind of fuckin' Indian's named Chester?"

Ray wasn't real sure how to answer that, so he decided to take it as rhetorical. Tyee missed this exchange since he was on the dock helping a customer fuel his boat, and Ray decided to go out and see if he needed any assistance.

With Ray and Tyee taking care of the business, Big Jack decided to have another beer, and settled into his rocking chair on the dock.

"You know Ray, this sprained ankle thing might actually be okay." Big Jack really should be mayor. He was perfectly happy sitting back and letting everyone else do the work, then taking credit for their efforts—the man was a born politician.

Later in the day, Chester showed up. He seemed like a very nice young man. Ray wasn't quite sure he was really related to Tyee—he was too nice. He and Big Jack hit it off immediately. It was clear very quickly that Chester knew a lot about fishing in general and fishing equipment in particular. He looked like he'd worked there for months after only a few hours.

Ray left to meet the contractor and felt like everything was moving in the right direction. Over the course of a couple of days he got bids from several contractors and decided on the two he thought were the best. Once he had a chance to meet with Tyee and Big Jack to discuss the bids, he was ready to get started.

# 29

*Wednesday*

Ray took Happy to the vet Tuesday for his checkup and decided to board him that night. He needed to leave for Santa Fe very early on Wednesday so he could meet with the Attorney General. The vet said that Happy still had some swelling and it would be good to keep him off of the leg for a while. Ray knew the dog wouldn't want to ride in the car for seven or more hours, so it made sense to let him stay at the vet's for the night.

Early Wednesday morning Ray was on the road headed to Santa Fe. He liked Santa Fe, though he knew some people thought it was pretentious. Ray just thought it was very expensive. It was beyond anything Ray could imagine to spend a hundred dollars on dinner—without even much to drink. Ray liked food, but to dress it up in small servings with fussy presentation and then charge that kind of money made the whole experience feel like robbery. So Ray was never going to be a food critic—he could live with that.

Finding the downtown state offices for the Attorney General, Ray pulled into the parking garage. It was cool in Santa Fe. The elevation was much higher than T or C, but something most people didn't know was that it was also much higher than Denver. This meant that most days started off very cool. Ray entered the building, found the office he needed, and took the elevator to the fifth floor. Unlike most government offices, this one had the feel of an upscale attorney's office—probably meant that few citizens actually saw the AG personally. Ray gave his name to the receptionist and took a seat. Just a few minutes later Tony Garcia emerged.

"Ray, how was your drive?"

"Very good, Tony. Good to see you."

"Yes. I was looking forward to our meeting today. Please come on back to my office."

Ray wasn't sure if Tony was looking forward to the meeting because he needed someone to yell at, or if that was just a general statement he made all the time. Ray smiled and followed Tony through the door and down the hall.

They entered Tony's office. It was obviously a power office—must've been the size of a small house. There was a large desk along one wall and an impressive conference table in the opposite corner. All in all, it looked more like a CEO's office than a public servant's.

"Nice office."

"Yeah. Actually it's a little embarrassing. You know me, Ray—I'm a simple guy with pretty basic tastes. That wasn't the case with my predecessor. He had a huge ego and not a lot of smarts. By all accounts he was a good politician, just not much of a worker bee. He held office for more than two years before he resigned to take a promotion to a federal position—and during that time he did almost nothing. But he sure liked nice things, and I've benefited from his excessive tastes. If I really wanted to make a statement, I'd sue him on behalf of the state for all of the money he wasted. But you have to pick your fights and he would be a tough one."

"Well, maybe you could sublet?"

Tony laughed.

"I always loved your sense of humor, Ray. Now, tell me, why were you using my name as authority to arrest the local sheriff?"

"Just trying to help you out any way I can."

This got some more chuckles, but the eyes didn't seem to smile.

"You know that deal worked out and nobody is going to say anything, including me. On the other hand, if Martinez hadn't been so obviously guilty, your actions could've put us in some hot water."

"Look, Tony, I know I shouldn't have handled it that way. I just had too many loose ends—I needed Martinez in jail so he didn't kill me or anyone else. I knew I was taking a big risk because at that point I still didn't have everything nailed down, but I also knew Martinez had to be part of what was happening. I know I'm no longer a sheriff and have no authority to act the way I did, but those were some pretty strange circumstances with the FBI being involved and a rogue FBI agent killing people and threatening to put me in jail. I did what I did because I thought it was the right thing—but it wasn't the most appropriate, and there's no question that I should have figured a better way of handling it rather than using your name."

"Well damn, Ray, I thought it was brilliant. I'm just messin' with you—it was brilliant. Who even knows what power or authority an AG has—nobody, that's who. Most of the time I'm not sure what I can and can't do. It was the perfect ploy.

When I heard what you had said, I thought it was hysterical."

"I'm glad you aren't mad Tony. I wasn't going to let any harm come to you. If it had gone bad—obviously it was just me bullshitting some folks."

"And that's why I asked you here today. I know you've started a private investigation business, and I know a little bit about your partners. But most importantly, I know you, Ray. You have that unique ability to do the right thing even when it's not obvious what that is—and I also know you're honest. That's why I want to hire your firm as a contractor to help me and my office get better control over the county sheriffs. You've seen it yourself. We have some people who are just out of control. Last session the legislature changed some administrative duties, and now the AG's office has a degree of authority over the county sheriffs. They're elected officials, but they don't and never have had carte blanche to do whatever in the hell they want—although some of them may think so. I don't have the resources to look at all thirty-three counties in the state. I want to use you and your team to do a little spying and research to help me pinpoint where there's good and where there's bad. Do you think that'd be something you'd be interested in pursuing?"

"Absolutely, Tony. That would get us excited. From a personal point of view I can tell you that most, maybe seventy percent, of the sheriffs are hardworking, honest law enforcement professionals. Some are more lazy than others; some are smarter than others, but by far the majority are trying to do their best—and they're the ones who will be the most pleased you're doing something about the others. The bad ones are often very bad. They abuse everything. Sierra County isn't a good example of much of anything when it comes to the sheriff's department, with two of the sheriffs in jail. But let me tell you the next sheriff, a deputy named Clayton, is as good as they come. So right there, with all of the bad, was a guy ready to step up and make things better. I think that can be true in many of the troubled counties. I'd be very pleased to work with you on that, Tony."

"That's what I wanted to hear, Ray. We'll set you up on a retainer and then put together a contract for professional services at an hourly rate plus expenses. I hope this works for both of us—I think we can do some good."

They continued to discuss the details—but it was obvious both men were excited about the possibilities. Ray left and was headed back to T or C. He was so excited about the news, he stopped to call the office—and got the voice mail. He called the storeroom phone at Big Jack's—and got the voice mail. They sure needed Sue to be part of this business—they needed to stay connected. He called Big Jack's number—and got Chester. Chester wasn't sure where everyone had gone. Ray thanked him and said just let them know he'd be back that evening. Ray got back in the Jeep and headed south.

It was early evening by the time Ray made it back to T or C. He went by the vet's and found there was still someone in the office. They'd waited on Ray because they knew he was picking up Happy. Small towns could be a real pain in the rear, but they could also sure be friendly. Happy was very pleased to see him. Ray gave him a good rub and took him out to the Jeep. He seemed less limber than when he'd brought him in, but Ray figured that was right since he hadn't gotten much exercise. They headed to the cabin. As Ray pulled in he was surprised to see Sue's car and a truck he didn't recognize. Ray parked and helped Happy get down. Happy then limped off toward his favorite spot in the yard. Sue came out onto the porch.

"Ray, it's about time you got back. Why didn't you call?"

Rather than trying to explain how irritating that question was, Ray just grinned.

"Didn't stop except for gas. But here I am—whose truck?"

"It's Tyee—he bought a truck. Come in, Big Jack is here too."

Ray gave Sue a hug and went in. He greeted everyone—told Tyee he wanted to hear the truck story in just a minute. He got Happy food and water and settled him down in the center of the room—his favorite spot. Ray grabbed a beer and settled himself.

"Man, that's a long drive in one day. Now, tell me the truck story."

"Can't bum rides forever off of White Man—Indian must be free to roam."

The room gave Tyee some laughter.

Ray told them about his meeting with the AG. Everyone was very excited. Sue even squealed a little.

"This is a big deal guys. The combined fees from the AG and FBI makes us a very viable business and we haven't even officially started. I think we're having some good luck. A toast to Pacheco and Chino, PIs."

Everyone took a sip of whatever they were drinking.

"Hey, maybe that should be Pacheco, Parker, and Chino, PIs—what do you think, Jack?"

"Well, not sure about that, but why not Pacheco, Lewis, and Chino—right, Sue?"

Sue looked embarrassed. She didn't want to have this conversation.

"I think we're all important to the success of our business. The name doesn't matter that much. But we need Sue as much as anyone. This is no doubt the wrong time and the wrong place, but I can't help it—this has been on my mind for hours. I have struggled with this issue about what is right and what is wrong—and I have made up my mind."

Everyone was looking at Ray, clearly confused. He had changed the mood, and they didn't know why or what he was talking about.

"Sue, I don't want you to just live here. I wasn't honest when I said I wanted you to live here with me—that's not what it is at all. Sue Lewis, will you marry me?"

Nobody had seen that coming, especially Sue. She looked stunned, not happy. Ray had just dropped a bombshell—not a smart thing to do in front of your buddies, surprise your lady by asking her to marry you.

"I don't want you to be my roommate, I want you to be my wife."

Sue ran out the door without saying anything. Ray still didn't know how he had screwed up. He'd been driving all day and he'd realized that he wasn't comfortable with Sue just living with him. He knew it was silly, but that's how it was—he wanted to get married. He wanted her to make the same commitment to him that he wanted to make to her. He had no desire to have an affair or a live-in mistress. Ray was tired of not being married and she was the person he wanted to be with. It started to dawn on Ray that he hadn't said all of the things he should have said—and it hit him hard when he realized he had just popped the question without any warning and had done it in front of Tyee and Big Jack. It became very clear to Ray that he was one big dumbass son-of-a-bitch. How could he be so smart at some things and so stupid at others?

"Ray, I think you better go find her." Tyee said this as gently as he could—he really wanted to scream it at Ray. Ray seemed to have shocked himself and now didn't know what to do.

He ran out the front door. Her car was gone. Oh, crap. What had he done? Then he noticed it was parked down the old road a ways. He started running. Ray got almost to the car and tripped. Mr. Prince Charming took a nasty fall. He hit the rocky ground pretty hard, scraped both hands and bruised his chin. After he stopped moving he sat up. If he hadn't been such a proud old fart he would've started crying. What more could possibly go wrong?

Sue walked up to him. She had obviously been crying.

"Are you okay, Ray?"

"I'm sorry."

"For what—being the nicest man in the world? Just because you didn't think about how I would react isn't bad, Ray. You said what you felt—right there in front of god and everybody. My answer is yes—I would be proud to marry you."

She fell into his harms and they tumbled over backwards and started laughing—maybe it was a mixture of laughing and crying.

# 30

*Fishing*

They decided they would be married in two weeks. The ceremony would only be for a few people, and it would be at the cabin. When Ray called his son and told him he was getting married, Michael reacted angrily. Ray said it didn't matter, but Sue knew that it did. Sue had history and family, but she wasn't inviting anyone who would actually come from that distant world. She would let a few people know from her family, but only if she was sure they wouldn't attend. She didn't want anyone from her past to interfere with her joy.

Ray, Tyee, and Big Jack met and decided on the construction plans for the new office and living quarters. The contractor said he could start in a week. They also discussed new security measures for the area around the office building. The plan involved installing cameras along the perimeter of the property.

Big Jack and Chester had established a working relationship that had Chester doing everything and Big Jack supervising—surprisingly this seemed agreeable to both parties. Big Jack's ankle was getting better, and he'd gone on a diet that still seemed to involve large quantities of beer.

"Ray, I know this doesn't make much sense considering that at some level I'm probably still hiding from some people—but I've decided to run for the mayor's job. Can I count on your endorsement?"

"Hell yes, you can. I think this is great Jack. We need to get Tyee going on putting together a campaign strategy. When's the election?"

"They haven't picked the date yet, but it'll be at least six months so we have plenty of time. You know, I don't want to get to sentimental here, but this is the first time I've felt like I belonged somewhere."

"I know the feeling, Big Jack."

Ray wondered if it was wise for Big Jack to run for the mayor's position. On the other hand, the risks seemed small. The FBI had done what they said and provided Jack Parker with all of the necessary documents to establish his new identity. It was very unlikely that anyone was even looking for the long gone Philip.

Tyee was meeting Ray at Big Jack's today to go over some last minute pointers before the big fishing tournament on the weekend. The El Paso paper even ran a story in the sports section about the Elephant Butte fishing event. They were predicting large crowds. Ray was still very unsure why he was doing this—so much had changed since he'd agreed. He now had a construction project to oversee and a wedding to plan. Of course, he knew all of that was just an excuse. What really bothered him was that he didn't want to be embarrassed—by catching no fish at all.

Big Jack had given Ray a cap and vest for the event. As Ray's sponsor, the cap and vest had Big Jack's store's name "Jack's Bait, Boats, and Beer" plastered all over. It was gaudy—maybe even ugly—but very visible. Big Jack was the organizer of the fishing tournament and no doubt there was some kind of conflict of interest in also being a sponsor, but Ray was pretty sure no one would care.

As the weekend drew closer, experienced-looking fishermen started to show up at Big Jack's store to register. Big Jack said it looked like they were going to have their largest number of contestants ever. That made Big Jack happy and Ray nervous.

Sue had advised Ray to turn off his macho competitive nature and just enjoy himself. What possible difference could it make if he won or not—or if he even caught a fish? Ray knew she was right, but the male competitive juices were hard to control.

"Ray, I have some lures I want to show you. Based on the temperature reports for this weekend, I was thinking we might try something a little different."

"Tyee, why don't I give you the cap and vest and you fish. Nobody will have to know it's not me. You like to fish, so it'll be fun for you, right?"

"This is getting a little tiresome, Ray. Why are you so nervous?"

"I really don't know. But all of these guys showing up—have you seen them? There was one guy yesterday who must have had twenty sponsors all over his boat and his vest—looked like a NASCAR driver."

"Trust me, Ray—these guys don't know any more than we do—and if you'll listen to me and do what I say, you'll have the edge. Those are the same guys I beat three years in a row, remember?"

Ray grudgingly shut up and listened to what Tyee was

trying to tell him.

There had been several election events scheduled for the week, but after Martinez was arrested he was officially removed from the ballot so Deputy Clayton was running unopposed. Turnout didn't matter any longer—he would soon be the sheriff of Sierra County. Everyone seemed pleased. Even most of the Mayor's old supporters were now claiming that they'd been in favor of Clayton all along.

After the mayor resigned he more or less disappeared. He put his house on the market and most people believed he had gone to Las Cruces to stay with his brother, a chili farmer in Hatch. Ray suspected that the mayor wouldn't be back—he had trampled on too many people with his mayoral power and had few real friends.

The opening day of the tournament was a cloudless, beautiful morning. Ray was still nervous but with all of the badgering by Sue and Tyee, he'd decided he would just enjoy the experience and stop worrying about embarrassing himself. Once he relaxed, he started to mingle more with the experienced fishermen. This was an interesting group, from full time pros to amateurs whose real jobs included a judge, a couple of doctors, and several schoolteachers. Ray started to enjoy their company and realized he'd been silly to have been so nervous. Almost immediately, people were giving him advice and tips—while it was technically a competition, for most of the participants it was just fun.

Ray's first day wasn't a disaster. While he didn't catch anything to keep, following Tyee's directions of releasing anything that wasn't large enough to be considered for the trophy, he did catch fish. He started to wonder if Tyee was right to have

Ray going only for the largest fish caught, but he stuck with the plan.

Also according to Tyee's instructions, he stayed in one place. This didn't seem right to Ray. He thought it made more sense to move around and look for that perfect spot. Tyee had said no to that. He had to stay in one place—there were plenty of fish all over the lake, so moving would just waste time and fuel. Tyee had become very bossy in the last few days before the tournament.

"Tyee, I did exactly what you told me to do today, and I don't have a fish."

They were sitting on Ray's cabin porch enjoying a beer.

"You're doing fine, Ray. Just keep doing the same thing tomorrow. You may not catch the biggest fish—remember no matter what anybody says, there is an element of luck involved—but on the other hand, you may. If you do it the way you want to it'll *feel* busy but you'll lessen your chances of winning."

"I don't remember you being so smug before."

"Probably you weren't listening."

Sue came out and put in her two cents.

"Boys, please don't fight—it upsets the womenfolk."

They laughed and said they sure the hell didn't want to upset the womenfolk.

Happy had noticeably improved over the last few days. The swelling was gone and he was walking normally. He was out in the yard chasing imaginary critters of some sort.

The contractor had moved material for the remodel into the yard, and it was beginning to accumulate a very large pile of various materials along the side of the outbuilding. They had approved the plans, and Ray was excited to see the completed project.

Sue had given notice on the house she was renting and had moved most of her belongings into the cabin. The transition to marriage was looking like it was going to be very smooth. Ray fretted a little over his son's reaction. The conversation had been very strained, and they never really talked much about who he was going to marry. Ray could imagine that Michael would be even less pleased if he knew it was someone almost twenty years younger than Ray—a lot closer to Michael's age than Ray's. None of that mattered to Ray at the moment. He had given thought to how difficult this could be for Sue in ten or fifteen years, but he wasn't going to give up years of happiness to protect her from the inevitable. He wanted to make sure the next however many years made Sue happy.

Sue had insisted that Ray know her history before they were married. He'd said it was unnecessary, but she told her story anyway.

"First, Ray, you need to know I have been married, twice. The first was mostly of no consequence. We were way too young and more than anything else I think we got married because we were bored. It lasted a little more than a year. His name was Allen, and I haven't seen or heard from him in twenty plus years. The second marriage was more serious. After my first divorce, I won a scholarship to go to a college in New York. I won it writing an essay on the importance of education. It was mostly BS, but I still I won. It wasn't a full scholarship, and my family didn't have the money to kick in any help, so I decided it was stupid of me to pile up a bunch of debt going to college. Even though I'd more or less decided I wouldn't go, they invited me to an orientation meeting at the school. I went and fell in love."

"Sounds pretty romantic."

"It was. Now don't go and get weird on me. I love you, Ray—this is something that happened a long time ago, so just listen."

Ray nodded. He wasn't real sure he wanted to hear any of this.

"He was an Assistant Dean. A little older than I was, but not much. He was absolutely gorgeous, and we were immediately attracted to one another. What followed was a whirlwind romance. We married and I moved to the university. Since I was now an employee's spouse, I could go to school for almost nothing—with the scholarship money, I had it covered. Our life centered on the school and time seemed to fly by. I got my bachelor's degree in three years. I had no job plans and was basically going to school because I could—so I entered a medical program. About three years later I had all of the requirements to be a physician's assistant."

"Things weren't working out as well for my husband, Ken was his name. He hadn't progressed as fast as he thought he should and had made some enemies in the school administrative ranks with his constant criticism of how they ran things. So I got my degree and he got fired. He was totally taken by surprise. To get to the point, he couldn't find another job. He looked everywhere, sending out hundreds of resumes. He thought he was being blackballed by the school's administrators, and maybe he was. To help us out, I took a job in New York City with a local doctor's group. The money was very good and we found a small place to live. Ken began to drink. He got

into arguments with everybody—the landlord, the postman—
anybody he saw. Then he started accusing me of having affairs.
He just became unreasonable. One night he got so angry at
me, he hit me."

"I left that night, went to a hotel. The next day I contacted
the doctor's office where I was working and told them I had a
personal emergency and would have to quit. Well, they weren't
happy. They had some knowledge of my husband's drinking
problems and no doubt guessed at what was really going on,
so they were understanding. I called Ken and told him I was
leaving. That was early in the morning but he had obviously
already been drinking. He yelled at me accusing me of being
with my lover and that I had left because he was a complete
loser. It hurt so much to hear the things he said to me. In hind-
sight I should've gone home or called someone to go see him,
but I didn't. I hung up."

"I didn't know about it for a few days, but that night he
killed himself. When I found out, I went into a tailspin. I just
left—all of my friends and my family—just walked away. I
drifted from town to town for years. Usually I got jobs in the
medical field. Sometimes as a PA or as a nurse—but many
times I worked as a waitress or a shop clerk. I just kept heading south, and eventually ended up in Florida. I got a job with
a large group practice as a PA. They also had the county contract for forensics, so that's where I learned about crime scenes.
After a while I started dating one of the doctors. He was very
nice, and it scared me. Emotionally I was still fragile even after
all of those years. I quit and hit the road to nowhere in particular. Just started running like I had before. It's been more than
eleven years since Ken killed himself, and you're the first man

I've been with. It's taken me a long time to feel anything, and I thought I would never feel love again—but now I do. I love you, Ray."

Ray was stunned. He knew that there had to be history to explain why such a smart, lovely woman was hiding in a diner in New Mexico—but it still surprised him. Ray hugged Sue and told her that she was the most wonderful person he'd ever known. They held each other for a long time.

They talked for hours. Ray became more convinced than ever that Sue was the person he wanted to marry. They both felt a new level of passion and commitment to each other.

The next day the weather was a little less pleasant—it was one of those cloudy, cool days, with falling mist that fishermen love. Ray knew he must not be a true fishermen because he hated this weather, but he kept his mouth shut. Tyee, on the other hand, was all excited. He told Ray this was the weather he had planned for, and today everything was going to go very well. Ray nodded his head, and wondered for the hundredth time how he'd gotten involved in this in the first place.

Per Tyee's directions, Ray went to a different spot. It looked more or less the same to Ray, but Tyee had been insistent that Ray had to get to this cove and not move. Ray wasn't going to argue with his mentor. Within the first hour Ray caught what looked to him like the biggest fish ever caught in the lake. It was huge and Ray was pretty sure it was a striped bass. Had to be almost three feet long. Ray had no idea how much it weighed, but it was a lot, and it had taken everything he had to get it into the boat. Ray leaned back and realized he was exhausted. Looking at his watch, he saw that the whole process had taken almost thirty minutes from the time of the first hit. He gave a fist pump and smiled.

Ray decided to return to the dock. Tyee would have said to stay out there and try for a bigger one, but Ray was done. He couldn't believe how big the fish was, and it was plenty big enough for him. It didn't matter if he won, he had the victory that mattered: catching the biggest fish he'd ever seen. Tyee was at the dock and helped him get the boat tied up. Ray held up the fish. Tyee started laughing and jumping up and down like a little kid. This was fun.

Big Jack and his helpers came over and took the official pictures. They helped Ray move the fish to the measuring area, where Ray had more pictures taken holding the fish. Now they just had to wait to see if Ray had won. The afternoon dragged on, but around three most everyone had reported in. There were two other fish close to Ray's in size, but Ray was still number one. The last fisherman to pull in was the previous year's champ, and his look said it all. Ray was the champion. Big Jack came up and made it official. He gave Ray his trophy. Nobody remembers ever seeing Ray smile so broadly.

Everyone was invited to the cabin for a celebration, including the other fisherman. The out-of-towners declined due to the long drive home, but even without them there were probably twenty or so people at Ray and Sue's cabin. Sue fixed enchiladas for everyone, and Ray realized that his wife-to-be was a great cook. With plenty of beer and Mexican food, the evening was a hit.

# 31

*Some Time Later*

Ray and Sue loved being married. Their lives were full of joy, with great friends and a thriving business. They were very busy and very happy. Sue had moments when she cried. That worried Ray, but she told him it was just something that happened occasionally.

Tyee moved into the office building even before it was completely finished. They purchased upgraded equipment, and it was beginning to look like a state-of-the-art computer center. Tyee had a satellite dish installed and was getting very fast access to the expanding world wide web.

Clayton became sheriff, winning by a landslide—since he was unopposed. Big Jack had become the de facto mayor. He began looking a little taller when people started addressing him as Mr. Mayor. Of course, he still had an election to win, but the final filing date was coming up and so far no one was running against him.

Sheriff Clayton had made some changes. A couple of the deputies who were Martinez's flunkies were fired. Clayton hired two new deputies who had worked in Dona Ana County back when Ray was sheriff. He'd asked Ray about them, and Ray had given both strong recommendations.

And Clayton was in the process of implementing the changes he'd talked about during the campaign to improve service for the lake residents. The sheriff's department took over the storeroom that Tyee had been using at Big Jack's and set up an annex station. The department rented the small space from Big Jack, and stationed a deputy there most days. This improved response times by up to thirty minutes over dispatching from the T or C office and was a big hit with the residents. It also pleased Big Jack. Nothing improved security more than a sheriff's station right on your property.

Chester was improving everything at the store. Without a complaint from Big Jack, he had almost completely taken over operations. He brought in new merchandise and cleaned out some of the old stuff. He offered specials for the slow times of day and had added an entire section with basic grocery items that was a big hit with the locals. Big Jack said Chester was a godsend and that hiring him had been the smartest thing he'd ever done—everyone just nodded as if that was what had really happened.

They decided to stick with *Pacheco and Chino, Private Investigations* as the business name. Big Jack thought maybe it wasn't wise to push things too far in relation to his new identity, and in a lot of ways it seemed like he was more comfortable behind the scenes anyway. Which is why Ray was surprised when Big Jack became interested in the mayor's job—but there was still a lot Ray didn't know about Big Jack.

Tyee was scheduled to spend a week in a training program with the FBI in Washington D. C. on computer technologies and accessing FBI files online. Crawford had been the one to get that going, and he was very complimentary about the few things they'd done for the FBI since they'd signed the contract.

So far, the work they'd done for the FBI was mostly research, and Tyee was becoming very adept at gathering all kinds of information using his computer skills.

Sorrow entered Ray's world when he learned that Mike Jackson had died. Of course it wasn't a surprise, but it still made him sad. He and Sue attended the memorial service in Albuquerque. They'd seen Monica not long before when she'd attended their wedding. Monica was upset by Mike's death, but she also said it was for the best—he'd been ready for it. Ray and Sue cared for Monica and told her so. They invited her to spend some time with them anytime she could get away, and she said she would.

Ray was sitting on the porch of his cabin when the phone rang. Sue was in town on errands, so Ray got up and went in to answer.

"Hello."

"Ray, this is Tony. Hope this is the right number—I have several for you and I wasn't sure which one was the business."

"It's fine, Tony. This is my house number, but you can call me here anytime. Sorry you couldn't make the wedding—we really wanted to see you and your wife." Ray had never met Tony's wife even when they both lived in Las Cruces. The rumor was that she was incredibly beautiful, but not the most pleasant person in the world. Ray had always felt sorry for Tony, whom he considered one of the nicest guys he'd ever met.

"Yeah. We wanted to come, but you know how it is. Ray, I wanted to talk to you about doing some work for us. I'd hoped to have this to you sooner, but there've been some disruptions in the office I've had to handle. Anyway, I'd like for you to look into some things in Lincoln County for me. This is about the sheriff's department. Sheriff Rodriguez took ill about two months ago and hasn't gotten better. He's currently in the hospital in Ruidoso. I've received some reports, or more like rumors, that the deputy who took over the department during Rodriguez's absence may be strong-arming some of the merchants. Don't know what's going on—maybe nothing. Ruidoso has a police department, but a really weak chief, so the sheriff's department is the major force in the area. This came to me directly from the governor. He wants us to move quickly on this if we can, but he also wants to keep it quiet and he doesn't want to be involved. What I need from you is reliable information. I need to know if there's something going on, and if not, why there are rumors. Is this something you can help us with?"

"Sure, Tony. Give me a few days and I'll get you some information. Let me know if you learn anything new—good to talk to you, Tony." Ray hung up.

Ray thought Tony sounded strangely distant, as if he wasn't telling Ray everything. Much colder than their last meeting. Maybe it was just his active imagination.

Ray hadn't been sure what their assignments from the AG's office would look like, but here was the first one—time to get to work.

# 32

*Late Evening*

The phone rang. Ray looked at it as if he could make it stop just by scowling—he wasn't successful.

"Hello."

"Mr. Pacheco?"

"Yes."

"Sorry to bother you at this hour, but Agent Crawford asked me to call. My name is Agent James with the FBI in Los Angeles."

"What can I do for you, Agent James?"

"Sir, Agent Crawford asked me to give you some information. This comes from a classified, internal FBI report, but he said he thought you should have all the facts that we have. At the same time he can't give you a copy of the report, so he asked me to relay the information to you. Is this a good time to do that sir?"

*Hell no, it is not a good time! I am tired and grumpy!* "Sure go ahead."

"This report covers matters that go back to the 1950s. Some of this I'll be reading—if you have any questions just let me know. It began with a man named Jim Emerson. He was employed by an Oklahoma bootlegger who was in charge of smuggling booze out of Mexico into Texas and Oklahoma. He was apparently responsible for moving large quantities of illegal liquor for his boss, the bootlegger. The report indicates that one day the bootlegger decided to quit and shut down his business. Emerson wasn't ready to quit and decided he could transfer his bootlegging skills to drug running."

Of course Ray knew Jim Emerson, the richest man in Dona Ana County. He'd always thought that there was more evil to Jim than met the eye, but drug trafficking—that was surprising.

"Emerson didn't have the connections that the bootlegger did to sell liquor in areas that were still dry long after probation ended in most places, so with the bootlegger gone he couldn't continue. But he realized that he could use the same skills he'd developed running booze to smuggle drugs—and the demand for illegal drugs was everywhere. Over the years this developed into a large operation. He made an effort to keep all of the pieces of the business separate so that no one person knew much about any other part of the structure. The first major piece he added to the business was the sheriff in Sierra County. Sheriff Hermes wasn't very bright, but he was eager to supplement his small sheriff's wages with illegal drug money. The sheriff recruited his even dumber deputy, Martinez, to handle most of the actual work. Also working for Emerson was Max Johnson, whose father had once owned a cabin in a remote part of Elephant Butte Lake. They were receiving the drugs from a group of people out of El Paso and moving them to outbuildings located on the same property as the cabin in T or C. Then they would fly them out to Albuquerque and Denver from a small strip close to the lake."

Ray knew about the sheriff—he'd been the one who'd arrested him, and of course Ray's own cabin was the one mentioned in the FBI report. Home sweet home had been part of a drug running operation.

The agent continued in his monotone voice, summarizing the report. "Emerson was doing well with his investments and had become one of the wealthiest men in southern New Mexico. But one day he was confronted by a young, very brash FBI man named Myers. Myers said he could prove Emerson was the head of a drug running operation moving millions of dollars of illegal drugs every year. Emerson tried to bribe the agent, but Myers just laughed at him and said that from that point on the operation was his, and Emerson was working for him. By this time Emerson was old, and he had no desire to go to war with Myers. Emerson's health declined fast, but before he died he told his son about the source of most of his wealth. His son, Bill, contacted the agent and said he wanted a place in the family business or he would expose the whole thing. Myers wasn't worried—he thought Bill was a joke—but he decided to bring him in anyway once Emerson died, just to make sure nothing would get screwed up after old man Emerson was gone."

Agent James paused for a moment, giving Ray a chance to ask any questions he had. When none were forthcoming, he went on.

"Myers had become the agent in charge of the Albuquerque office and had expanded his criminal operations to include smuggling forged documents into the US. As that business grew, he brought in hired goons to work as collectors. Myers continued to expand the business and spent more and more time running his illegal operation. Based on several reports, Myers had little respect for his superiors at the FBI and thought it was a joke that he could run a major drug smuggling operation under their noses.

"Myers had been abusing drugs for years and there had been a toll on his personality. He'd become more and more abrasive, with the result that people stayed away from him, and that may have been a factor in his ability to keep everyone in the dark about his activities. At its peak, it's estimated that his operation was handling well over twenty-five million dollars in illicit drugs and forged documents every year."

"He must have had quite an empire," Ray said.

"As of this writing, little of the money has been recovered. Myers had an unusually opulent lifestyle for an FBI agent, but there still are large sums of money missing. There's speculation that some of it was sent to partners who remain unknown at this time. One guess is the Mexican Mafia in L.A. There is some evidence that the illegal document operation may have been a partnership with people in L.A., at least in the sense that someone there was the source of the materials. The investigation is ongoing."

Finally, James began wrapping things up.

"That's a quick summary of a rather extensive, detailed report. Most of the information came from interviews with Sheriff Hermes, Max Johnson, and Bill Emerson. I hope that gives you the information you need. I am sorry to have called so late, but Agent Crawford insisted that I contact you as soon as possible."

"Thanks Agent James, I appreciate you calling. Good night."

All of that going on right in his backyard when he was sheriff of Dona Ana County. The FBI should be embarrassed, but Ray was too. He went to bed and snuggled with Sue. If that FBI report remained a secret, it was fine with him.

*Keep reading for a free preview of...*

# THE BOOTLEGGER'S LEGACY

*Meet Ray Pacheco, pre-retirement, in this prequel to the* Pacheco & Chino Mysteries.

*When an old-time bootlegger dies and leaves his son Mike a cryptic letter hinting at millions in hidden cash, Mike and his friend Joe embark on a journey that takes them through three states and 50 years of history. What they find goes beyond money and transforms them both.*

*An action-packed adventure story taking place in the early 1950s and late 1980s. It all starts with a key, embossed with the letters CB, and a cryptic reference to Deep Deuce, a neighborhood once filled with hot jazz and gangs of bootleggers. Out of those threads is woven a tapestry of history, romance, drama, and mystery; connecting two generations and two families in the adventure of a lifetime.*

# PROLOG

*Oklahoma City, Oklahoma, 1952*

Deep Deuce was swinging tonight. The Billy Parker Band was hitting every note. The sound was magnetic, attracting dancers young and old. Blacks and whites alike were enjoying great rhythms from one of the best big bands of the time.

John Giovanni didn't come for the music, though—he'd never been accused of being cultured. He was in town to meet one of his customers. He hated all of his goddamn customers, but what the hell—if he killed them all he wouldn't have any business. Giovanni was originally from Brooklyn, but he'd moved to Dallas at the urging of his uncle. Uncle Tony had made it clear that Giovanni should move or Tony would cut his throat. The threat was accompanied by an easy-to-understand gesture. Giovanni had slept with Uncle Tony's ugly daughter, and Uncle Tony was pissed. She was only fourteen.

Giovanni realized his options were limited, so he moved. He started selling illegal liquor to the shitkickers who lived in the backward world of Texas. God did he ever hate Texas.

Tonight Giovanni was in Oklahoma City, another useless shithole. The only people who could tell the difference between Texas and Oklahoma were the assholes who lived there, and to them the distinctions were enormous. To Giovanni the only good thing about this ugly part of the country was they still had prohibition—at least Oklahoma did, and parts of Texas.

That's why Giovanni was here: to feed the beast all the illegal hooch it wanted.

Giovanni had dreamed about being alive in the twenties and thirties, raising hell like Capone. Man, what a wonderful time to have been alive. So when Uncle Tony said to get lost fast before he sliced Giovanni up real bad, Giovanni did a little research and discovered gangster nirvana in the southwest.

Using all of his well-honed skills, which mostly had to do with killing anyone who got in his way, he became the major wholesaler of liquor in the region in just a few years. If Uncle Tony hadn't hated his guts, he would have been proud.

Why he was meeting this creep in the black section of town, he had no idea. Giovanni wasn't particularly prejudiced—he just mostly hated everybody who wasn't Italian, so color didn't really matter. As a matter of fact, being up to 1950 standards of racial harmony, his favorite whore was black. Her name was Lacy, and Giovanni liked screwing her almost as much as he liked killing fuckin' Texans. She was with him tonight, along with three bodyguards and his dumber-than-dirt cousin, Marco.

"Marco what the hell kinda music are they playing?"

"That's jazz Johnny. Really cool jazz."

"What the fuck do you know about jazz? What the fuck do you know about anything?"

"Hey, why do you talk to me like that? I'm your goddamned cousin—you shouldn't talk to me like that."

"How about I just blow your fucking brains out, right here in this stupid jazz hip-hop joint, how would that be, shithead?"

Marco was never sure how far Johnny might go. He had seen him do some pretty horrible things.

"Okay, okay, sorry Johnny. It's just sometimes you make me feel like I'm stupid or something."

"Well, yeah. Maybe I'll be nicer. How's that? Maybe you should take Lacy out to the car and get a little—how would that be Marco?"

This caused Lacy to give Johnny a *never-turn-your-back-on-me-asshole* look. One way or another Johnny wasn't likely to make old age.

"Why are we here Johnny?"

"I'm expanding. Dumb shitkicker who runs the largest Oklahoma bootleg operation is going to retire. We've been selling him some of his booze for a while, but now he's decided to buy from those Mexican fuckheads out of Juarez. Can't have that, so he's going bye-bye."

"You going to kill him?" Marco seemed nervous. You never knew with Johnny. He might do it right here, right now.

"Don't worry baby Marco, it won't be tonight. But once everything gets transferred over to me, he'll be dead. I'll be the booze king of fuckin' Oklahoma."

# CHAPTER 1

*Oklahoma City, Oklahoma, February 1987*

Depression seemed like an old friend. There was comfort in being able to describe, with medical precision, the reason you weren't successful, weren't particularly happy, were overweight—you get the picture.

Joe Meadows was a CPA who'd experienced only minor success as an accountant and hated every aspect of his tedious life. His wife Liz was mostly pleasant, although she was preoccupied with her own activities. These centered around their two teen children, who seemed totally absorbed in their own realities, and her church, The Church of Christ. Joe often thought that it was possible that his family wasn't fully aware of his existence in the sense that he wasn't a distinct individual to them. He was the family provider, but there was little doubt that they didn't give a shit about Joe the person.

Joe's appearance was mostly unremarkable. Some people said he was handsome, with his longish, dark hair. He was just under six foot—never said five eleven. He used to have sparkling eyes that seemed full of mischief, but the years of tedium and boredom—and a little too much drinking—had toned the gleam down some. His best quality still remained: an engaging smile.

It was February, 1987. Joe lived in Oklahoma City with a bunch of cowboy rednecks who enjoyed beer, big-breasted women, guns, and pickups—not necessarily in that order. Everything about Joe's life felt foreign to him, like he was visiting from another planet. Where he was supposed to be in this world, he didn't know, but it sure wasn't where he was right now.

By the standards of the American dream, Joe was doing just fine. He had a nice looking wife and two beautiful kids, he was a professional with his own business, and he had a house, two cars, and probably a dog somewhere—what the hell was the matter with him? He wasn't sure. It just seemed like there should be something more to life. What that something was, he didn't know. Nor was he making any effort to find out. He showed up for his life each day and clocked in, and he anticipated that nothing would change.

Monday morning, and Joe was headed to a client's office to discuss the company's financial condition. The client was Mike Allen, owner of Allen's Hardware. Mike's business had lost a bundle the previous year and he wanted Joe to tell him why. Joe knew why: Mike was an idiot—or at least acted like an idiot.

Mike was either drunk, or getting ready to get drunk, and almost certainly chasing a woman who wasn't his wife, leaving very little time to focus on the hardware business. And he'd been Joe's best friend since grade school.

They'd become best friends in Mrs. Smith's second grade class at East Side Elementary. They had formed a bond on the playground to improve their defenses against the girls—especially one girl. A second grade boy's worst nightmare is the inevitable bully girl on the playground. It's one thing to be beat up by some boy—but by a girl? That's just terrible. Jane Waters was their nemesis. She was meaner and tougher than most of the boys in the school. Rumor had it that she'd been held back in second grade—twice.

Jane had been tormenting the boys for months. Recess had become hell. Much of it consisted of threats, but the boys had seen her in action. She had pummeled Ray M so bad he had to go to the nurse's office. He was out of school for three days. Jane was gone for a few days, too—to everyone's relief.

The only way to improve their position was to form an alliance. Once the boys made their bond, cementing the deal with a ritual handshake and spit, they stood up to her in a frightening display of little boy courage. She left them alone from that day on, and Mike and Joe had been best friends ever since.

Joe parked in front of the hardware store and sat in the car for a while, not wanting to tell Mike how bad things really were. The store had belonged to Mike's father for more than twenty years and something of a town institution. The original owner, before Mike's dad bought it, opened in the current location sometime in the 1930s. But times change, and a new Walmart down the street had cut the store's business in half overnight. Mike's dad had died about ten years ago, so at least he hadn't had to see what had happened to the "best little hardware store in OKC." As the store declined, Mike's drinking increased. There was probably little Mike could do to help his business, but what he was doing was the opposite of helping.

Joe entered the store and was once again struck by the feeling it had to be hundreds of years old. Everything about the place seemed to be from another era. Even the old cash register was more antique than functional. The store was crammed full of a variety of merchandise, some of which hadn't been moved in years. On the other hand, if you needed a part for a thirty-year-old washing machine they just might have it. There was comfort in being inside the store—like it was a wonderful part of your past you had forgotten.

"Joe, come on back and give me the good news." Mike was standing in the doorway of his small office and didn't look so good. His eyes were bloodshot, and he hadn't shaved. He had a strange look about him these days, like he wasn't quite real. There were times it seemed like Mike was an actor in a movie, playing himself. Never a real sharp dresser, now he looked like he should be sitting on the sidewalk outside the store with a bottle in a paper bag rather than occupying the owner's office.

Mike had inherited a strong physique. Standing at least six foot two, he was often mistaken for an ex-football player, though he'd never been good at sports. Wearing his hair cut short gave a no-nonsense quality to his demeanor. Developing a small stomach was about the only change to Mike's physique since high school.

Joe went into the office and took a chair at Mike's desk. He began, "The loss last year was a lot more than you can stand. You have no cash, you're past due with your suppliers, you owe back payroll taxes to the IRS, and the bank note is four months past due. Mike, you're broke. I'd be surprised if the bank doesn't call your loan and put you out of business." So much for small talk.

Mike just stared off into space. After a short while he turned to Joe, "What can I do?"

"You're going to need to get some cash—I would say

somewhere around $25,000—in order to keep things from imploding. You don't have much time. The most important thing is to stop the losses—you can't keep digging a hole and filling it with borrowed money."

Mike looked dejected. He was quiet. It was evident that this was hard for him to take. His expression reflected something worse than just disappointment.

"My gut tells me you need to shut the business down. Use the $25,000 to buy some time to get a plan in place. I don't think you can sell the store. So, more than likely, your only option will be bankruptcy and liquidation." Joe was Mr. Doomsayer today.

Mike erupted "What kind of fuckin' friend are you? Is that the best you can do?"

"Look, if it was up to me I'd wave a magic goddamned wand and make everything perfect—but I don't have a wand and, if I did, I'd use it on my own fucked up life." Joe and Mike shared some stress issues.

"Mike, you can just walk away and lose everything, or you can try to get some cash and have an orderly closing—maybe save your house and some of your other assets. But I think the store is gone. The climate for your type of business has just changed too much. There are plans for a Home Depot only ten minutes from here—what would that do to your business? You need to try and protect as much of what you have as you can and then get on with something else."

"Something else? Listen to you—you know there's nothing else for me. I've worked in this stupid business since I busted out of college. I don't know anything else. Maybe I could get a job at Walmart and slowly starve to death. Samantha—I'm sure she'll understand. We'll just have to downsize and learn to like living in a mobile home. None of her snotty friends will even notice we're suddenly white trash."

Samantha Allen, Mike's wife, had been his high school sweetheart. She was the prom queen, football queen, home coming queen—pretty much queen of everything. And she was gorgeous. Mike had always felt lucky that she was his wife, but he was also intimidated by her beauty. He'd developed serious insecurities about himself because he hadn't lived up to her standards.

The room was quiet. Joe felt bad for his friend and at the same time thought he had done very little to prevent the mess he was in. Mike had always lived way beyond his means. If he had a good year and made $50,000, he would spend $70,000—mostly on things and people he could live without. Mike's wife seemed to think that they actually had money, and she lived just that way.

"Mike, I can loan you maybe $5,000 or so. I'm only going to do that if you can come up with more, so you can have a chance to work out a plan that will let you get out of this business without a complete collapse."

"I don't want you loaning me money. Why make you more miserable just to give me a few more hours before I go down the tubes? I need a way to make some big bucks, and fast—not just keep borrowing and struggling from one month to the next. I need a plan."

Joe agreed: Mike needed a plan. They made a plan to meet for a drink around four that afternoon at Triples, a local bar and restaurant down the street from the hardware store. That wasn't really a plan at all—it was more like an old bad habit that should be broken—but it was the best they had right now.

Driving back to his office, Joe began to think about how Mike could make some quick money. They were both forty-four—the perfect age for nothing. If you were going to be one of the successful people you read about, it would have already happened. Now there wasn't much to do except wait for some sort of miracle or death. Joe knew his fate. Working late, drinking too much, and wondering what might have been. The problem Joe had was that even if he was able to start over, he wasn't sure what he would do differently. He had no vision of what an ideal life would look like, although he was pretty sure lots of money would help. He just wasn't very interested in much of anything.

Joe knew that Mike thought he'd hit his peak when he married Samantha. She was the most beautiful girl in their senior high school class—Mike had hit the jackpot. But it seemed to Joe that Mike had never really been happy after they were married. He'd won the prize, now what did he do? After all, there was something very contradictory about the fact that he worked in his father's hardware store and was married to the most beautiful woman in the world. It felt unreal, and Mike seemed almost to be waiting for her to leave him—or maybe his behavior was a way to get her to leave. The pressure of his marriage seemed to be all in his head, but it was as real as could be to Mike.

Although they lived beyond their means, Mike and Sam still lived a modest lifestyle. They didn't have a mansion or drive fancy cars. They lived a few blocks from the hardware store, on Hudson just off Eighth. Their house was older, in a nice neighborhood. Mike had always planned on fixing it up more than he had. Someday he'd get around to that—well, maybe. Their whole life had a demoralized quality to it that made itself felt in every one of their interactions. Everything was stretched very thin. They were waiting on something, but they didn't know what.

# CHAPTER 2

*Oklahoma City, Oklahoma*

At 4:15, Joe walked into the darkened confines of Triples looking for Mike. He was over in a corner booth, obviously already headed toward drunk, sipping his usual scotch and water. Joe slid in and waved a finger at the bartender, who immediately begin fixing a gin and tonic—his usual.

"How long have you been here?" Joe wasn't sure he would stay if Mike was already beyond discussing anything.

"Just a little while. I have had only a couple of drinks—so don't get all high and mighty on me!" Mike made an ugly face as he said his piece. Under more normal circumstances, Joe would have left to avoid the conflict headed his way. He'd seen Mike like this before. But today he felt he needed to help Mike the best he could.

The bartender brought his drink, and Joe sat back and sipped without comment. In a little while the tension seemed to let up some. Mike was still sulking, but he was doing it with a more pleasant expression on his face.

Joe had given thought to Mike's financial problems. Without some surprise he didn't think there was much hope. Mike was like a lot of people, including Joe—he had borrowed as much as he could in order to live the life he wanted to live, right now—to hell with the future. Credit cards had been a way to live beyond their means and enjoy the good life. Everyone did it—why not him?

Joe had counseled Mike several times about the debt and the declining revenues of his business—even when he felt like a hypocrite doing it. Mike would just shrug his shoulders and say, "Everything'll be better next month." It never was.

"Let's get to it, okay?" Joe prodded Mike. "Do you have any assets you can sell?"

"Everything is hocked to the max. Even if I could sell something, it'd just go to pay off debt—there wouldn't be any cash." While not a surprising answer, at least Mike seemed lucid and over the anger Joe had encountered when he first arrived.

"How about Samantha. Does she have any assets or family money she could get?"

"Well, even if she did, I wouldn't ask. I'm sure she's already planning her life after we're done. My guess is that she's hidden a tidy sum somewhere that I can't reach so once everything starts to collapse she'll have a nest egg to use when she starts over without me. I know she got some money from her brother's estate after he died—she never told me how much, although I'd guess it was considerable."

"Well shit, what kind of deal is that? She's your wife. That's as much your money as hers, and you need it—now!" Joe was stunned that Sam would have her own funds and not be helping deal with the family's financial woes. She and Joe had never got along, so it was easy for Joe to think ill of the bitch.

"Maybe legally, but I'm not going to pursue it. I just don't want to talk about that—it's not going to happen."

Mike was beginning to lose interest in the conversation. You can only talk so much about your failures. Eventually it becomes pointless.

"There is something that could be—oh never mind, that's crazy." Mike seemed to be drifting again.

"Crazy? This whole conversation is crazy. Listen, Mike, I know we're different. I'm not much of a risk taker, but crazy is the mess you're in right now. You have big financial problems, and we're in an expensive bar sucking down costly drinks. Is that crazy? If you have any ideas, even crazy ones, now's the time to hear about them."

"Okay, okay stay calm. This is a strange area for me. You know my father kind of lost his mind before he died. My mother stayed with him until the last few months, when she couldn't take it anymore. She asked me to help her with him. During his last years he and I had become a little closer, although he was always distant with me. Or maybe I was a little bit distant with him, I don't know. Anyway she asked me to help."

"I looked around for a place he could be moved to. There just wasn't much that was very pleasant. Then there was an incident with him and my mother and I started to worry about her safety. So, I decided he had to be moved to a nursing home. Putting him in that nursing home was the hardest thing I'd ever done. It felt like I betrayed him. Because of that I didn't want to be around him, and when I was he seemed to just talk nonsense."

Joe knew some of this about Mike's dad. He'd heard from other people that Mike's whole family was just a little weird. Mike's dad, Patrick Allen, had been something of a legend in the 40s and 50s, when he'd been the biggest bootlegger in Oklahoma. Joe had always thought the stories were exaggerated, because the man he'd known was a grandfatherly, easy-to-be-around kind of guy. He was much older than Mike's mom, although he was always energetic, very outgoing and friendly.

"Come on Mike, what's the crazy part?"

Mike looked worried, then finally spit it out. "My dad kept telling me he had buried millions from his bootlegging days, but that he couldn't remember where."

"Millions—as in dollars?"

"I guess. Much of this I think was just him losing his mind toward the end. I mean, I knew the stories, that he'd been a big time bootlegger in the past. I thought they just amounted to him arranging a few bottles of something for his neighbors. I asked my mother, and she said he never was into selling whisky. That was just a bunch of rumors made up by people who were jealous of my dad's success selling insurance and buying his own hardware business. Anyway, I never knew what was true."

Mike decided to order another drink, so to be polite Joe joined in. Millions buried in Mike's backyard—that would go a long way toward solving Mike's problems. And, of course, he would give some to his best friend since the second grade. Why not relax and see where this was headed?

The bartender brought their drinks over and asked them to clear the tab since he was going off shift. Joe flopped out his American Express card and gave it to the bartender, mentally noting that this was a business expense since Mike was a client. Of course, Mike hadn't paid him in about six months—maybe with his dad's millions things would look better.

"I know you're thinking this is nuts, but the strange thing is that after he died I received a package from a lawyer in Dallas with a letter from my dad and a key." Mike took a drink and eyed Joe to see if he was snickering or actually listening.

"Go on—tell me what was in the letter." Mike had his attention.

"Some of the letter made sense and some didn't. I have it out in the car in my briefcase—wait just a minute and I'll go get it."

While Mike went to his car, Joe decided to take a bathroom break and use the payphone to call Liz.

"What the hell are you doing out drinking with Mike? Didn't you just tell me he was broke and would probably be going out of business? No doubt you'll be picking up the tab. Sometimes I wonder about you Joe. It's like you're smart and stupid at the same time. I don't want to hear any made up stories about why this is important—if you want to go waste your money drinking and carousing with your lowlife friends, you go right ahead. I'm sick and tired of it—unless you want to consider living alone with no family, maybe you ought to give ol' Mike a hearty goodbye and get your ass home. This is just about the last—"

Click. Calling home may have been a mistake. She hadn't even given him a chance to explain how important this was to Mike. But of course she thought Mike was scum, so she didn't really care. Hanging up on her was going to create a serious problem. Her threat to divorce him had been going on since about the six-month anniversary of their marriage. Well, he would deal with her later. The first trick was to avoid her until morning, so he'd stay out late, sneak in, and sleep on the sofa in his home office. He kind of liked it there anyway.

Mike returned and slid into the booth. He handed Joe the letter.

*Dear Son,*

*I know we've had some rocky times, all my fault and I'm sorry. This letter is to let you know that I loved you and you have always meant the world to me. Maybe I didn't show it the way I should have. It was just easier for me to let your mother handle everything. I was too old to be your typical dad—more like your granddad—but you gave me great joy and made a lot of the things I had done in my life seem okay.*

*Since you're reading this, my time will have come to an end. Don't overly grieve. I had a good life and have no regrets.*

*With this letter you will receive a key. I cannot tell you what this key is for or I will risk other people discovering my secret. I know you may think that I've lost my mind and that this letter is nonsense, but trust me, this is important. I know you know I was a bootlegger before I retired and started running the store. Well, son, I was a very successful bootlegger. I stockpiled a shitload of cash. It is waiting for you. You'll think this is the madness of an old man, but let me assure you, it's true.*

*I couldn't just give you the money without creating problems. If you can discover what you need to find the cash, you'll have demonstrated that you're clever enough to figure out how to use the money without causing problems.*

*You may or may not want to pursue this. If you do and you're successful there will be a big reward. If you decide that this is too crazy and you're not interested in my far-fetched stories, I understand. Just do what you think is best. I only want you to be happy and have a good life.*

*I think you are a lot smarter than I ever was, so I'm sure you can figure out what this is about.*

*Dad*

*P.S. Don't talk to your mother about this. She'll just tell you that I always had a screw loose—and she's right. And remember your path to financial independence goes through Deep Deuce at the St. Francis.*

Mike gave Joe the key.

Joe sat quietly for a while. He wasn't sure what to make of any of this. If Mike's dad had millions to give his son, why make it so difficult? *Dear Son, here is the secret number to a Swiss bank account that has millions for you. Thanks, your Dad.* But this seemed almost crazy—just like Mike had said.

"How in the hell can you find out what this key is for? Didn't he tell you any more toward the end?"

"Well, that's what I mean. He did tell me more, but it never made any sense. After I got the letter, I was curious. I don't know. It just went into the back of my brain as some nutty thing my dad did at the end. I wanted to forget the whole thing."

"Let's start over. He told you he had buried millions, right?"

"That's what he said, but Joe he was out of his mind—it was just nonsense."

"Did you contact the attorney in Dallas?"

"Nope—didn't do anything except run the store into the ground and drink a lot."

"Did he give you any hints where it might be buried?"

"Joe, listen to you. You're starting to believe. It was all

nonsense. My father lost his mind before he died. He was just making up stuff. Complete and absolute bullshit."

"Stop feeling sorry for yourself—I think this is worth exploring further. After all, you may not believe it, but my dad told me that your dad was once one of the wealthiest men in the city. I always thought he was just joking. Maybe he wasn't."

"Yeah, I heard some of those stories. They never made sense. He was old from my first memories. There was no way him being a bootlegger made sense to me. And we lived okay, but we were sure the hell not rich. Why would we live the way we did if he had millions? He worked his butt off every day in that hardware store, waiting on grumpy old farts who needed a bolt. Why in the hell would you do that if you had millions?"

"Well, yeah, that's a fair question. One that I don't have an answer for. I know it doesn't make much sense—but there's something so odd about all of this. So odd that I'm not sure someone would make it up. I think we need to see if we can determine what this key is for. What does this mean about Deep Deuce at the St. Francis? Does that make any sense to you?"

"Well, I'm not sure. Although I seem to remember that the black area just east of downtown was called Deep Deuce. Least I think it was, not real sure. I think my dad had even mentioned that area many, many years ago as a part of town that had lots of nightclubs with live music way back when. He said he had gone there a couple of times. But St. Francis doesn't mean anything to me."

Joe thought about what that might mean. Was Mike's dad trying to give his son millions of dollars after he died by sending him a strange letter and key? This didn't seem to fit the picture he had of Mike's dad. The guy sold nuts, screws, and shovels for goodness sakes.

"Regarding the key, the guy who supplies our key-making kiosk would probably know how to figure that out—if there's any way to actually do that. Could be this is just an old key he left me for no reason at all except he'd lost his mind." Mike's mood was getting worse. If they were going to decide anything tonight, it would have to be pretty soon, before Mike slipped into a deep depression.

Joe responded, "Okay, you're right—this is probably just some kind of strange joke, and your father was lost in a different world toward the end. We just have to make the effort and see if this is nonsense or not. When can we contact your guy about the key?"

"I'll go call him right now and see if he can meet us in the morning."

Mike returned quickly after making his call. "He said no problem, he'll be there tomorrow morning at ten. Will that work for you?"

"Sure, I'll see you at your store. I think I'll hang out here for a while. Better if I can sneak in later without having a battle with Liz tonight. She's no doubt beyond pissed since I hung up on her earlier right in the middle of her 'Joe's a shithead' speech. See you tomorrow."

Joe sat in the booth alone and gave some thought to his life. He remembered his school days with Mike, when everything had seemed possible. They'd always thought they were going to be something—something special. But it didn't happen that way. Joe had periods of success. He didn't want to be an accountant, but when he passed his test and got his CPA license he felt successful. It was just that the work didn't suit him—he wanted to be creative, build things, not track other people's success by crunching numbers.

He and Mike had stayed close after school, and that was an important part of Joe's life. Mike considered him the smart one, and Joe liked that. Joe thought Mike was more daring than he was—often that wasn't a good thing for Mike, leading him to make risky decisions. After his father died and Mike took over the business, Joe thought that the change would be good for Mike, but now he wasn't so sure. Failing at running your dad's hardware store was a heavy burden, one that Mike wasn't handling well.

Joe wondered what things would be like for them in ten years. He guessed he'd still be doing taxes and hating it, and Liz would still be yelling at him, or worse yet ignoring him—basically the same as now. For Mike, he didn't know what was going to happen—it worried Joe.

# CHAPTER 3

*Oklahoma City, Oklahoma*

Liz had had it with Joe. He was a drunk and he was a terrible husband and father. She had worked every day at making their marriage a success. She was exhausted from the effort. How many years can you be married to someone who seems to always be in a fog?

When they were first married, Liz had had real hope. She thought Joe could be a success. He worked hard and, except for his drunken nights out with his useless buddy Mike, he was a good provider. Liz had used every alluring skill she'd had to get Joe to propose to her—but once he did she immediately stored her charms away for some future use. Liz had never really enjoyed sex, and Joe's constant need repulsed her. After years of her coolness he began to leave her alone—of course by then they had two children.

While sex wasn't vital to her life, her children were. Somewhere in the recesses of her brain it was as if the children had nothing to do with Joe, as if they'd been conceived and born only of her. With the kids her life took on a new meaning, and Joe started to blend into the background.

Like most people in Oklahoma, Liz was a Christian. Her beliefs, based on the Bible as the literal word of God, grew as her children grew. She took them to church at least twice a week, often more. They participated in extended Bible school in the summer and attended summer camps devoted to their faith. She knew it was vital that the sinful ways of their father be cleansed from her children.

Liz's first impulse to divorce Joe probably came within a year of their marriage. But the birth of the children and Joe's ability to provide financial comfort were barriers to her ever taking action. While she'd never asked for a divorce, sometime in the early years of their marriage she effectively divorced herself from Joe. He was necessary for her to have a means to support herself and her children, so he stayed. She knew that without her constant nagging for him to apply himself he would more than likely fall into an alcoholic stupor and become an even more useless drunk. She had to stay to make sure that didn't happen.

There was a constant pressure on Liz to steer her children in the right direction and to keep Joe working and earning money. She never relaxed, knowing that without her unwavering dedication to making sure that everything was done in the way she prescribed, it would all fall apart. She also knew no one appreciated the sacrifices she'd made for her family. She was alone, but she wasn't about to be stopped.

Liz sometimes dreamed about what her life could have been if only she had married someone she could have loved. She hadn't had that luxury, though. Her family was poor. Her father had been a drunken bully who beat her mother, until one day he left and never returned. Her mother was broken-hearted when the bastard left. To this day Liz couldn't understand why her mother was so devastated. After her husband left, her mother became the family drunk—and ignored her kids. Liz had hated her family and spent part of each day planning how to escape.

As a teenager, Liz was attractive. She knew she was no beauty queen but with a little make-up and some borrowed clothes she could be very appealing. She wasn't particularly good at school and knew her best hope for getting away from her mother and their mind-numbing poverty was to marry. Every day of high school, the goal was to find a husband. Liz's best friend was Judy. Liz suspected that Judy had been having sex since the eighth grade, and she was the class expert on attracting a man. Judy had told stories to Liz and her friends that had made Liz blush and hide her face. Liz listened to Judy and was soon walking and talking differently. They had spent hours working on how Liz could use her eyes to flirt. Liz thought much of this was silly, but before she knew it boys were noticing her. Her first reaction was disgust at the fact that these guys could be so easily manipulated. Judy declared gender victory.

After a period of practice, Liz focused all her new skills on a single target: Joe Meadows. She chose Joe based on a very non-scientific method involving his looks, the fact that he seemed to have some money, his car, and that he was in her homeroom. Joe was obviously smart and made reasonable grades in school. She knew he was on a pre-college path, and had heard he was expected to graduate a semester early and enroll in the local college. This, she felt, made Joe a good prospect to succeed at whatever he decided to do and be able to provide for his family. Plus, in an it-really-doesn't-matter way, she kind of liked him.

Once Liz set her sights on Joe, he had little chance. He wasn't very experienced, and she was able to control him easily throughout their senior year. Once Mike, his idiot best pal, got engaged, it was inevitable Joe would want to marry Liz. But Joe's parents stepped in and insisted on a delay until Joe finished college. This was not to Liz's liking, although she mostly lived with Joe his last two years in college.

After Joe graduated, they were married. Joe was offered a great job right out of school at the local box manufacturing plant. He was an assistant controller. Liz thought that sounded important. She'd never really cared what Joe did, as long as he was making money—and leaving her alone. It had been easy to turn Joe's sex drive on—it turned out to be a little harder to turn it off.

Joe spent a lot of time at work. He also spent many evenings out drinking with his work buddies. Liz thought that was fine, as long as he gave her his paycheck every two weeks. Joe was quickly promoted into more responsibility and money. After a short while they had plenty of money. Liz was very happy.

Once Joe passed the CPA exam, he started talking about opening his own accounting practice. Liz wasn't supportive. She just wanted Joe to continue to make money and not risk anything. Joe didn't listen. But it worked out. Joe knew a lot of people, some of whom he met drinking and hanging out at bars. His business grew quickly, and he was a success.

While Joe was growing the business, Liz was having children. The world according to Liz couldn't have been better—of course, Joe wasn't a factor in that world, except to provide money.

Liz had sacrificed so much to make everything better for everyone. She knew they didn't appreciate what she'd done, but it didn't matter. She had kept her family together all of these years, and one day her children would thank her for it.

Liz prayed every day for the strength to continue to make the world a better place for her children and herself. She knew that the day was coming when she would leave Joe. He just didn't have the same moral standards as Liz and her children. In some ways she regretted ever marrying Joe, but she'd done what she had to do—there hadn't been a choice. She knew she would leave Joe, but it would have to wait until she had more financial security.

Joe's accounting practice was growing every day. One day soon she would get a divorce and get half of all of the assets, including the business. She dreamed about that prospect: half of the money and no Joe.

The other aspect of her life that was important to Liz was associating with important people. Of course, they were also rich—that's why they were important. This had begun at church. She'd organized several charity events that had been attended by the high society of the community, and she'd quickly become enamored. Coming from dirt poor people, she'd never dreamed of hobnobbing with the elite, but here she was sipping wine with the upper echelon of society. She was hooked. It was like a drug. She wanted to attend every event and couldn't get enough. Of course Joe wouldn't go. "Who gives a shit about the high and mighty?" he'd say rudely. It made her realize how much she had grown, while Joe had not.

Liz attended one society event after another—Joe never went. Liz spent money like it was free—Joe worked until he went to drink, never doubting that he was digging a hole with his credit card that he could never fill. It couldn't go on much longer—but it continued without changing. One of these days it would have to.

# CHAPTER 4

*Las Cruces, New Mexico, March 1987*

Ray Pacheco had been the Dona Ana County Sheriff for over nineteen years. A good life. He had always taken pride in his job and his department. Ray didn't just give lip service to his role serving and protecting his community—he lived it. These were his neighbors and his neighbors' kids, no matter how bad or rotten they sometimes were.

Law enforcement was Ray's life. He had lost his wife to cancer more than five years before, and his only son had moved to Boston to take a job with a top-notch law firm. Ray was proud of his son, but he also agonized over a deep resentment he felt toward him for moving so far away.

Ray was originally from Macon, Georgia. That was where he met and married his wife. His first years in law enforcement were in Macon. He'd also spent a short time with the Jacksonville, Florida, police force before he answered an ad in a law enforcement magazine for a Chief Deputy Sheriff in Las Cruces, New Mexico. Ray and his wife debated the craziness of moving to New Mexico—the distance, the difference in cultures, all the various risks. They were excited about the opportunity for Ray to advance in his career, but also concerned about moving so far away to such an unknown place.

Even when the Dona Ana Sheriff's office offered Ray the job, the mixed feelings remained. After heart-searching discussions, their decision was made. They took the plunge, and they fell in love with Las Cruces and Dona Ana County. Ray's wife became active in civic matters almost at once and began to feel connected. She had made Las Cruces seem like home to Ray.

He did well in the department. He and the Sheriff made a good team—the Sheriff was very political, while Ray knew law enforcement—so the Sheriff could spend time at meetings and political events, which he enjoyed, while Ray ran the department, where he excelled. Ray formed some great relationships with the deputies, and they learned to trust him. He always backed his men, and he became a resource for everyone in the department on the best way to handle any matter.

The job of Sheriff opened up rather suddenly when the old Sheriff was seriously injured in an auto accident. Unable to perform his duties, the Sheriff resigned. The county commissioners scheduled a special election. Many people encouraged Ray to run, and he decided to give it a shot. His biggest hurdle was that he was totally non-political. He answered every question as truthfully as he could, and if he didn't know the answer he said so.

Ray's last name was Hispanic—Ray was not. He'd never paid much attention to his Spanish heritage when he lived in Georgia. He'd never much cared what tribe people belonged to—he treated everyone more or less the same. The old Sheriff had made a mistake when he hired Ray, sight unseen, based on his Hispanic last name, although it had worked out well for everyone.

There was a three-person race for the Sheriff's job and both the other candidates were Hispanic, one from the department and the other a car salesman with local political connections. They attacked Ray for being white and an out-of-stater. The white part was never said outright, but often implied. The other candidates captured the majority of votes, but Ray got the most votes of any individual candidate. There was no process in place for a runoff—Ray was Sheriff.

His first year was a little rough. Ray tried the best he could to be a little more political, or at least diplomatic, but on occasion he still ruffled some feathers. Soon, though, it became obvious to anyone who was paying attention that there had been an overall improvement in the department. After that, he was entrenched in the job. His ability to successfully run a Sheriff's department and fairly represent everyone's interests overrode his sometimes less-than-politically-correct, direct manner. He won the next race in a landslide.

Ray was generally described as burly, about six feet one and just a little on the heavy side. He'd recently grown a mustache, which gave him an old west cowboy appearance. He dressed in his sheriff's uniform every day, except Sundays and the one other day he took off each week, which rotated. On those days he was most comfortable in jeans, an old work shirt, and a cowboy hat.

Nothing felt the same to Ray after his wife died. She had kept him connected to the world outside of the Sheriff's department. Her death and his son's move across the country to Boston caused him to withdraw from most civilian activities. The department became his family and law enforcement his life. The county was his sole focus. He made it his goal to know everyone by name, and to make sure they knew him.

Still, the last few years had presented some problems. The

new deputies he was hiring seemed different. Where Ray saw neighbors and friends, most of the new people saw threats and danger. The world was changing, and Ray wasn't sure he liked what he saw.

Dona Ana County covered an area about the size of some states back east, with a population of a little over 150,000 that was concentrated in Las Cruces. With a major college located in town—New Mexico State—there were another 25,000 or so visiting students. Like most of New Mexico, the majority of the population was Hispanic and proud of it. Green chilies and Mexican food were the cuisine of choice—the hotter the better. Most people described this part of the country as unique, picturesque, and extremely friendly. To Ray it was home and very comfortable.

Ray had been reelected Sheriff about two years before to a three-year term. At sixty-four, he'd decided this would be his last term. He still hadn't given much thought to what he might do when he retired—he'd made up his mind to retire the previous year during a very difficult time dealing with the county commissioners over changes they wanted made to the department. Every commissioner except one, in Ray's opinion, was a complete asshole. A couple of the new commissioners were in their thirties and acted like they knew everything there was about running a Sheriff's department. It was during this period of confrontation, while dealing with complete morons, that Ray decided it was time to step down. He loved his job. The politics were something he couldn't handle any more.

The biggest jerk on the county commission was Bill Emerson, the son of the richest man in town, Jim Emerson, bank president and owner of about one third of all Las Cruces real estate. Not only was Bill a complete know-it-all, his dad was the biggest piece of shit Ray had ever had to deal with. He would not miss any of the dealings he'd had to endure with the Emerson family.

Today Ray was headed toward downtown Las Cruces for a Kiwanis club executive committee meeting being held in the board of directors' conference room at Citizen's Bank. The Bank owned by Jim Emerson. Civic activities like this, which came with the job, were the least enjoyable part of Ray's duties.

The Citizen's Bank was located in one of the oldest buildings in Las Cruces, dating from the late 1800s. The stories about the building included years as a brothel, several murders, and almost eighty years as a bank. The beginnings of the bank were rumored to be rooted in substantial deposits from some rather unsavory citizens of Mexico. Ray was of the opinion that the building itself had much more character than its owner.

The ornate conference room had the distinct atmosphere of a different time. Ray could imagine sitting in this room seventy years before discussing the major events of 1915. The room still had a certain flair about it that gave any gathering a grand feel. The attention to detail that showed through in every aspect of the bank building, and in particular in the conference room, was something from a different time. The level of craftsmanship in the construction was breathtaking.

Ray sat back and tuned out a discussion about the Kiwanis club's plans for the annual Spring Arts Festival. From his perspective this meant overtime for his deputies, dealing with crowds, and a very popular beer tent that had grown over the years to cover almost a whole city block.

"Hey, Ray, looking forward to retirement? Going fishing

every day. Boy that sure is what I'd do. Hear the fishing is really good right now at Elephant Butte. Maybe you should move up to Truth or Consequences and enjoy the good life." This burst of wisdom was directed at Ray by Max Johnson. Max owned several car washes in town and seemed to mostly do very little except empty the coin machines a couple of times a day. He was also very active in the county Republican Party. Ray had never really figured out where Max had come up with the money to build those car washes. Rumor had it that someone in his family had died and left him some substantial cash, but Max had never confirmed that as far as Ray knew.

"Yeah, maybe that is what I should do alright Max. The biggest problem is that I always hated fishing. But living on the lake up at T or C might be just the way to go when I retire. Don't you have a cabin or something in that area, Max?"

"My family used to—dad sold that a long time ago. We used to use it some after he sold it, because the guy who bought it was never there. My dad had a deal where he could use it if he looked after it. But after my dad died we lost contact with the guy—I think he lived in Oklahoma somewhere." What the hell was he doing chattering on like this to the Sheriff? Shut the fuck up you moron. Max's eye started to twitch. Hell, it didn't matter, the stupid Sheriff was never going to go up there anyway. "Gotta run. I can hear those quarters calling me now. See ya later, Ray."

Ray always figured Max was not the sharpest knife in the drawer, although he'd done okay for himself. He had a lot more money than Ray, that was for sure. He gave some thought to what Max had said. Living at the lake in an old run-down cabin actually sounded just fine to Ray. His needs were mostly on the Spartan side of things. Moving an hour away from Las Cruces and out of Dona Ana County might also simplify his remaining years.

Later that same day Ray dropped by Owen's Realty to see his old buddy Chuck, who'd been selling real estate in New Mexico for as long as Ray could remember. He'd made a fortune doing very little except acting as Jim Emerson's realtor. Ray always thought the real talent Chuck had was sucking up to Jim to maintain those commissions over the years. All in all, Ray thought Chuck was an alright guy.

"Afternoon Chuck, what the hell's going on."

"How the hell would I know Ray? All I do is sit at this desk and talk on the phone. There are days when the whole town could sink into a black pit and if it didn't affect my office or the phone lines, I wouldn't even know. If it wasn't such easy money, I'd give it up."

"Well, you could always become Mayor and go around kissing ass for nothing. At least you're paid well."

"Not sure I like that kissing ass remark—but shit, you're right. If you're going to have to be nice to all of these assholes, might as well make some bucks, right? What brings you to my playpen? Somebody accuse me of a crime?"

"Not yet. I'm sure you know this is my last year as Sheriff, and I don't really have a good idea of what I'm going to do next. A couple of things have come up and I wanted to run some stuff by you."

"I say use your authority and steal as much money as you can in the next few months, then head off to a Mexican beach with the prettiest, youngest senorita you can find—how's that for advice?"

"Sounds like that might fit someone else's fantasy. My situation is a little less exciting. You know I have that big old house out by Hatch, and I was wondering what you thought I could get for it? Also I had a chat with Max at the Kiwanis meeting this morning and he suggested I should look at maybe buying something on the lake up in T or C—what do you think?"

"Okay, I'll keep the senorita fantasy to myself. As far as your house in Hatch, I'd have to do some research. That area has some appeal with the newcomers moving into Dona Ana. Let me run some numbers and then I can give you a good idea what you could get and how long it'd take. There are lots of cabins in T or C for sale, some dirt cheap and some very expensive. Did you have a price range?"

"Once I see what I can get for the old homestead I can make a better estimate of what I'd want to spend. Max mentioned something about an old cabin his dad used to own. Said he'd sold it to some guy in Oklahoma years ago—maybe fifteen or more years back. Said they were allowed to use it to compensate his dad for some upkeep he did, but then once his dad died they lost contact with the Oklahoma guy. Maybe you could do some research and see if that might be something I'd be interested in?"

"Sounds like it could be a dump by now. Let me check the records, see what Max's dad used to own up there, and then track down the current owner. Give me a couple days, and I'll see what I can do."

"Okay. Thanks, Chuck."

# CHAPTER 5

*Oklahoma City, Oklahoma*

Waking up on the small sofa in his home office was less than comfortable. Joe's head hurt and he was cold. On the other hand, there was one real benefit—he hadn't had to deal with Liz. He'd heard her and the kids in the kitchen while he remained in the office, hoping she wouldn't come in and start one of her lectures about his shortcomings. After a while he'd heard the garage door open and close. Feeling a little guilty about hiding out until they left, he also felt a sense of relief that he didn't have to start his day off with more confrontation. He headed toward the kitchen, looking for coffee and aspirin.

Joe called in to the office and told Lucille, his office manager, that he was meeting with Mike again this morning and would be in the office about noon. Lucille didn't say anything. "Hello, did you hear what I said, Lucille?"

"I heard you, Mr. Meadows. You'll be in about noon."

"Thanks, Lucille."

What a pain in the butt she was. Joe had thought about firing her hundreds of times, but she was just too good at what she did to let her go. She was the best bookkeeper and organizer Joe had ever seen. But in her world there were the good guys and the bad guys. The good guys went to church, didn't drink, didn't dance, didn't cuss, didn't... well, just about everything they didn't do, including and especially anything to do with sex. How children came about in Lucille's world, he wasn't sure. Joe and most of his clients were the bad guys in her Bible Belt concept of reality. So Joe just put up with her thinly veiled disapproval—one more person damning him to hell probably didn't make a whole lot of difference.

After a little coffee and some toast, with the aspirin starting to kick in, Joe was beginning to feel more human. His depression wouldn't leave him alone, though. Some days were worse than others. Just for a while this morning he'd felt like he couldn't go on any more. But the feeling passed. He knew he wasn't suicidal, although if he'd told someone about his feelings they might have thought that was exactly what he was. He didn't want to be dead, what he really wanted was to be someone else. With a coffee go-cup in hand, he headed out to see Mike and maybe find out about the mystery key.

"This is for a bank lock box." Mike's key guy, Fred, looked even worse than Joe felt. *My gracious, this guy looks like he slept in a dumpster.* But Mike seemed to think he knew what he was talking about and they sure didn't know anyone else who might be a key expert.

"These guys have a unique design. They have special security measures to make it difficult to duplicate the keys, and if they're not inserted along with the bank's key, they can break off in the lock. I used to work on these for some banks in town—well, before my little slip."

Joe'd heard that Fred's "little slip" involved theft, followed by four years in prison. Good thing he hadn't had a big slip.

"Can you tell what bank this key came from?" Mike looked like he was starting to believe the key was some kind of magic wand. Joe thought it was just a little key to a bank lock box issued by one of, say, five thousand banks. *I suppose narrowing it down to banks is progress, but how can we figure out which bank?*

"Not really. On the front you can see the lock box number: 487. And on the back there are letters stamped right into the metal, CB. Maybe that's the initials of the bank—like Commerce Bank, City Bank, Citizens Bank, Colorado Bank, Connecticut Bank. Or maybe Central Bank—no way of knowing. Could be those are the initials of the manufacturer of the lock boxes—Columbus Boxes, California Beaches—anything. Sorry, Mike. I'd like to help you more, but I have no idea how you'd narrow it down."

Joe spoke up, "Well, since this was your dad's key, I think we can assume it was an Oklahoma bank, and maybe even an Oklahoma City bank. We have a Commerce Bank in the city, a Cattleman's Bank, a Central Bank, and a Citizens Bank. That's four banks—not hard to go by each one and see if this is their key."

"Well hell, Joe—you make it sound easy. At least it's something to do. If it works, great—if not, we just give up since we could have hundreds, if not thousands, of banks after the short list is exhausted. It makes sense that dad would use a local bank, so let's get going."

Mike was looking more like a believer today. Maybe he'd dreamed about the millions and how they could make all, or almost all, of his problems go away.

"Mike, you know I want to help, but I've got a ton of things that I need to do today. How about you visit the banks and see if you can learn anything. If I can help after that, you give me a call." Mike didn't look happy that his playmate couldn't play anymore, but he cheered up quickly and agreed that he'd go see the banks that day and the next, then give Joe a call to let him know what had happened.

"Hey Joe, not much luck in my bank visits."

"What did you find out?"

"It's a pain in the butt to drive all over town in this heat and humidity and with the crazy Oklahoma drivers."

"Anything about the banks?" There were times Mike made conversation difficult.

"Yeah. Well I visited all four banks. Basically got the same answer everywhere. Not their key. They said as far as they knew no one in this area ever had CB on their keys. Their keys always had the bank's full name stamped on the back because there were other banks in their market with the initials CB. One guy suggested that I look at banks in smaller markets where the CB would be unique to one bank in that town. Basically this has been a waste of my valuable time. Oh wait, my time is not worth crap, so no harm."

"Shit, what now?" Joe wasn't sure they would ever find out about the key.

"Well, that isn't all I learned. They told me even if it had been their key I'd have to have a bunch of legal shit before they'd allow me to access the box. One guy said that alone could take months. Plus, if the box rental hasn't been paid after a certain period of time then the bank can open the box and, if there's anything of value, they turn it over to the state."

Mike went on, "So, if they'd opened the box and found a bunch of cash, they would have given it to the state. Who, I imagine, would contact the police or the IRS or somebody who would have come snooping around to try and find my dad and arrest him, or tax him, or something. That never happened. I think this whole thing is a waste of time—nothing more than Dad losing his mind and giving me an old key he probably found somewhere."

"Yeah, well it does kind of sound like a pipe dream. You need money and suddenly the strange things your dad did at the end of his life start to sound less strange, maybe a solution to your money problems. I think we're just fooling ourselves into believing something magical is going to happen that will fix the world—but we both know it's not."

"How about I meet you at Triples?"

When in doubt, drink.

They met at Triples, but rather than talk about the world's problems—including Mike's impending financial woes—they discussed football at great length, with special emphasis on the OU Sooners and how they were expected to fare the following year. Kind of hard to live in Oklahoma and not be an OU fan. Discussing sports at length can be a balm to a wounded male ego. *Might be a complete failure in life, but I sure the hell know a lot of useless information about sports teams and their players.* It's amazing the depth of knowledge a beer-guzzling lowlife might have about some long ago college football game or long dead baseball hero.

Months passed, not much happened. Joe was preoccupied with tax season and more or less kept his head down and concentrated on work. Liz and the kids went about their business without much interest in what he was doing or not doing—as long as the bills were paid and the credit cards worked. Joe gave some thought to seeing a doctor about his depression, but the idea of being put on some kind of happy pill for the rest of his life was—well, depressing. Instead, he decided to continue occasionally self-medicating with a little gin and hope for the best.

Joe talked to Mike almost every week, helping him gather information about his finances. The bank had been more understanding than Joe had predicted and hadn't foreclosed or forced much of any action on Mike's part. The store was generating enough cash to spread around among the parties and keep anyone from taking any immediate action. Mike knew this couldn't go on forever, but he had little motivation to force anyone to do anything. He would follow the Joe mental health plan—he would occasionally self-medicate with a little scotch and hope for the best.

Neither of them forgot about the letter, or the key, or what Mike's dad had said—they just had no idea how to proceed. They discussed the possibility of finding someone else to look at the key, but it seemed like a waste of time. Mike's father's ramblings seemed increasingly likely to be meaningless the more they thought about them. Without some further hint, their search for the buried millions would stop before it really began.

Maybe it was for the best. They both needed to face the reality of their day-to-day circumstances and deal with them. Dreaming about millions would only delay the inevitable pain of facing life and its various problems. So long to get-rich-quick fantasies.

# CHAPTER 6

*Las Cruces, New Mexico, April 1987*

"Ray, this is Chuck—give me a call when you get this message. Think I have the name of the owner of that cabin up in T or C you asked me to check into a couple of months ago. Sorry it took so long, but looks like I have a lead now and I was wondering if you wanted me to pursue it. Talk to you later."

Ray was not real sure what he thought of Chuck. The man was annoying, but also oddly likable. Chuck had gotten back to him real quick on an estimated value on his house—no doubt because there was a real chance of a fee on that deal. Ray still couldn't make up his mind if he wanted to move or not. The old place sure held a lot of memories, but it was about five times the amount of space he needed. A small, simple cabin would be something he could take care of by himself for many years without having to deal with housekeepers or pay a bunch of people good money to keep the place in reasonable condition. It made sense to move into something smaller and to get away from all of the nosy gossip that went on in Dona Ana County.

"Chuck, this is Ray. What do you have for me?"

"Glad you called back, Ray. You've been giving some thought to listing your house—now's a good time as we move into spring."

God, you could not have a normal conversation with this

guy. He was always in salesman mode. "Well, I'm still thinking about it. What did you learn about that cabin Max's dad used to own?"

"Yeah, sure. But, remember, don't wait until you're ready to move to put your house on the market. More than likely it'll take a few months to find a buyer. So as soon as you're sure, we need to get a listing signed."

In an ideal world Ray would just hang up on this annoying little pest and go take a nap. "You bet, Chuck. As soon as I decide, I'll give you a call. How about the cabin?"

"Well, I was able to get the records by searching for Max's dad's name, so I found the details of the sale. You may not remember this, but Max's dad was Bud Johnson—he was something of a mystery man."

"What do you mean mystery man?"

"Well, this is old gossip, mostly from my grandfather. He thought Bud was a crook. He was long gone before you became Sheriff. I think he died in the sixties—not real sure, but I think that's right. Anyway my granddad said all of Bud's money was from illegal liquor. Mostly he was talking about the late 1920s and early 1930s, when there was prohibition. My granddad said that Bud was a big shot in this area and also had a bunch of holdings in El Paso. He said the rumor was that he was connected with some of the wealthiest Mexican families in Juarez. How much of this is true is kind of beyond me. Seems like there are a lot of unsavory stories about a lot of our best citizens. But who am I to gossip, right?"

The wiseass answer would have been *you're the biggest gossip in town—that's who you are*. But this was interesting stuff— why not let him continue? "Wow, that's interesting Chuck. So when did Bud sell the cabin, and who did he sell it to?"

"The records indicate he sold it in 1953. That means this cabin could be nothing, just a pile of trash by now. Even if Bud or someone was taking care of it into the sixties, that's still a long time to just sit up there abandoned. It's kind of an intriguing story, but I really don't think you want to retire and spend your last remaining years restoring an old broken-down cabin, do you?"

"You're probably right, Chuck. Did you get an address? Maybe, just as a lark, I'll run up there this weekend and see if anything still exists."

"Sure, 405 North Deer Trail. This is actually a Hot Springs address, before they changed the name to Truth or Consequences. I have no idea if that street—or trail, or dirt road, or whatever—still exists. But let me know if you find anything."

"Thanks, Chuck, will do." Ray hung up and debated whether this meant anything to him or not. But the weekend was looking to be unusually warm, and this would be a good excuse to get out and spend some time doing something other than dealing with one bureaucratic screwup after another at the department. It occurred to Ray that Chuck hadn't told him who Max's father had sold the property to. He debated calling Chuck back, but the thought of listening to him drone on some more persuaded him to leave it until later. It might not matter—there was probably nothing left of the cabin to buy.

The Saturday morning was as promised: sunny skies and warm temperatures. Spring had arrived in the high desert. Ray had only lived in this part of the country for about twenty years, but he'd learned to love the desert and mountains as much as if he'd been raised here. The trip to T or C was an easy drive of about fifty minutes. It was early morning when Ray reached the town and he decided to stop at the Lone Post Café, which many locals considered one of the best breakfast places in New Mexico.

Ray was in his civvies, so he didn't expect anyone to bother him. He settled into one of the well-worn wooden booths and ordered coffee and a breakfast burrito with lots of green chili. The smell of the place alone was worth the visit. He had grabbed an El Paso paper from one of the boxes outside and settled in to wait for his breakfast.

"I'll be damned, is that Ray Pacheco? How the hell are you, Ray? Kind of a long way to come for breakfast."

What luck. Staring down a long cigar was none other than Hector Hermes, the county sheriff for Sierra County. Not one of Ray's best buds, Hector complained to anybody who would listen that his county got the short end of state and federal money because they weren't considered as important as Dona Ana.

"Hey, Hector. How're things going?"

"As well as can be expected I guess. What're you doing in my neck of the woods on such a beautiful Saturday morning?"

Ray understood that Hector's friendly act was just that— the man wanted to know what the hell he was doing in his private domain. Ray decided the best approach with this guy was to be honest. What he was doing up here had nothing to do with their less-than-friendly competition. Plus, maybe this jerk didn't know he was retiring—that ought to make him happy.

"Well, Hector I've decided to retire at the end of my term. So, been thinking maybe I would move into your county and become an old fogey livin' in a remote cabin, just enjoying my remaining years." Ray was starting to annoy himself.

"Retiring—no I hadn't heard."

"Well, it's not a secret—not anymore. I just recently decided. Could be you'll want to run for the opening."

"Golly, I don't know. Wow, this really is sudden."

"By the way maybe you can help me with an address. I was looking for an old cabin that was owned by a Las Cruces resident a long time ago. His son mentioned it to me, and I thought I would check it out in case it fits my needs. The address is—let me see—four zero five North Deer Trail. Know where that is?"

"Hmmm... North Deer Trail. Sounds familiar, but I'm not sure. Let me run out to the car and radio the station and have them look it up for you. Just take a second."

Before Ray could say anything Hector had gone out to his car and was on the radio. Ray hadn't been sure how he was going to proceed once he got here, so running into Hector had turned out to be a good piece of luck, at least once the man had gotten past his initial suspiciousness.

While Hector was gone, the waitress brought Ray's breakfast. The burritos were large enough to feed a family of four, but Ray was willing to give it his best shot. Spicy and delicious. He was about halfway through when Hector came back in.

"You going to need any help with that, Ray?"

"Just might, but I'm going to give it a good college try. What'd you learn?"

"Kind of strange, we don't have a North Deer Trail anywhere in the county. You know a lot of those older names were in areas that no longer have any residents, usually due to fire or flooding. So the names just get dropped. Sorry for your wasted trip Ray. I'm sure you can contact a realtor up here or in Cruces—there are a lot of cabins for sale around the lake. Good to see you, though."

Hector left. Something about their exchange struck Ray as odd. Hector had seemed nervous and eager to leave. Maybe it was just his imagination. But now how was he going to find the address if the county had no record of it?

Ray decided the best solution was the one he often used in Las Cruces, the public library. He was a frequent visitor to the library to research anything that had happened years before or to locate information about something that was going on in the area. He found the main library just a few blocks from the restaurant. He had visited the T or C library once before when he was assisting with a federal operation at Elephant Butte Lake.

"Hello, I was wondering if you could help me find an old address from back when the town was Hot Springs."

"Sure no problem." The woman behind the counter could have posed for a Norman Rockwell painting of a small town librarian. She guided Ray toward the back of the library and began pulling down books of maps. She quickly went through them and gave Ray instructions on how to use the map book to search for the address he needed. After she thought he had a good idea of what to do, she went back to her post at the front desk.

Ray spent considerable time going through the books, looking for the right year and then searching for the street name. Eventually he found the street on the map. He took the book up to the librarian and asked if he could get a copy of the map.

"Sure, I can do that right now. It'll just take me a minute." She was gone for just a few moments, then came back with a copy and gave it to Ray. She told him that she was fairly familiar with the area since she'd lived around the lake her entire life.

"This was an area that had a massive wildfire and most of the high-dollar cabins up there burned to the ground, although a few survived. After the fire there was a huge rainstorm and it washed out almost all the roads in the area. Once that happened it was mostly just abandoned." She was pretty sure that the county didn't maintain any roads up there since there was nobody living in the area. "If you go up there, you need to be careful—it can be a dangerous area."

Ray wasn't real sure he wanted to venture off into an unknown area. The wise thing to do would be to just forget it and go back home. Although after that mega-calorie breakfast a little walking might be just the thing he needed. And it was still a beautiful early spring morning.

"Well, thanks for your help and the map. I was looking for an old cabin that probably isn't there anyway—but still it's a beautiful day for a hike—so I guess I'll go have a look. Thanks again."

It took Ray almost an hour to find the spot the librarian had pointed out on the map. While the area wasn't deep wilderness, the roads turned out to be horrible. This alone caused him concern about moving into the area. Maybe Sierra County wasn't getting its share of state money after all, or if it was it sure wasn't being spent on road maintenance. He rocked along in his old four-wheel drive Jeep for a very uncomfortable mile or two, then decided to stop, get out, and explore a little.

The area felt much more remote than the distance from town could justify. It was for sure there wasn't much up here. Ray hadn't seen any houses or cabins for at least a half hour. There were no other cars on the in-need-of-repair road. And while there was a comfort in being away from people, there was also an unease in being away from people. He would have been embarrassed if someone had seen his jumpiness, but it didn't matter—there was no one around. He reached into his glove box, removed his service revolver, and stuck it in his belt. Alone or not, it made him feel better.

Off to one side, about fifty feet from where Ray had parked, there was a gate with some kind of sign. He hiked over in that direction. There was no path, and the gate looked out of place as a result. When he got closer he could see that on the other side of the gate was a very primitive road. The sign on the gate wasn't much help: *Keep Out*. The whole area seemed to be fenced off. The fence wasn't high and it wasn't very strong—obviously just a boundary, not a serious attempt to keep anyone out.

Ray wasn't sure of his legal ground, but given what the librarian had said there was every indication that it had been abandoned—he could at least make an argument that he was allowed to enter. Besides, he'd mentioned it to the local Sheriff. Hector hadn't dissuaded him, and openly talking to the sheriff like that was evidence that Ray wasn't being surreptitious. All in all, that was enough of a rationalization for Ray.

Quickly hopping over the fence, he began walking up the makeshift road. The terrain was rough, and there was ample evidence of water damage over the years. If Ray was serious about buying something up here that he would actually live in there would have to be some fairly major improvements to allow him reasonable access. Once again it crossed his mind that this was something of a wild goose chase and probably a waste of time. But as soon as the thought occurred to him, he realized that that was pretty much all he had to do today: waste time. He relaxed and started to enjoy the hike and the day.

About a quarter of a mile from the gate, Ray could see some kind of structure off the road a hundred yards or so. There didn't seem to be a driveway or any kind of path toward the structure, although there might be something on the other side of the cabin or whatever it was. The more Ray looked, the more it seemed like some kind of outbuilding, maybe used for storage. He decided to stay on the road, which curved, and see if maybe it went around to the other side of the building. Anyway, he felt better staying on the road than blazing his own trail through the trees.

Ray remained on the road. It did slowly curl around to the other side of the outbuilding, and once he got clear of that he could see a pretty good-sized cabin further along. Sticking with the road, he soon came upon a small road or driveway that looked like it led to the cabin. There was no gate and no indication of the address or who might own the cabin. He started up the driveway.

After a walk that probably seemed longer than it really was, Ray reached the cabin. While it was obviously very old and in need of some repairs, it was, at least from the outside, in surprisingly good shape. It was a large structure made of logs. The rustic nature of the original construction had allowed the building to maintain its condition, even though it looked like it had been many years since anyone had been here. He climbed the few steps up to the large wraparound porch. On his right, he saw numbers on the cabin: 405. The five was dangling, and looked like it would fall any minute, but there it was, proof that this was the old cabin once owned by Max's dad. He felt like he'd just discovered a lost land or something.

Ray stood back and examined the outside of the cabin. It was an impressive structure—two-story, with an elegant design. The quality was obvious, even after being neglected all of this time. He was impressed.

He walked the length of the porch trying to look in through the windows, but they were all boarded up from the inside. The last person to leave this place wasn't expecting to come back any time soon. Although he still felt like he was likely wasting his time, he was also intrigued by the mystery of the place. Not sure what he wanted to do next, he made some detailed notes and a new map of the location of the road, gate, and cabin.

The time had slipped by and it was now almost noon. Ray had spent several hours poking around and making his notes and diagram. Deciding that his next priority of the day was a nap, he settled on heading home. Walking back down the road everything was quiet, but he had an eerie feeling that he was being watched. He made up his mind that it was just the result of being out in a remote place and brushed it off. Normally when his instincts raised a red flag he heeded them, but who would be watching him up here?

He headed back home. The trip had been uneventful, and once home he enjoyed a long nap—a habit that had been his

Saturday afternoon secret for some years now. He awoke at the sound of his phone. Slightly embarrassed that someone had caught him napping, he took his time picking up so he wouldn't sound sleepy when he answered.

"Ray Pacheco, is that you?"

Ray hadn't even said hello before the person started talking. "Yeah, this is Ray Pacheco. Who is this?"

"Pacheco, nobody wants you sticking your fucking nose in Sierra County business—if you're smart you'll find another place to retire. It could be real dangerous, got it asshole?"

"Max, is that you?"

Click.

What the hell was that about? Ray was used to some strange calls but seldom at home. His number was unlisted. Of course other law enforcement people and agencies had it, so maybe it was more available than he realized, but why tell him to stay out of Sierra County? It was strange, but Ray had thought it sounded like Max Johnson. It was his father's old cabin—why would Max threaten him? No question it was time to consider retiring—maybe it should be somewhere that no one knew him.

## *Praise for The Bootlegger's Legacy:*

"... superb character development ... vivid backdrops, brisk pacing, and meticulously researched ..." —*Kirkus Reviews*

"A rollicking good time." —*Self-Publishing Review*

"... interesting characters, true-to-life situations, and intriguing twists ..." —*Stanley Nelson, Senior Staff Writer, Chickasaw Press*

## *Where to find The Bootlegger's Legacy:*

Available from Amazon.com at:
www.amazon.com/gp/product/B014TFC9AK

Available from Barnes&Noble at:
www.barnesandnoble.com/w/the-bootleggers-legacy-ted-clifton/1122600076

Available on iTunes at:
itunes.apple.com/us/book/id1039073183

Available from Kobo Books at:
store.kobobooks.com/en-CA/ebook/the-bootlegger-s-legacy

Or ask for it by name or ISBN at your favourite bookstore.

# ABOUT THE AUTHOR

Ted Clifton has been a CPA, investment banker, artist, financial writer, business entrepreneur and a sometimes philosopher. He lives in Denver, Colorado, after many years in the New Mexico desert, with his wife and grandson.

## Keep in touch

Once a month, I send my readers a newsletter with a little of everything in it: southwest US culture, be it art, recipes, or local sights; my thoughts on writing and reading; book recommendations; updates on my current writing project; and from time-to-time a short story.

To sign up, visit TedClifton.com and either wait for the pop-up window, or scroll to the bottom of the page. Everybody who signs up receives a mystery gift, with my compliments.

You can also learn more about me and my latest books by visiting TedClifton.com or emailing me at ask@tedclifton.com.

# OTHER BOOKS BY TED CLIFTON

## Pacheco & Chino #1: Dog Gone Lies

Sheriff Ray Pacheco returns from his introduction in *The Boot-legger's Legacy* to start a new chapter as a private investigator, along with his partners: Tyee Chino, often-drunk apache fishing guide, and Big Jack, bait shop owner and philosopher.

## Pacheco & Chino #2: Sky High Stakes

Lincoln County, New Mexico was best known as the site of The Lincoln County Wars, featuring the likes of Billy the Kid. Martin Marino, the acting sheriff, is also short in stature, just like The Kid—and no doubt also like The Kid, Marino is crazy. Lincoln County survived Billy the Kid, but Martin Marino might be a different matter.

Ray Pacheco and Tyee Chino have been asked by the state Attorney General to find out what the hell is going on in the Lincoln County Sheriff's department. Ray is sure there's some big trouble waiting for them and his gut is right: murder, lust, madness and greed are visiting the high country.

*Coming in early 2016.*

## Pacheco & Chino #3: Four Corners War

Navajos, Apaches, militias, good sheriffs, and bad sheriffs are all drawn to a small town by millions in stolen money and a small army's worth of stolen military equipment. Is this the start of a Four Corners War? Nothing is as it should be as Ray Pacheco and Tyee Chino try to untangle the mix of greedy businessmen, corrupt politicians and a slightly unhinged sheriff—along with the usual dead bodies.

Farmington, New Mexico's unique mix of cultures is the backdrop for Ray and Tyee's most dangerous assignment to date from the bombastic Governor of New Mexico.

*Coming in late 2016.*

CPSIA information can be obtained
at www.ICGtesting.com
Printed in the USA
BVHW031653050819
555087BV00002B/243/P